But there it was: T̶h̶e̶ ̶c̶a̶s̶t̶e̶l̶l̶a̶n̶ ̶d̶i̶d̶ ̶n̶o̶t̶ ̶l̶i̶k̶e̶ ̶h̶i̶m̶, and Garak doubted very much that she trusted him either. When the castellan looked at her ambassador to her people's closest ally, Garak was under the unhappy impression that she did not see the patriot and the servant of the people—she saw the liar, the torturer, the killer, the man without boundaries. No wonder she kept him as far away from Cardassia as she could.

And this, really, Garak knew, was the source of his sense of injury. The post of ambassador to the Federation had been an obvious one for him, offered to him by Ghemor and taken gladly, because he knew how much Cardassia depended on the Federation's goodwill, and he knew how well he could do it. The job played to his strengths: his charm, his sociability, his taste for intrigue. He had developed an excellent relationship with Bacco, and being on Earth allowed him to continue his long love affair with Bashir's civilization. But, at the back of his mind, and as the years rolled on, Garak could not shake off the feeling that the position was, in some way, another exile. Sometimes, on Earth, staring out of the window at the gloss, the profusion, and the too-bright sun, Garak was filled with a profound sense of dislocation that was crushingly familiar. Perhaps it was time to come home. Perhaps it was time to retire to his garden.

Don't miss these other exciting novels in

THE FALL

Revelation and Dust
David R. George III

A Ceremony of Losses
David Mack

The Poisoned Chalice
James Swallow

Peaceable Kingdoms
Dayton Ward

STAR TREK®
THE FALL

THE CRIMSON SHADOW

UNA McCORMACK

Based upon *Star Trek* and
Star Trek: The Next Generation®
created by Gene Roddenberry
and
Star Trek: Deep Space Nine®
created by Rick Berman & Michael Piller

POCKET BOOKS

New York   London   Toronto   Sydney   New Delhi   Coranum

Pocket Books
A Division of Simon & Schuster, Inc.
1230 Avenue of the Americas
New York, NY 10020

This book is a work of fiction. Any references to historical events, real people, or real places are used fictitiously. Other names, characters, places, and events are products of the author's imagination, and any resemblance to actual events or places or persons, living or dead, is entirely coincidental.

First Pocket Books paperback edition October 2013

POCKET and colophon are registered trademarks of Simon & Schuster, Inc.

For information about special discounts for bulk purchases, please contact Simon & Schuster Special Sales at 1-866-506-1949 or business@simonandschuster.com.

The Simon & Schuster Speakers Bureau can bring authors to your live event. For more information or to book an event, contact the Simon & Schuster Speakers Bureau at 1-866-248-3049 or visit our website at www.simonspeakers.com.

Cover design by Alan Dingman; cover art by Doug Drexler

Manufactured in the United States of America

10 9 8 7 6 5 4 3 2 1

ISBN 978-1-4767-2220-7
ISBN 978-1-4767-2228-3 (ebook)

To Jenny,
for guidance

Historian's Note

The main events in this story take place just after the castellan arrives for the dedication of the new Deep Space 9 (*Star Trek: The Fall—Revelation and Dust*) on August 24 to September 4, 2385 (CE).

THE CRIMSON
SHADOW

Part One

The Emotion

"Earth is the goal. She stands at the end of all things."

—Preloc,
Meditations on a Crimson Shadow,
Vol. III (Earth), 3, iv

One

My dear Doctor,

I was sorry not to see you on your last trip home, but by all accounts it was a hasty visit, and my own availability was also sadly limited at that time. The ambassadorial life proves more hectic than that of a tailor, and these days my lunches are neither as lengthy nor as entertaining as those we once enjoyed in the Replimat.

I left your world ten days ago and am now en route home—and upon the *Enterprise,* no less! To gain admission to your flagship is surely a great honor. As you know, my spirits lift merely at the thought of returning to Cardassia, a luxury denied me for so long. And while I must admit that your world fascinates me more and more as I grow to know it better, the desire to be surrounded by my own people, to feel the hot sun of my own world upon me once again, is as strong as ever. You asked me in your last letter whether I had considered returning home again for good, and it is true that this thought is never far from the back of my mind. But the alliance between our civilizations remains still uncertain, and I believe that there is more that I can do yet. Duty to Cardassia will always drive me—never, I hope, to the excesses of the past. . . .

We will be welcoming your president to our world. Is this the first time that a serving president of yours has visited us? I'm sure that your brilliant brain would be able to answer that question in an instant. Whether or not she is actually the first, I hope that she will find herself most welcome. I have seen a great deal of Nan Bacco in the past few months as we negotiated the terms under which Starfleet would finally remove its personnel from our world. I respect her vision for our peoples and admire her breadth of literary learning. She has proven an acceptable substitute lunch partner in your absence.

Keep well, Doctor. And do keep an eye upon your news services. Very soon the eyes of the whole quadrant will be able to see your president standing alongside our castellan, and, while you will not catch a glimpse of me (I am, after all, in the habit of living in the shadows), you can rest assured that they have been brought together, in part, by the hand of:

Your affectionate friend,
Elim Garak

*   *   *

Before the fire, before the fall that destroyed the Cardassian empire and all but obliterated that clever, subtle, proud people, their capital city was a sight to behold. Coming down from lower orbit in a shuttle-craft (as this world's most forgiving, most forgiven son—Elim Garak—often had cause to do in the course of his long career), you could see the whole of the city rising up before you. Here, on the south side, nestled by the river and harassed day and night by the screech and roar of shuttles, lay the Torr district where ordinary lives were lived out in tenement blocks crammed close together, and the bittersweet scent of *gelat* drifted irresistibly from the corner houses.

Beyond rose up the steel-and-glass towers of Barvonok, gilt-edged and glitzy, where the money acquired from empire was transmuted by some strange alchemy into more wealth for the district's financiers. If you turned your head to look west, you could spy the long, low lines of the warehouses and factories of Munda'ar, receiving goods and materials from client planets, distributing them throughout the homeworld. In Akleen, long coppery lines of well-kept *ithian* trees signaled the avenues along which the Cardassian military had so proudly paraded for many long years. And, last of all, there, to the north, on the high ground, far above the city, was Coranum, where the rich and (thus) the powerful watched from their mansions distantly but assiduously over the great empire that was their chief possession. All this you could see as your shuttle made its descent; and if, like Elim Garak, you loved this place—your home—so deeply that you would oppress the best part of yourself in its service, then your heart would quake at the sight, because it was everything to you.

The city was gone now, long gone. The fire had taken it all and not discriminated. Old or new, rich or poor, building or person, the occupiers had not cared. As long as you were Cardassian, you were to be destroyed. You were to be wiped out, as if you had never existed. And so it was that all the tenements and towers, all the mansions and counting houses—they all came tumbling down.

Yet there is something indestructible about the Cardassian spirit (as that people's most unquenchable son, Elim Garak, can tell you). And from the bones and the cinders a new city was coming into being: bravely, and uncertainly, and not without setbacks. New towers were being raised, and between them ran new alleys, leading to new opportunities and new bolt-holes. Yet something of the old remained, haunting the half-formed city like a revenant.

Take the northern part of Torr (not chosen at random, for some of this story concerns that district closely). Once this had been an area of densely populated tenements, whose inhabitants traveled daily by tram out to the munitions works in Munda'ar. At the end of the Dominion War, when the Jem'Hadar came calling, they found many to murder here, and the narrow dead-end streets did not facilitate escape.

In a few short days, this busy life-filled district was reduced to rubble and ashes and corpses. Then the Federation arrived, their hands open, offering shelter, food, and medical assistance. When the rubble was shifted, and what remained of the corpses was buried, new buildings popped up, little prefab affairs, gray and functional and uniform. The survivors clustered gratefully within them. And slowly, slowly, they began to put their mark upon them.

Something of the old was imprinted upon the new. The prefabs somehow arranged themselves in memory of the old streets and walkways, and the old murals reappeared on the sides of the new buildings. The survivors brought back with them what was left of their old friendships and rivalries, their tattered possessions all the more prized for having almost been lost for good. This new corner house was where you went because it stood on the rubble of your old haunts; this walkway ran along a route that had been out of bounds for you and your family for time immemorial, so you did not cross that space. And above all, the old ethos survived—the old belief: that to be Cardassian was to be (despite all evidence to the contrary) the very best that there was. The old way of life—with its reliable work, steady patterns, and close-knit groups—was largely gone, but the northerners did their best to re-create it.

North Torr was militant too—always had been. Northerners were different from the peaceniks that clustered around the east side of the district, and they held these people largely in contempt. North Torr supplied the soldier boys who served the Union—not the legates but the ranks—and had done so proudly for generations. Northerners couldn't understand why it was these days that talk about their service wasn't so welcome, why the military didn't seem to want their sons anymore. Hurt pride, dispossession—this was rich soil for demagogues in search of a constituency. There were plenty in the new Cardassia with their eye on this opportunity.

North Torr was never the easiest place on Cardassia Prime for a newcomer trying to find a home, and that had not changed much. Yet it was here, nonetheless, that a young man by the name of Rakhat Blok had, for the last couple of months, been trying to make such a home for himself.

Blok had the tired and bewildered look shared by many Cardassians of his generation that resulted from the early and savage extermination of a deeply inculcated romanticism about his culture. If anyone had asked (and nobody did), Blok would tell them that he had been born on one of the empire's agricultural worlds and, desperate to get away from a life of boring and backbreaking work, joined up during the first recruitment drive that took place when Skrain Dukat seized power and handed over the empire and its people to the Dominion.

Blok had taken to soldiering. Although he was only a foot soldier, he was used to repetitive tasks and doing what he was told. Blok could say (if he'd been asked) how he'd liked the company, and the sense of purpose, and having more money in his pocket than ever before. He'd liked feeling part of something bigger than himself. In fact, he'd liked the whole business right up until he'd been deployed to the Romulan front. He hadn't liked that at all, and by the time the war was over, the question of likes and dislikes seemed something from a different age. The war ended in the blink of an eye, and in the space of a few hours—Blok could tell you—he went from proud servant of the Union to refugee from the Jem'Hadar to Romulan prisoner of war. When the Romulans finally released him, he went home, where it turned out that everyone was dead. He'd liked that least of all.

A story countless Cardassians of his generation could tell, if anyone asked. And, like many of them, the man called Blok had not wanted to drift around the ruins of his old home among the ghosts of so many dead families, so somehow he'd ended up on Cardassia Prime, in the capital, looking for work. The locals pegged him immediately as an outsider (there were enough of them about these days, taking the jobs), and proceeded with caution.

He found digs in a block built from old Cardassian stones and new Federation plasticrete. This space he shared with an old woman who muttered constantly under her breath and a male of indeterminate age who stank of *kanar* and didn't say a word, but could be heard most nights through the flimsy walls yelling in his sleep about choking, choking, choking. . . . Blok took to staying out late, pounding the alleys and walkways, and sleeping through the day. The dust that lay on the city wasn't so bad at night.

Every night he passed a *geleta* house on the corner of his street. He didn't at first dare to enter, but at last, late one long and lonely evening, he went inside. The regulars took one look at him, moved closer together, lowered their voices, and ignored him. But Blok went back every night and sat by himself on the periphery, listening to the camaraderie of their tight circle, building up a picture of their connections, and wondering how he could get inside.

They talked a lot, these people, more freely than they ever had under the old regimes, and more freely than they realized. They talked about the hound racing, and what they'd heard on the day's 'casts, and how you couldn't get decent *kanar* anymore. They talked a great deal about how things weren't as good as they used to be. They talked about the new young politician who understood how they felt and said things they liked to hear. They talked about the trouble last week in the southern city of Cemet, and how those students didn't know how lucky they were.

One night, about four weeks after his arrival on Prime, Blok sat listening to them, silently counting the coins lined up in front of him. If asked, he could have described how an army pension wasn't anywhere near enough to cover the cost of living in the capital these days, and how he couldn't find work. Doors seemed to shut in his face. Sitting and counting coins and listening to the unfriendly company complain how you could only get four days' work in five at the moment, Blok decided not to hold his tongue any longer.

"Four days out of five!" His accent, off-world and rural, sounded clumsy and out of place among these fast-talking locals. "What I'd do for that, eh! I haven't worked since I got here. Nothing! There's nothing for me. What's someone like me supposed to do, eh?"

There was a silence. Blok could tell what they were thinking: *If you don't like it here, son, you can always go back to where you came from.*

"It's not like there's anything back home. I don't just mean work. There's no people. No buildings. Do you know what it's like on some of the client worlds, eh? Do you have any idea? I fought the Romulans for the Union—"

That got a reaction. "Everyone's had hard times," said a man at the back, who had a thin white scar cutting down sharply through one of his eye-ridges. He was cradling a heavy glass in both hands and looking down into it, as if contemplating what other uses he might make of it.

"And I don't see why we should put up with it any longer," said Blok. His voice got shriller as he strove to convince his audience that he meant every word of what he was saying. "There'd be work for everyone, if it went to Cardassians. But it doesn't. The government is at the mercy of Starfleet officers and Federation officials! They don't want us to get the jobs. They'd have nothing to do. If we did what they were all doing, they'd have nothing to do. We're becoming dependent on them. Like servants. Like slaves. You know the worst of it? The other day, I saw a Bajoran, strutting around as if she owned the place! A *Bajoran!*"

The room was quiet for a moment, and then a low rumble of agreement rose up, ending on a growl of discontent. That old enmity had not been forgotten, not here in North Torr. Many of its old boys had lost their lives to the Resistance, trying to protect the Bajoran people from themselves.

The boundaries shifted and—suddenly, dizzyingly—Blok knew he'd been admitted. He'd put the key in the lock and this time it had turned. He looked down into his glass, which had been filled, and then people asked for his story. So he told them a version of it, and his glass got filled again and again, and Blok was admitted into the brotherhood of North Torr. At the end of the evening, when they all reluctantly left the warm little space for their less than satisfactory homes, Blok stood on the step of the *geleta* house, wavering slightly from side to side, and felt a steady hand upon his shoulder.

Turning, he found himself face-to-face with a male he'd noticed now and again throughout the evening, who hadn't spoken but who had been listening to everything closely. His grip was firm, Blok noticed, and he didn't smell of drink.

"You're a man who deserves better," he said to Blok.

"I am," Blok said, firmly, if with some slurring. "I do."

The man pushed a data card into Blok's hand. "You go home," he said, "and have a good sleep, and contact me tomorrow. I can put work your way. Good work, steady work. Work I think you'll like." He smiled, all teeth, and winked, and then turned and walked down the street, leaving Blok to weave his way unsteadily home, back to his cot and another man's nightmares. But he did what he was told, and slept well, and the next afternoon the data card was still there, so he thought he might as well use it.

Captain Jean-Luc Picard was not accustomed to realizing that the person he was addressing was no longer paying him attention. Particularly not when the person was sitting in the captain's own damn ready room.

"Ambassador," Picard said, "is something the matter?"

The Cardassian ambassador to the Federation, who hitherto had been a most conscientious audience, started and drew in a soft breath. Opening a palm, the ambassador gestured toward the observation window. Picard, turning to see what sight could possibly have proven so riveting, saw a pale brown disc, pocked and marked with dark shadows, around which two moons were suspended like weights hanging heavily upon a scale.

Cardassia Prime.

A prickle of apprehension ran along Picard's spine. The ambassador, however, was looking tenderly at this hard bare world, as if he would take hold of the whole planet with both hands and caress it, if he could. *Would I look at Earth in the same way?* Picard wondered. *With love, yes, and with longing— but with a devotion as fervent as this? I hope not. I hope I am not so intemperate.*

Garak, perhaps sensing the other man's disapprobation, gave a self-deprecating smile. "Forgive me, Captain," he said. "But the sight never fails to move me. There have been times when I thought I would never see it again."

Exile might do that to a man, Picard reflected, not to mention the attempted extinction of one's species. "Quite," he said gently. "I understand."

"And now you have my undivided attention," Garak said, with a smile. Picard was in no doubt of the truth of that. The ambassador's bright blue eyes, when turned upon you, seemed to pin you to your chair. But Picard was an old hand at this game too, and he had suffered Cardassian scrutiny in the past, and he had come out intact.

"All the documentation concerning Starfleet's withdrawal from Cardassia is now with the president's office," Picard said. "They assure me that this is simply a matter of looking over the final wording of the agreement, and they don't see any particular problems arising."

"Nor do we," Garak said. "Our news organizations have been instructed to keep the details under wraps until after the event."

"As have ours. We understand the political significance of this event for the castellan, and we wish to . . ." Picard pondered his wording. He could hardly say outright that the Federation wanted to assist Rakena Garan in her reelection in any way that it could, but that was the bottom line. The current castellan was by far the friendliest option.

Garak was watching him, a twinkle in his eye. "Quite," he said, obviating any need for Picard to say any more. The two men smiled at each other. It was helpful, Picard thought, how well the ambassador understood subtext.

"By the time she and our president join us here on Cardassia Prime," Picard said, "we should, I hope, be able simply to enjoy the moment of watching them sign the agreement."

Garak let out a deep breath and relaxed into his chair; he was a man about to see months of work come to fruition.

"This has been a remarkably smooth process, Ambassador," Picard said. "You and your staff are to be commended."

Garak waved a nonchalant hand. "Impossible to have achieved any of this without the goodwill of your president, Captain. Nan Bacco is a remarkable woman. A force to be reckoned with, as my memoirs will assuredly one day record. I know there were many within the council who believed that Starfleet was unwise not to keep one foot upon our soil, despite our much closer relationship these days."

"Indeed," said Picard, who had had his own private reservations about Starfleet's complete withdrawal from Cardassian space. Were these allies as solid as hope made them? The ambassador himself had not at first been an unequivocal supporter of the Union's entry into the Khitomer Accords. How long would his support remain? As long as it was expedient? And on Prime itself, how long would the will to continue as friends last? The experiment with an open society was still in its early days on Cardassia: its expression unconventional and its outcomes unpredictable. Cardassia was stony soil for such a graft, and there was no guarantee that it would flourish. And if it failed, what would grow in its place? Would these new allies remain allies?

"I believe," Garak said, "that only Nan Bacco could have persuaded her opponents that not only was it the right thing to do, it was also the most efficient use of your resources." He smiled. "Expediency combined with morality is, as ever, an unbeatable argument."

And that, really, was the truth of it. No matter how much Picard, and many others, might prefer to keep a small presence in Cardassian space, Starfleet needed the people back. The Dominion War and the Borg Invasion had taken an inevitable toll. There weren't enough experienced officers around these days. And, whatever the past, their two civilizations were now allied. One couldn't police one's allies, not on a permanent basis. Eventually you had simply to trust that they weren't, in fact, going to stab you in the back.

Garak was looking at him steadily. "This alliance is as new to us as it is to you, Captain," he said. "We have not been in the habit of thinking of the Federation as friends. But . . . our habits have not served us well." His mask slipped for a second, and Picard glimpsed the weary man behind the polish. "Quite simply," Garak went on, "we are tired of war—and I believe that to be true of you also. Therefore, we must endeavor to break the habits of a lifetime and make peace with each other." He smiled. "Friendship may take a little longer, but I remain hopeful. And I remain hopeful because, despite everything"—he turned his head once more to look at his home—"I live to see Cardassia yet again."

Rising from his chair, the ambassador offered Picard his hand to shake. Picard, gripping it, felt the rough scales upon un-human fingers. So very, very different. Garak, smiling, released his hold, and then something seemed to occur to him. "Ah, yes, I mustn't forget . . ." Reaching, he drew out a small parcel, neatly wrapped. He pushed it across the desk. "For you, Captain," he said.

Picard, frowning slightly, picked up the parcel. Unwrapping it, he found a small red book, about the length of his hand and the thickness of his thumb, bound in the hide of some animal he did not know and covered in small spots—burn marks, he realized. This book had once had a brush with fire.

"A small token of my appreciation for your hospitality on this journey," Garak said, "and for all that signifies for our alliance." Looking straight at Picard, he said, "I believe that my previous career leads you to hold me in some suspicion. I do not blame you for such sentiments. My past was not a pretty one. Therefore—" He pointed at the book, letting it say the rest.

Picard examined the volume more closely. Was the ambassador trying to charm him? Certainly this kind of gift was a sure means of attracting his attention, at least. Although he was by no means a collector of Cardassian first editions, his eye was experienced enough to see at once that this was an object of some provenance. "I would guess this has some history behind it."

"It was from my father's library," Garak said. "Although I doubt Tain ever read it."

Picard ran his hands slowly over the supple binding. "Not much of that library must exist now."

"Not much," Garak agreed.

"How did it survive?"

"I was reading it in the basement of my father's house while the Jem'Hadar destroyed the city. Everything in the upper levels of the house burned, but the cellar, in the main, survived. You, as an archaeologist, will know that burial has saved the fragments of many civilizations in the past. This was no different."

Picard put the book back down on his desk, resting his fingertips lightly on the cover. "Ambassador, I am honored by this gesture, but this is clearly an item of great significance, both personal and cultural." He pushed the book slightly back toward its owner. "I cannot accept—"

Garak held up both hands to silence him, and, to his own surprise, Picard acquiesced.

"I insist," Garak said. "Whatever our history, Captain, I believe that the future of our peoples is tightly bound together. We cannot stand alone. We *must* be friends—somehow. More and more I am certain that if we do not secure our friendship, if we do not make a habit of it, we will surely fall alone."

So the gift could not be refused. It really was very beautiful, all the more so for being rare and damaged. "Then I accept. Thank you."

"The pleasure is mine," Garak said, and Picard found he was prepared to believe him. Once again, he opened the book, but the close-printed characters inside were undecipherable. Picard gave a short bark of laughter. "I can't read it yet, of course. Not even the title!"

Garak smiled. "It's called *Meditations on a Crimson Shadow*," he said, "by Eleta Preloc." He gathered up his padds and papers. "I think that when you begin your researches you'll learn that it's a rare example of a Cardassian speculative novel. Our literature has tended toward the historical—one might even say the nostalgic. And indeed Preloc wrote many superb books of that kind. The tetralogy set during the fall of the Second Republic is surely the most exquisite of its type. Your own Tolstoy or Mantel would recognize those works. But with this book, she broke the mold." He smiled. "Preloc was a visionary, not to mention a genius. And if Preloc could see a future for our civilizations, who am I to deny genius?"

"I am extremely honored by this gift, Ambassador."

"It is by no means as grand a gesture as I would wish." Garak's padds and papers were now neatly stacked. "Our capital city is hardly the center of sophistication that it once was, Captain, but I hope that you and your excellent wife will join me for dinner at my home." He glanced around covertly, and Picard instinctively leaned inward. "The castellan's cook," Garak whispered, as if handing over a state secret, "is not a man of great talent."

Picard laughed. He might doubt the veracity of that statement, but he did not doubt that the invitation would be accepted.

"And when this agreement is signed," Garak said, "and the beaming faces of our leaders have been transmitted across the quadrant for all to see—allies and enemies alike—come again, and we will toast our alliance. Our friendship."

To police a city, one must know it: know its walkways and alleyways, its hidden corners and dim back streets. Once upon a time Arati Mhevet, senior investigator in the city constabulary, had known her capital as well as a Bajoran *kai* knew the prophecies. Born in North Torr's free hospital, she grew up in one of its tenements, playing along the walkways and in the tiny stone gardens set between the residential blocks. She knew the shortcuts down to the river, raced along the narrow footpaths that ran beside the tram tracks, and, with her playmates, kept open the gaps in the fences that let them slip into the industrial estates of Munda'ar, or gawp at the distant, radiant heights of Coranum. As she grew older, the city broke her heart again and again. But when the battle came to its streets, she stood and fought the Jem'Hadar building by building, alley by alley, as they razed her city to the ground, because to know a place so well is to love it, despite all, and to wish to keep it alive.

Now, like everyone else, Mhevet was learning this city again. She'd been a quick study. Crime doesn't wait for the police to catch up. It finds its niches and sets up its stall. Black market medicines lifted from the clinics? Certainly we can do that for you. Plasticrete panels to add another room to your new shelter? As it happens, Starfleet has left one or two lying unattended on the back of a transporter. Something to ease the pain, the particular acute pain of survival? We would be glad, so very glad to supply. No, no— there is no need to pay now. We can come and collect later. We know where you live.

All of this Mhevet was prepared to learn again, because her love for her city was undimmed, however little it resembled the place where she had grown up.

The geography might have altered, but something of its spirit had remained, however shell-shocked and bewildered—as if the Cardassian people, looking around at the destruction, called upon the strength that had always let them survive on this dry world, and said to themselves: Never again. *Meya lilies,* so the old saying went, *can flower in the stoniest of ground.* But they need nurture—and they need someone to stop the spread of weeds.

Mhevet, leaving Constabulary HQ, felt the grit in the air coat her eyes and nose, and she slid gladly into her skimmer. A wave of clear air and the babble of a newscast hit her the moment she started the machine. She lifted the skimmer up and out onto the boulevard and relaxed back into her seat. She was a confident driver, comfortable with the machine, swinging it easily into the fast lane. On the 'cast, two voices quarreled over the significance of last night's political missive from Cardassia First.

"*What you have to understand,*" said one, "*is that Cardassia First represents a new voice in our democracy, one that hasn't really ever been heard before—*"

"*And this is where you're fooling yourself!*" replied the other. "*Cardassia First is nothing more than the old chauvinism masquerading as something new. Evek Temet's a young man, but he's telling the same old story.*"

"*Yet I'm willing to bet that when the election cycle begins next month, he'll give Rakena Garan a run for her money—*"

"*He hasn't put his name on the ballot yet—*"

"He will."

Mhevet shifted uncomfortably in her seat. Everyone watched or listened to the newscasts these days. Everyone wanted to talk about them all the time. But doing so made Mhevet feel guilty. Her father (murdered when the Jem'Hadar walked into their tenement shooting anything that moved) wouldn't have approved, nor would he have approved of the political missives that were ubiquitous these days, and becoming more so as the deadline came closer for candidates to put their names on the ballot for castellan.

Her father would have hated all this: not because he didn't put Cardassia first, but because the whole idea of free elections would have terrified him. *Why would I want to choose?* Mhevet's father had said once to a friend (quietly, one didn't know what the Order might take exception to). *What do I know about running an empire? I'm a builder. It's good work, honest work, and I do it well. So long as those fellows up there keep the work coming in, I don't mind what they're doing, because they're doing right by me.*

Little good all his hard work and loyalty had done him in the end. The Jem'Hadar couldn't have cared less. To be Cardassian was enough. Brushing her fingertip across the companel, Mhevet found a different 'cast. Music this time, something catchy and mindless that had been a summer favorite. *Love!* the singer advised her confidently. *It's what we want! It's what we need! It's all we need!* Mhevet was mumbling mindlessly along when the 'cast cut out and the request

came for someone to head out to Munda'ar. Calling
in to say she was on her way, she swung the skimmer
around expertly and set the klaxon blaring. The traffic
peeled away to let her through unhindered. Her compatriots were still Cardassian enough to obey that
instruction from authority without question.

The Munda'ar sector was hardly the bustling area it
had once been. Gone were the huge silos and warehouses, the big cargo skimmers carrying in materials
and goods from the spaceport. Cardassia was nowhere near the industrial powerhouse it had once
been, although the green shoots of recovery could
be glimpsed here and there: some new light units;
the distinctive thump of a reconditioned industrial
replicator. Immediately after the war, all you could
see in Munda'ar were a few small buildings thrown
up wherever the rubble had been cleared and centers
for distributing charity to the survivors. All she remembered of the exhausted time directly after the
war was standing in lines outside those distribution
centers. That, and the burials.

   The new buildings here were more in the Cardassian style: a touch extravagant, although nothing
like the swagger of the Union in its heyday, but dis-
tinctively indigenous nonetheless with their curves
and spires and spikes. The materials were not from
here: these buildings were Federation beige and gray.
Living in the Cardassian capital was like inhabiting
two cities at the same time: one a ruin, the ghost of

the past; the other new, half-formed and fragile, but growing. Laying foundations; setting down roots.

The southeast quarter of the Munda'ar sector was still as flat as the Jem'Hadar had left it, however, and here Mhevet stopped her skimmer next to the single remaining wall of what had, from the look of it, once been a vast grain store. The presence of a couple of other constabulary skimmers told her that she'd come to the right place. Tret Fereny, another investigator, much junior to Mhevet, emerged from the shadow of the wall.

"Hi, Ari," he said. Mhevet didn't bother much with formalities like titles as long as people did what she said, when she said it. Fereny glanced back over his shoulder. "You're not going to like this."

Behind the ruined wall a familiar, depressing scene was unfolding. A handful of forensic officers were beetling around what was presumably the corpse, while a couple of constables, uniformed and impassive, stood by. On the ground near them sat two small girls.

"Those two found the body?" Mhevet asked, nodding at the girls. "What were they doing down here?"

"They'd been playing—playing *here*!—and stumbled over it." Fereny tutted his disapproval. "They should be in school. Kids these days are practically feral! I blame the parents. Gone soft, living on Federation handouts."

Mhevet smiled to herself. Fereny couldn't be more than twenty-five. He would have grown up on Federation handouts. There hadn't been much else to live off for the best part of a decade. She gave the two girls a quick look-over. One was pale gray and shivering—not so adventurous now. The other was looking around with dark, inquisitive eyes. They'd have to be questioned, of course, and that would be a nuisance. Not so easy to question children these days. Not so easy to question anyone these days.

"All right," she said, heading over to where the body lay, hidden beneath a gray covering. "What have we got?"

One of the forensic team bent down to reveal a gray uniform beneath the cover. A distinctive uniform, recognized across several quadrants, with a bright blue stripe across the top. Mhevet closed her eyes for a moment and cursed her luck. If only she'd left HQ a little later. . . . If only she'd taken the slow lane. . . . Right now, this could be somebody else's problem.

"Is that a Starfleet uniform?"

One of the little girls, the nosy one, not the shaky one, was standing at Mhevet's elbow, peering at the corpse with a keen interest unsavory in one so young.

"It is, isn't it?" the girl asked. "He's dead, isn't he?" She all but licked her lips. "My dad says the only good Starfleet officer is a dead Starfleet officer—"

"Yes, well, your dad is an idiot," said Mhevet.

"I know *that*," the girl said scornfully. She nodded at the corpse. "How did he die? Did someone whack him? I bet someone whacked him. What did they whack him with?" She looked around hopefully, perhaps to see whether there was something she could use to experiment.

Mhevet gestured to one of the officers to cover the body again. "Isn't anyone here taking care of these kids? Don't we have a counselor on call or something?"

"If you want a counselor," said Fereny, "you'll need to get in touch with Starfleet. You ready to do that yet, Ari?"

She was not, and therefore the pair would have to remain uncounseled a while longer. Nonetheless, they did not need to remain so close to the cooling corpse of a Starfleet officer who had, by the look of things, most certainly been whacked several times around the head and shot in the back for good measure.

"Someone put them in the skimmer and give them a padd to play with," she said. "And get their parents' names."

"I'm not telling you any names," said the girl firmly. "My dad'll kill me if he finds out I've been down here—"

"We've already established your dad is an idiot," said Mhevet. "So get in that skimmer with my nice friend Fereny, and don't let me hear another squeak from you." She looked across at the other girl, still sitting on the floor and trembling, and said to Fereny in a low voice, "Get the pair of them back to HQ and rustle up some parents as soon as possible, please."

Fereny nodded. Putting his arm around the little girl, he tried to maneuver her away from the barrier and in the direction of the skimmer. The kid dug in her heels. She grabbed hold of a nearby strut and hung on for dear life. One of the constables who had been minding her friend walked over, picked her up, and tucked her under his arm. "Consider it done, ma'am."

"Thanks," said Mhevet, and turned her attention back to the corpse. Behind her, she heard the kid yell, *"You'll never take me alive!"* before the constable bundled her into the skimmer.

With some semblance of order now restored, Mhevet nodded to the forensic team. Again, the covering was taken off, and one of the officers rolled the body over. She groaned at the sight of the face: the ridge across the nose and the long earring.

Marvelous, Mhevet thought. *That's all we need.*

Two

My dear Doctor,

I am home.

I will never tire of writing those words, and I hope you can continue to indulge me each time that I write them.

I am *home*.

Autumn is coming to our capital. Only last week one would not have been able to walk about in the midday sun and would keep to the shadows, while the dust rolling in from the plain would be a permanent plague. Now the heat is bearable throughout the day, and in the evening people must go long-sleeved. The rain comes sometimes—a few showers here and there, the storms will not come until autumn proper—but enough to clear the air now and then so that one might on occasion breathe freely. Autumn proper will bring respite from the harshness of our seasons—but only briefly. In a few weeks' time the first cold wind will come down from the mountains, and the city will begin the long freeze.

Spring and autumn are short here. We exist, in the main, in the glare of summer or the bite of winter.

As ever, on returning to my city after an absence, I am conscious of all that has changed. And although the ghost of the place that this once was still lingers, I see more new buildings lifted, more new homes, more tramlines connecting the outer districts. I can see the end of the bad times and the promise of better times. But I still see poverty, alas; and here and there I catch glimpses of suffering—and its bedfellow, despair. For all the growth and renewal, much about my home has not changed. We must watch for this. It may threaten us if we allow it to take root, for disparity causes envy, and envy causes hate. It is not enough for only some of us to prosper. We all came through the fire. And I have seen much of your world now, and I desire some of that peace and prosperity for all my people.

If you take, as I believe you do, a passing interest in our politics, you will know that very soon elections will open for the office of castellan. We all know that Rakena Garan will stand again as the most progressive candidate, and the friendliest toward our alliance. She has enjoyed an unprecedented run of popular support, and there is no candidate among her coalition that commands the respect she does. But now that I am home, and can watch the newscasts and read the broadsheets firsthand, I cannot help thinking that there is more than a rumble of discontent being sounded about our castellan. Perhaps it is simply that familiarity breeds if not contempt, then certainly displeasure—and our castellan is the subject of the disappointment that any politician earns after a while in the public eye.

But you know me—I always imagine the worst, because the worst has happened to Cardassia. I see a new face on the political scene, Evek Temet, and a new party, Cardassia First, arising from the ruin of the old Directorate. Certainly they speak smoothly, sounding all the right notes about free speech and democracy—but when I listen closely, I'm sure that right on the edge of my hearing, like the high-pitched whistle that one uses to train a riding hound, I catch some notes that trouble me. Let us hope this is not some kind of signal. Let us hope this does not mean trouble for our castellan, and that the visit from your president will boost support for her. The alternatives could alarm me, should I let them.

Coming home is, therefore, as ever, bittersweet—because I cannot forget what has been lost, and I cannot stop myself hoping for more, and I cannot help fearing that we are not yet free from the past.

I still hope too that one day you visit Cardassia Prime, Julian. Come in the spring, or in the autumn, when my home is at its most forgiving. You will be welcomed here by:

Your friend,
Elim Garak

"Bajoran?"

Guessing that her direct superior, Reta Kalanis, was not going to like the news she was bringing, Arati Mhevet had stopped on the way back to HQ to collect some *ikri* buns as a peace offering. She'd stopped too at a small eatery near the Starfleet compound that served its homesick officers food and drink from home. Kalanis and Mhevet, like many Cardassians since the Federation had arrived, had acquired a taste for coffee. The achingly long hours both had by necessity worked directly after the war, trying to set up a functioning police force in a post-apocalyptic city, had been enough to turn a taste into a habit.

For now the buns sat forgotten in their box and the coffee cooled in the cups.

"I'm afraid so," said Mhevet.

"A Bajoran Starfleet officer?"

"A lieutenant, to be precise."

"In the Munda'ar sector?"

Mhevet held up her hands. "I wish I could make this go away, Reta, but it won't. His name is Aleyni Cam, and he was part of the Civilian Outreach Program at HARF."

"Civilian Outreach?"

"You know the kind of thing. Help set up schools. Smile at children so that they don't think Starfleet officers are monsters."

Turning her attention to the buns, Kalanis ate one slowly and meticulously, with small, precise bites. She was a steady woman who did not let much rattle her. She made decisions calmly and then lived with the consequences.

"Well, then," she said. "A dead Bajoran Starfleet officer it is." She picked up another bun, demolishing that one in exactly the same way, biting around the outside before finishing up the center in two quick bites. She dusted the icing sugar off her desk and wiped clean sticky fingers. Picking up her coffee, she wrinkled her nose. "Cold," she said.

Mhevet reached for an *ikri* bun of her own, licking the sugar from the top and biting straight into the fruit at the center. "I had to go past the Starfleet compound to get it," she said. "For some reason they're not serving it in the canteen anymore."

"No?" Kalanis raised an eye-ridge. "How unhelpful."

Mhevet agreed. Almost everyone on Cardassia Prime was used to human food and drinks now. Would it all disappear once Starfleet left? She didn't want to have to ship this stuff in.

Kalanis put aside her misgivings about the coffee and drank it nonetheless. "I'm going to have to ask you to do something you're not going to like, Ari."

Mhevet sighed. She had seen this coming. Someone was going to have to head the murder investigation, and given the potential sensitivities that might arise with the Federation president's visit, she feared it was going to be her.

Kalanis and Mhevet went back years. Mhevet had served under Kalanis at the very start of her career, during the reforms of the police under Meya Rejal's ill-fated civilian administration. She'd been inspired by Kalanis's firm refusal to allow the politicians to use the constabularies to suppress unrest. Both had watched with horror when Rejal finally asked Skrain Dukat to use the military instead. Kalanis had stayed after, but it had been too much for Mhevet, and she had quit. Kalanis had never blamed her for that and they'd stayed in touch. After Rejal's fall— when the Dominion, by Dukat's invitation, occupied Cardassia—Kalanis, like many senior Cardassian police, was sidelined in favor of Vorta supervisors brought in to run the police. Mhevet became her eyes on the ground. She'd brought Kalanis advance warning of the Jem'Hadar massacre, and they'd both defended the people of their city when the death squads finally went on the march.

Later, after the war, when Cardassia was in chaos, Kalanis asked Mhevet to come back, to help her in the creation of the new constabulary. This was the time that had cemented their friendship, working together to satisfy the Allies that they were free of the kind of extremists that had been willing to carry out Dukat's orders and flourished under the Vorta. Under

Kalanis's guidance, and with Mhevet's loyal support, this city's constabularies had been rebuilt from the ground up.

Mhevet didn't like to dwell much on this time. It had been tough: removing people whose loyalties were uncertain, recruiting people whose reputations were unblemished. By necessity they'd worked closely with the personnel of the Allied reconstruction forces, leaving Mhevet with many friends at Allied headquarters, HARF, and a reputation for being Federation-friendly. These days that reputation was becoming something of a double-edged sword. Being known to be pro-Federation didn't sit well with those of her colleagues who were starting to tire of Federation overseers. It also meant that sometimes Mhevet got stuck with sensitive investigations, particularly if there might be tensions between Starfleet personnel and the Cardassians whose reconstruction they were overseeing. There had been many such cases over the years. And now there was this one.

But Mhevet had other work on her mind. "Reta, this isn't a great time to move me to something new. I've got someone embedded in North Torr right now, and we're building up a clear picture of the extremists operating there. We've got to press on with this—they're getting out of control. Some people are too scared to walk around North Torr these days. They had Cemet in flames last week."

"I know how hard you've been working in North Torr. I know how much it means to you to get these people, but I also know that it's going to be a long, slow process. In the meantime, we have a dead Starfleet officer and frankly, Ari, you're the one person I trust in this department to investigate this murder properly. Tell me, what do you think is behind it?"

"First instincts? Racially motivated, surely. All the anti-Federation sentiment that's being stirred up these days, a Bajoran officer is an obvious target."

"I agree entirely. And so you see already that putting you on this case isn't really taking you off your current one at all. You're investigating extremist activity in North Torr. All I'm asking you to do is come to them from a different angle. If they're guilty of this, you'll connect them to it." She lowered her voice. "If you can stick something on those bastards from Cardassia First while you're at it, you'll have my undying gratitude."

Mhevet looked back over her shoulder, making sure the door was shut. She lowered her voice nonetheless. Directive 964 of the charter of the reconstituted Cardassian constabularies stated: *Political affinity has no place in the work of the reconstituted constabularies. Political discussion is not appropriate within constabulary buildings or between constabulary members.* The idea had been to prevent partisan disputes dividing the organization as they had done in the past.

"The problem is," said Mhevet, "I'm not sure who to trust to look after what's happening in Torr. You know there are CF sympathizers in the department?"

"Unfortunately, Ari, that's their democratic right, however much it shows them up to be idiots of the first order. If it makes you feel any better, I'm going to ask Istek to take over the investigation in North Torr."

"*Istek?*" It wasn't that Mhevet didn't like the man, and she knew that he shared her dislike of the nationalists in North Torr, and suspected them of much more than the usual troublemaking. But while there was no doubting his good intentions, he was not blessed with much in the way of subtlety. Mhevet could see months of painstaking work being ruined.

"I'll keep an eye on him, Ari. But this murder case is important. I can't afford any mistakes."

Reluctantly, and with a fair few misgivings, Mhevet agreed.

"Thank you," Kalanis said. "All right, off you go. I've got to tell the people at the top. We've got the Starfleet flagship here already and the president herself due to arrive soon to sign this agreement. Imagine how well it's going to go down with the castellan's staff when I tell them someone's going around killing Starfleet officers."

"Only one, Reta."

Kalanis claimed the last bun. "So far."

Afternoon settled upon the Cardassian capital. The red sun was hidden by gray dust. In the private office of the Cardassian ambassador to the Federation, the lamps had been lit since lunchtime. The ambassador's secretary knew how her superior preferred things slightly brighter than most, as if all that time spent amongst humans had made his eyes adapt.

Shadows quietly lengthened across the room. Everything was still. Elim Garak, sitting at his desk, listened to the quiet and was at peace. His desk was, as ever by this point in the day, fastidiously neat. To his left a pile of padds—contents thoroughly read, digested, and responded to—sat in a tidy stack. To his right, a cup of red leaf tea gently cooled. Before him was a flat, square parcel, still wrapped in packaging from the long journey from Earth. Garak's hands rested protectively upon the parcel. He had two more calls today, after which he would open the parcel and carry out the usual ritual. Then he could go home and see how his garden had fared in the time he had been away.

The comm on his desk chimed.

"Put him through, Akret," Garak said to his chief aide.

But Akret herself came on the line. *"I'm sorry, sir, but Director Crell's office says that he regretfully must postpone your call."*

"Postpone?" Garak drummed his fingertips against his desk. Prynok Crell was the current head of the Cardassian Intelligence Bureau, and Garak had numerous questions to ask him in advance of the arrival of Bacco and her team. This call had been arranged for more than a week. "Did he give any reason why?"

"I'm afraid not, sir. He said he would get back to you as soon as he could. He said he was sure you understood how busy he must be in the run-up to Bacco's visit."

"Well, yes, that was rather by way of being the point of the conversation!" Garak tidied up the pile of padds, which now seemed slightly in disarray. "I suppose I'll have to wait for our diaries to be in alignment once again. Perhaps you could reopen negotiations with Crell's office before you go, Akret."

"Consider it done, sir."

Garak cut the comm. This was tremendously frustrating. As well as the arrangements for the upcoming presidential visit, he also wanted to discuss the possibility of increasing his own security. Some of the anti-Federation noises he'd been hearing since his arrival home had alarmed him rather more than he'd indicated in his letter to the doctor. Not that there was anything directed toward him specifically—the castellan was the chief target—but Garak was long past the days of taking risks with his own safety. Crell, however, while not openly hostile, was not the friendliest of colleagues. Whenever Garak spoke to the man, there was, beneath the conversation, the dislike that many in the CIB held for their predecessors in the Obsidian Order. And then there was the question of territoriality. *Keep out*, Crell seemed to be saying whenever Garak appeared to be coming too close. *This isn't your business.* He wasn't the only high-ranking official on Cardassia that did this.

With a little time now on his hands, and feeling a

need to be soothed, Garak turned his attention to the parcel in front of him on the desk. Slowly, with great care, Garak began to remove the packaging. Eventually, the contents were revealed. He raised it in front of him at arm's length to admire it: an abstract painting, combining elements of Cardassian and Bajoran design, created by a young woman at the start of a promising career. In the bottom left-hand corner, a single initial acted as the artist's signature: *Z*. Tora Ziyal had painted this. It was the only relic of her that Garak possessed, and it traveled with him between Earth and Cardassia Prime every time he made the journey.

With a sigh, Garak stood up from his chair and, carrying the painting carefully between both hands, went over to the wall opposite his desk. There, in a little alcove, stood a small table upon which, at his instruction, there was a vase of freshly cut *perek* flowers, scarlet bright. Leaning over the table, Garak hung the painting on the wall. Sitting at his desk, he would be able to look up and see it, and take courage from it. He stood for a while studying it. Focusing on the detail, he picked out delicate meya lilies, and *mekla*, and long winding *elta*, and copper *ithian* leaves, narrow and elegant. There were Edosian orchids too, for him, and from Bajor there were lilacs for Colonel Kira, and leaves from the *moba* tree, and spiny twists of basil. When Garak moved his head back to capture the whole, the intricate pattern of flowers and leaves swirled and intertwined.

"You're remembered," he said to her, as he did every time he performed this quiet ceremony. He often talked to Ziyal. "As long as I live, you'll be remembered."

Returning to his desk, Garak pondered his next call. He was waiting to speak to the castellan, currently visiting Deep Space 9 for the dedication of the new station. As ever, the promise of a conversation with the castellan weighed heavily upon him.

Garak did not understand why he and the castellan had never quite become friends. Their goals for Cardassia were in alignment; he respected her dedication, her common sense, and particularly her political longevity. Yet there was nothing of the camaraderie that had marked his relationships with other leaders. Even Damar, whom he'd had good reason to hate, Garak had eventually come to respect—to like, even. But then one had to get on with someone with whom one was stuck in a cellar; otherwise one would simply murder him. . . . Alon Ghemor Garak had served willingly as friend and confidante, and he missed that time profoundly. Perhaps this was what colored his relationship with Rakena Garan? Regret that she was neither Corat Damar nor Alon Ghemor? But Garak also sensed a hesitation on the castellan's part. If he didn't know better, he might think that the castellan didn't like him.

"Really," Garak muttered, "whatever is there not to like?"

But there it was: The castellan did not like him,

and Garak doubted very much that she trusted him either. When the castellan looked at her ambassador to her people's closest ally, Garak was under the unhappy impression that she did not see the patriot and the servant of the people—she saw the liar, the torturer, the killer, the man without boundaries. No wonder she kept him as far away from Cardassia as she could.

And this, really, Garak knew, was the source of his sense of injury. The post of ambassador to the Federation had been an obvious one for him, offered to him by Ghemor and taken gladly, because he knew how much Cardassia depended on the Federation's goodwill, and he knew how well he could do it. The job played to his strengths: his charm, his sociability, his taste for intrigue. He had developed an excellent relationship with Bacco, and being on Earth allowed him to continue his long love affair with Bashir's civilization. But, at the back of his mind, and as the years rolled on, Garak could not shake off the feeling that the position was, in some way, another exile. Sometimes, on Earth, staring out of the window at the gloss, the profusion, and the too-bright sun, Garak was filled with a profound sense of dislocation that was crushingly familiar. Perhaps it was time to come home. Perhaps it was time to retire to his garden.

The comm on his desk chimed.

"Ambassador," Akret said, *"the castellan is on the line."*

Garak steeled himself. "Do put her through."

The screen blinked, and then the castellan appeared.

She was a small woman, with graying hair, wearing a beautiful set of amber *reta* beads that could only be an heirloom. Even at a distance, she conveyed a great deal of personal strength and courage. And she didn't like him, and she didn't trust him, and she was totally immune to his charm.

"Madam Castellan," Garak said with a tilt of the head. "I trust you're well?"

"As well as ever, Ambassador. How was your journey home?"

"Very pleasant. The *Enterprise* is a most hospitable environment." He glanced beyond her, trying to get a glimpse of the place that had, once upon a time, been his unwelcome home. Cheerfully, he said, "And how is the old place?"

The castellan gave him a puzzled look. *"It's brand new."*

Garak sighed. Ah, yes, that was the other problem. They did not share a sense of humor. *Oh, to be talking to Bacco. She at least knows how to spar. . . .* "Well, it certainly looks very comfortable."

"It is, but I'm on the Trager.*"*

There was a pause. They had no small talk. "How can I help, Rakena?"

"I wanted to check how the final stages of the negotiations were going."

Garak felt his impatience rise. He had been sending her, twice daily, meticulous and—though he said so himself—very elegant summaries of all that was happening. Not that anything was happening. Everything was proceeding like clockwork toward the withdrawal. All the castellan had to do was turn up, write her name, and hand the stylus over to Bacco. And all Bacco had to do was turn up, take the stylus, and use it.

"It really is a done deal—"

"A deal isn't done until it's done. I know you've only recently arrived home, but I'm sure you've seen the pictures from Cemet."

"I've seen them." A sudden explosion of violent emotion between nationalists and radical progressives that could surely please nobody except the perpetrators.

"And I imagine you've heard Evek Temet on the 'casts about them. 'That the castellan should choose to go away at such a time reflects badly upon her judgment.'" She did a fair impression of her young opponent's voice—slick, but with a breathy urgency behind it. *"'She cares more for the alliance than for her own people.' I don't like not being there to counter it."*

"Aren't your people here on top of that?"

"I hope I'm not going to have to make some kind of gesture to prove my credentials as a tough negotiator."

"Such as?" Garak said, uneasily.

"Such as asking Bacco for concessions."

Garak listened with some alarm. Surely she didn't mean this? At this late stage, it would be outrageous to have to go back to the Federation team and reopen discussions on the withdrawal agreement. Just in time, Garak stopped himself from retorting that if she wanted to ask for concessions, she could find herself a new ambassador to ask for them. He didn't want to retire just yet.

"Maybe I shouldn't have gone away. Maybe I should simply have sent Vorat. I wonder if I should return home. There are parts of the agreement that are going to take some careful explaining—"

That was certainly true, and they'd been gambling on being able to do that. "The full details won't be available until Bacco is here. With any luck our estimable press will be so busy gossiping about the president that they won't be bothered with the minutiae. It's a long document, after all, and they have short attention spans, and I know I'm certainly more interested in what colors Nan Bacco is wearing this season." He saw her eyes narrowing, but he couldn't stop himself. "Emerald is very good on her, but I think she's been wearing it too often in recent months. I'd like to see some signs of blue in her repertoire. Nothing navy—that would be *far* too dull! I mean something more on the lines of electric blue. Mark my words, Rakena, that will be next season's color. My advice to you, as well as to remain where you are, is to start wearing electric blue."

She was looking at him as if face-to-face with a blithering idiot. The only person who Garak could think of who had been this immune to his patter was Worf. Even Kira had laughed occasionally, although probably more for Ziyal's sake than his.

"What I am trying to say," Garak said, in a steadier tone, "is that I think your being on DS9 is a unique opportunity for you. Stand in a line with all those other heads of state and think of the images appearing on every screen across the Union. Evek Temet can't manage anything like it. And when you return home, you'll be there to oversee the last Starfleet personnel leave Cardassia Prime. You'll be the star of the show. Temet will look amateur beside you: a parochial man clamoring for an agenda that *you* have delivered. You'll be the castellan who oversaw the final liberation of Cardassia."

That earned the makings of a smile. *"Very well. Thank you for your time, Garak. I know you think I'm bothering you over details, but we've both put a great deal of work into this, and I don't want to see us fail at the last hurdle."*

"On that we are entirely in agreement."

There was no more mention of concessions or her return and, when the conversation finally ended, Garak leaned back in his chair and sighed with relief. Now, he hoped, the withdrawal could continue as planned, and the castellan of the Cardassian Union and the president of the United Federation of Planets could shake hands and smile at each other like the allies they must be and the friends they might be.

The comm chimed again. "What is it, Akret?"

"Reta Kalanis on the line for you, sir."

"Who?" he asked, starting his own quick researches via the companel.

"She's the director of the city constabulary. She says she needs to speak to you. Urgently."

His garden, it seemed, would be waiting for him a while longer.

Lieutenant Aneta Šmrhová had come to Cardassia Prime without preconceptions. Yes, there had been the war, but that was a long time ago now, and the Cardassian people had suffered unimaginably, and, as far as Šmrhová could tell, had then taken seriously the task of understanding what had brought them so close to the brink of self-annihilation. Besides, Šmrhová didn't like to generalize. She only knew one Cardassian well, and she liked and admired him. Glinn Ravel Dygan had served on the *Enterprise* with distinction and even turned out to be good company beneath the seriousness. When it came to Cardassians, Aneta Šmrhová had a data point of exactly one—but it was on the credit side.

Her immediate impression of Dygan's homeworld was admittedly less positive. She and Commander Worf beamed down in front of the main building on the Starfleet compound in the capital city and both immediately began to cough. The air was full of dust. A spare woman in Starfleet uniform, wearing the pips of a commander, strode over to meet them, palm raised in greeting Cardassian style. She wore a face mask. Clearly this was someone who knew the place well.

"Margaret Fry," the woman said when she reached

them. "Commander, Allied Reconstruction Force, Cardassia Prime. You're our visitors from the *Enterprise,* yes?"

Worf, still coughing, nodded. Fry gave a wry smile and offered a couple of masks. "You'll need these on the tour of the base."

The compound that comprised the Headquarters of the Allied Reconstruction Force on Cardassia Prime (or HARF, as this mission was more generally known) housed a mixture of Starfleet personnel, Federation relief workers, and their opposite numbers from the Cardassian military and civil service. Commander Fry, driving them around quickly in a small open-topped skimmer, gave them a brisk history of HARF's operations on Prime.

"Obviously there was a substantial military presence here directly after the Dominion War," Fry said, "but over the years, the balance has shifted significantly toward the relief and reconstruction work. Most of the personnel still stationed here have expertise in medicine, construction, scientific research, education, health policy, and so on."

"The base is much bigger than I would have guessed," Šmrhová said as the skimmer reached the perimeter. They were up in the hills of what had once been the prestigious residential area of Coranum. Šmrhová, looking out, saw the sprawl of the new city: the low buildings, the haphazard spiderweb of the tramlines, the sudden patches of devastation. She rubbed her eyes, which were full of grit.

"We've been here a long time," Fry said, swinging the skimmer around and down one of the compound's main streets. "As well as offices and residential blocks, we have our own shops, our own mess, and we can keep ourselves entertained if we choose. To all intents and purposes, this is a city within a city."

"Probably wise," said Šmrhová.

Worf, however, frowned. "Have you limited all contact with the Cardassians?"

"Absolutely not," said Fry. "This isn't a fortress and the intent is certainly not to divide the peace-keepers from the locals. If you walked into any building on the compound you'd find Cardassians working closely alongside Starfleet or Federation personnel. Even in the early days, the security risk was minimal. The Cardassian people were simply too exhausted. There was no fight left in them. All people wanted was shelter, something to eat, and, most of all, a reliable source of clean water. We supplied that as quickly and as fairly as we could. But we knew that that wasn't the whole story."

They were driving past a playground and the children ran across to watch them go past. Šmrhová waved, and laughed at the roar she got in return.

"There are Cardassian kids there," Šmrhová said, in surprise. She'd assumed the schools would be for the Federation families.

"School exchange," Fry replied. "And some of them will be the children of Cardassians who work here. We've had an integration policy since we arrived.

There are young adults on Cardassia Prime who will have been entirely educated in mixed schools. You see, we've understood reconstruction in the broadest terms possible," Fry explained. "It's not just about putting up buildings and installing infrastructure. It's about revitalizing Cardassian institutions—the civil service, the constabularies, the military. We've had experts on hand to assist the Cardassians in creating these organizations from scratch. How do you inspire trust in institutions that have brought a civilization to the edge of destruction? How do you create new organizations to replace the old ones? This is as significant a part of our work here as getting the water running and the clinics out there. Not as desperate a task, perhaps, but with the long term in mind."

Reaching their starting point outside the main command center, Fry stopped the skimmer and led them inside. Šmrhová was relieved to find that reconstruction had got as far as full scrubbers. The security officer took off her mask and breathed deeply. Her hair, when she ran her hand through it, was coated with dust, even after so short a time outside.

"Then there are the civilian projects," Fry said, leading them through the busy building. "New farming and irrigation initiatives, R&D, bringing scientific colleagues together to work toward a common goal, whether Federation or Cardassian. Bear in mind that HARF has bases like this across the whole of the Union—not just across Prime, but pretty much on every client world, if the need was there. It's my dearest hope that there's not a single citizen of the Union who has not had a positive encounter with a Starfleet officer."

"Your work here is a byword for success, Commander," Worf said. "Do the military exchange programs originate here too?"

"The military is one of the great success stories," Fry said, "when you think how the Central Command was organized and operated before it was contained by the Rejal administration, and think of the alacrity with which it got behind Dukat. But of course, there were elements in the military that never supported entry into the Dominion, and personnel who joined Damar's resistance as soon as they could. These are the traditions that have been built on to create the new Guard."

"If Dygan's anything to go by," Šmrhová said, "the Cardassian military is in safe hands."

They entered Fry's office, a comfortable but not ostentatious space that already showed signs of being cleared; packing cases stood around, and some of the shelves had been emptied.

"How long have you been here?" Šmrhová asked.

"Ten years," Fry said, with a smile. "I came here with the second wave of forces assigned to the reconstruction."

"Will you find it hard to leave?" asked Worf. Šmrhová, rubbing at the grit in her eyes, thought that she would never have unpacked. With all respect to Ravel Dygan, his home planet was a dump.

"I don't think I'll ever do work as meaningful as this again," Fry said frankly. "It's an amazing world, and the Cardassians have been courageous and tireless. It's been a privilege to help them rebuild their world."

The office, on the third floor, offered a view marred by the reddish haze that hovered over the city.

"What's with the dust?" Šmrhová asked.

Fry offered them both bottles of water, which they gratefully received. "Cardassia Prime's most distinguishing feature," Fry said. "Prime was aggressively over-farmed, Lieutenant, generations ago. Famine was a problem here right up to the Dominion Occupation. That's what drove their expansion and the conquest of Bajor. What you see is, in part, the ecological effects of such farming practices."

"Dust bowl," said Worf.

"Exactly that. This city stands right on the edge of the northwest plains. The wind blows across them, collects the dust, and dumps it here. You should have been here earlier in the summer. You can't get your hair clean. When the rains start, you'll know autumn has arrived."

"You said ecological 'in part,'" said Šmrhová. "And the rest?"

Fry looked sadly through the haze at the piecemeal city. "The rest? The rest is what the Jem'Hadar left behind. You can't destroy a civilization without leaving some trace."

Šmrhová shuddered, and swallowed some water gratefully.

"Preparations for departure look well under control, Commander," Worf said. "But are you quite sure that the Cardassian Union is ready for us to depart?"

"You're thinking of the recent trouble over in Cemet, I think?" Fry asked.

"A city on fire was our impression."

The commander took a sip of water. She seemed unperturbed. "Cardassian newscasts can be fairly melodramatic, and civilian unrest makes people here jumpy. Not surprising, given recent history. It reminds people of the period before Dukat seized power. I don't want to downplay what happened in Cemet, which was certainly a breakdown in order, but it was by no means as bad as the 'casts made out."

The *Enterprise*'s first officer pressed on. "Our understanding is that at least one politician is attempting to gain from it."

Fry gave a dry laugh. "Ah, you've come across Evek Temet, have you? A nasty piece of work, but clever. He's good at saying what people want to hear. That's propelled him to a seat in the Assembly and leadership of his party."

"But is he a serious threat to the castellan?" Šmrhová asked. "Could Rakena Garan lose an election to him?"

"I don't think so," Fry said. "Temet makes a lot of noise, of a particular type, but I don't think there are enough people here prepared to listen." She looked out lovingly across the city. "I know this seems counterintuitive, but you have to see these debates as a positive aspect of Cardassian democracy. I'd rather a hundred Temets than the whole Union back under the heel of the old Central Command or, worse, the Obsidian Order. These voices may sound strident to us, but they do provide an outlet for certain sentiments that still have a hold in some parts of Cardassia."

Worf rumbled his concern.

"I have a great deal of faith in the Cardassian people," Fry said. "I don't believe for a moment that they want someone like Temet in power. Finally, after so many years of instability, Cardassia is really beginning to feel stable once again. Think about where they once were, and think about where they are now. A castellan who has actually survived long enough to seek reelection. Admission into the Khitomer Accords. And now we at HARF are saying: 'We trust you. We believe you're ready to mind your own affairs again.'" She smiled slowly. It transformed her from someone rather brisk and sparse to someone with great warmth. "The Cardassian people are different now. They aren't going to elect Evek Temet. They're wise to what he's peddling."

Worf's frown wasn't doing too great a job disguising his doubts. Šmrhová took a swig of water. Perhaps Fry was being optimistic, but she had been here a long time, and presumably knew what she was talking about. Still, Šmrhová picked out the boundaries of the compound, took into account the surrounding terrain, and mused upon how it might be defended.

The comm on Fry's desk chimed. Excusing herself, the commander took the message. Šmrhová watched her expression turn grim. "Bad news?"

"I'm afraid so," said Fry. "One of our officers has been found dead—murdered, in fact. Lieutenant Aleyni Cam."

Worf's frown deepened further. "The name sounds Bajoran."

"Yes, Cam was Bajoran. He'd only been here eighteen months. Recently married too. Poor Zeya. . . ." Fry headed toward the door. "My apologies, we'll have to continue our discussions later. I should be the one to inform his wife."

"Of course," Worf replied.

"Our facilities are at your disposal. Do speak to my staff if there's anything you need." And with that, she strode out of her office.

"Not such a smooth departure after all," Worf remarked.

Šmrhová noted her commander's concern. "We don't know the circumstances," she said. "He could simply have been walking down the wrong street at the wrong time."

"We'll see, Lieutenant. But I fear that Commander Fry has spent too long here. She may be blind to the obvious."

"The obvious, sir?"

"That under the surface, perhaps Cardassia has not changed."

*   *   *

Garak, having spoken to Reta Kalanis, stiffened the sinews and summoned up the blood to inform Picard of the death of Aleyni Cam.

"Of course I understand that this has nothing to do with our current mission," Picard said. *"We have no desire to make any capital from this—that would be an insult to the family of the young man concerned. Rest assured, Ambassador, Starfleet has no interest in delaying the withdrawal from Prime any longer. Your city constabulary is surely best placed to investigate a murder, and we shall of course give every assistance needed to bring the guilty party to justice."*

The conversation concluded with the usual mutual assurances of friendship and support, and when the comm cut, Garak leaned back in his chair and breathed a sigh of relief.

The door opened, but Akret, ominously, stood on the threshold and didn't come any closer. "You're not going to like this," she said.

"What now?"

"The text of the withdrawal agreement has been leaked." Akret took a step back. "I hate it when you do that face," she said. "It makes you look like you want to kill someone."

"Oh, Akret." Garak gave a heartfelt sigh. "Let us not even *joke* about that. . . . How much of the text exactly has been leaked?"

"The full document."

Garak put his head in his hands.

"Do you want to see how the 'casts are handling it, sir?"

"No, Akret, I want to go home, where I have not been for months. But do what you must."

Akret switched on the screen at the far end of the room. Garak's jaw clenched as the 'cast blared out with its brash presenters and garish colors. Garak's heart quailed at the thought of all that uncontrolled information flooding past. He thought longingly of the productions overseen by the Order's Office of Vision. They had been stately affairs, authoritative, soothing, and largely devoid of anything approaching the truth. Whereas this . . .

On the screen, a fresh-faced young man wearing a Cardassia First badge was letting his opinion of Garak's carefully wrought agreement be known: *"What I can't believe is this section here! A limit on military spending for the next ten years! The Dominion War was a decade ago! We're signatories of the Khitomer Accords! Are we really still being made to pay for the actions of one dead madman? Haven't we suffered enough? Lifting that clause alone would put hundreds of jobs directly into North Torr. No wonder the castellan has tried to conceal this. The people of North Torr will be rightly furious to hear about this, and no doubt will want to make their opinion heard—"*

"Who," Garak muttered, "will rid me of these turbulent priests?"

Akret, who took the time to read whatever her boss happened to be reading, asked, "Is that an instruction, sir?"

"No. Or, at least, not yet. First, I want to speak to

whoever produces this excuse for a news broadcast. Immediately."

While Akret busied herself arranging this, Garak sat at his desk and fumed. *This,* he thought, *would never have gotten past the Obsidian Order.* Nobody would have dared to transmit something like this; no, nobody would even have dared to *know* something like this. . . . And so soon after the trouble in Cemet? So much for Crell and the CIB.

The face of a young woman appeared on the screen in front of him. *"Ista Nemeny for you, Ambassador,"* Akret said smoothly. Garak launched straight in. "Young woman, do you have even the *slightest* idea how much damage you're causing right now?"

"Sir, if you could give me a moment—"

"Months of work have gone into this agreement! *Months.* On both sides. Months of delicate negotiation—!"

"Sir, if I could speak—"

"In a few days' time, the president of the Federation will be here to sign an agreement that will send her people home. I would be happy, she would be happy, and the chances are that the entire population of the Union would have been happy. But, no. You couldn't wait. You couldn't resist the bait offered by those third-rate hooligans in Cardassia First—"

"Sir, I insist you listen to me!"

"You insist, do you?"

"Yes, I insist!"

All of a sudden, Garak wasn't angry any longer.

He was very tired, and he was desperate to go home. "Well," he said, opening a palm, "if you insist. I shall, at your insistence, endeavor to listen."

The woman took one deep, shuddering breath. She pressed her thumb into the concavity at the center of her forehead. *"You do know your reputation, don't you, sir?"*

"I wonder," Garak purred, "what you could *possibly* mean by that?"

"Ambassador to the Federation? Adviser to Alon Ghemor? Last man standing with Corat Damar? Not to mention your previous career. . . ."

Softly, Garak asked, "What about my previous career?"

"Let me just say that having you on the screen there makes me want to run home and hold my children."

Garak closed his eyes. "Young woman—"

"If you didn't want a free press, Ambassador, you shouldn't have let Alon Ghemor set one up."

There was a pause. Then: "I must apologize," Garak said, more calmly. "You are entirely correct. This . . . *debacle* is of course exactly what I have been trying to achieve for the best part of a decade. I suppose now I have to live with the consequences. You are naturally well within your rights to inform the Cardassian people of the full details of the withdrawal agreement."

"Thank you."

"If I may, however—you might have considered some of the potential consequences."

"I'm sure the castellan's media team will cope," Nemeny said.

"That's not what I'm worrying about," Garak said. "It's what the public response might be. None of us wants a repeat of what happened in Cemet."

Nemeny blinked. She looked as if she hadn't thought about that. *"I suppose,"* she said slowly, *"that in fairness I should tell you that we're inviting Evek Temet from Cardassia First onto the program tomorrow morning to debate this. You might want to warn your friends in the administration. Assuming you have friends in the administration? I've been hearing rumors that the relationship between you and the castellan is strained—"*

The woman's nerve was incredible. "Your concern for my popularity is touching. The castellan and I are in perfect accord when it comes to the benefits of this agreement for the Cardassian people. Forgive me, but I need to attend to clearing up the mess that you are currently creating for me—and I would so *hate* to keep you from making further mischief."

"A pleasure to speak to you too, Ambassador," she said.

Garak cut the comm. Then he braced himself to speak once again to the castellan.

She was, as expected, horrified. *"Where has this leak come from, Garak?"*

"Who knows? A disgruntled underling at Foreign Affairs? A young hopeful trying to curry favor with the press? An enemy set upon doing us harm? The head of the CIB himself?"

"There are significant differences between all those! Some are considerably more alarming prospects than others!"

"My team is being interviewed—" He surreptitiously tapped out a message to Akret to tell her to get onto it. "I suggest you conduct a similar investigation of your own." Sweetly, he added, "Or ask Crell to do it."

The castellan glared at him. Garak was not the only one out of favor with the head of the CIB. Crell's son had died in the forgotten war with the Klingons, and he was not well disposed to that particular alliance.

"Is there a problem?" Garak asked. "I only ask because, as I'm sure you know, a castellan at odds with the head of her intelligence service could end up facing difficult questions in the Assembly—"

"Therefore you can be sure that I'm very much in control of that situation." The castellan shook her head. *"Really, Garak, I wish you would stop trying to make every single aspect of government your business. Your responsibilities as an ambassador are quite clear and are surely enough to tax even the most energetic of men. Worrying about the governance of the entire Union will probably kill you."*

There was a pause while Garak tried to determine whether that was an expression of concern, a brush-off, or a threat. Unable to come to a conclusion, he pressed on with all of his bad news. "Rest assured that I'm in excellent health. But if I might trouble myself with domestic politics a little longer, you might like to know that Evek Temet intends to make as much political capital out of this as he possibly can. Starting with a debate on Edek Mayrat's newscast tomorrow morning—"

"*That's it,*" said the castellan. "*I'm coming home.*"

"That . . . strikes me as an overreaction. It's not as if you'd be back in time to debate with him. All you'll be doing is signaling that you believe matters really are spiraling out of control. Better to sail serenely above all this and return home on your own terms and according to your own timetable—"

"*While Evek Temet takes to the airwaves to stir up who knows what kind of trouble? No, Garak, this really is getting out of control. I'm coming home.*"

"The other signal that will send," said Garak quietly, "is that you do not have faith in your ambassador to the Federation to handle this affair."

She hesitated. "*Your responsibility is the diplomatic fallout, not the political fallout. That's my business—*"

"You have a deputy to handle that."

She sighed. Garak sympathized. Her second in the Assembly, Enevek Vorat, delivered a number of significant critical rural client worlds, but he was not fast on his feet in debate. "*No, Garak, I need to be there. Evek Temet is not going to hold back.*"

"Who," Garak murmured, "will rid me of this turbulent priest . . . ?"

"*What was that?*"

"Nothing. Perhaps you're right. . . . Very well, I'll expect you home. But while you're en route Evek

Temet will be taking to the airwaves to call you and your administration craven and under Bacco's heel. May I ask what you intend to do in the meantime? Put Vorat out there?"

The castellan shook her head. *"I'll be asking Vorat to come here to take my place. Besides, this is not a partisan issue, and we should try to prevent Temet from making it a partisan issue."* She looked him straight in the eye. *"I think you should debate with him."*

"Oh, no! Under no circumstances—!"

She spoke quickly. *"Think about it. You're not allied to any political group and you know this treaty better than anyone. Who else can convincingly argue that this withdrawal is good for all Cardassians, regardless of their political allegiance—?"*

"You know I prefer not to be in the public eye—"

"If you didn't want to be a public figure, Garak, you shouldn't have become a public figure."

This was turning out to be a revelatory day on that score. Garak had the unpleasant feeling of having suddenly discovered that there was a huge target painted on his back.

"You say that my returning home sends a signal that I don't have faith in my ambassador. So let me demonstrate my faith in you. You're the one I want out there defending this treaty." The ghost of a smile passed over the castellan's face. *"Temet won't know what's hit him."*

Despite himself, Garak found his own lips twitching. "Oh, very well," he said. "I suppose it can't do any more harm."

"Excellent. That's decided. I know you'll do a marvelous job."

"Thank you."

"I'll assign one of my aides to assist you."

So not that marvelous a job, then, Garak thought.

"There's nobody who understands the terms of this agreement better than you."

And nobody better placed to take the flak in such a way that the castellan's administration was not implicated. *I'm a fool to let myself be persuaded to do this,* Garak thought. *But somebody has to. . . .* With a sigh, Garak conceded that he had been outmaneuvered. Perhaps it really was time to retire. "You realize one of us has to speak to Captain Picard?"

There was a pause.

"I've not really worked with him," said the castellan.

"Oh, very well. . . . I suppose it won't be the first difficult conversation that I've had with the captain today."

"I appreciate this, Garak."

Garak cut the comm, took a deep breath, and prepared himself, for the second time that day, to speak to Picard. Outside, the daylight was quickly fading, and his garden would soon be covered in darkness.

Three

My dear Doctor,

In one way my home does not change: she never fails to surprise me. What was meant to be a smooth path to the signing of our agreement has now become fraught with complication. And suddenly I find myself in the limelight—surely no greater service has Cardassia ever requested! I do not know how closely you follow our news, but you may wish to keep an eye upon it tomorrow. You may see something to amuse you, not least:

    Your friend,
    Elim Garak

As he waited in his ready room for the call from Admiral Akaar to come through, Picard leafed through the book that Garak had given him. He had read two-thirds already and wanted to be finished by the time that he and Beverly went to the ambassador's home that evening. The story was fast-moving, like a glancing blow in fact, following events as a future Cardassian Union swept through the quadrant, conquering all that lay in its path. The second act (where Picard had put the book aside the previous night) had ended with a critical defeat of Starfleet. Now the armies of the Union were poised to occupy Federation space and set foot on Earth.

Where was this going? Picard wondered, as he flicked back through the pages, reviewing what had happened so far. *Why had Garak given him this particular book?* The ambassador was a subtle man: there must be meaning to this gift-giving somewhere, if Picard could only decipher what it was. A story in which the Cardassians conquered all? Not a warning, Picard was sure; that was far too obvious an interpretation and incongruent with the man's actions over recent years. So what else? Of course, he hadn't finished reading yet. The story might have a completely different meaning once he had come to the end.

On the inside front page, a name had been inscribed. Only a part of the signature remained now: scorch marks and other damage accrued during the fall of a civilization had obliterated the rest. Still, there was enough left that when Picard put the thin translator film in front of the page, he could see clearly who had once owned this book.

—*bran Ta*—

It sent a shiver up Picard's spine. Even though Garak had told him who had owned this book, there was something frighteningly immediate about seeing the man's own handwriting, thick-stroked and blocky, impressed upon the page. Enabran Tain: the most ruthless and successful head of the now defunct Obsidian Order, and the man whose unprovoked and genocidal assault on the Founders' homeworld had been the opening move in the game that ended with the near destruction of his own people. Garak had played a part in that too, Picard recalled. Underneath what was left of his father's mark, Garak had written, in a precise and elegant hand (in Federation Standard too; Picard had not needed the translator to read this):

> *To Captain Jean-Luc Picard, in the hope that while past deeds cannot be forgotten, future acts may in time outnumber them.*
> *With respect, Elim Garak.*

A relic from a burned civilization. A fragment of a name. An offer of friendship from a duplicitous man. A story in which Picard's own civilization stood on the brink of ruin. How did one decipher all this? The chime of the comm saved him from further reflection.

The Commanding Officer of Starfleet Command did not waste time. *"This leak of the text of the agreement is very unfortunate, Jean-Luc. Any idea where it came from?"*

"None as yet."

"Just as long as it wasn't one of our people."

"We're conducting a thorough investigation. But you know as well as I do, Admiral, that these leaks are almost impossible to pin down to a single source."

Akaar grunted his agreement. *"Still, I have to say that from where I'm sitting I'm getting mixed messages about Cardassian enthusiasm for this withdrawal—"*

"Starfleet's withdrawal from Cardassian soil is by no means unpopular," Picard said. "At least according to our experts at HARF. It's the specific terms of the withdrawal that are causing complaint. What concerns me, sir, is the effect this might have on popular support for the alliance."

"Not to mention the danger faced by our personnel in the meantime. Is there any news from the constabulary on the death of Lieutenant Aleyni?"

Picard shook his head. The death of the officer was preying on his mind and he could only hope that this was not a sign of deeper trouble. The young man's death was tragedy enough. "None as yet."

Akaar frowned. *"Should we be pressing to carry out our own investigation?"*

"I understand why that's tempting," Picard replied. "Nevertheless, Commander Fry insists it's vital at this point that we signal our trust that the Cardassian constabularies will investigate this murder fully. I agree with her. What message would it send if we indicated that we don't believe they are either willing or able to find Aleyni's killer? Fry tells me that she knows the investigator assigned to the case and trusts her to get a result."

"Then your advice is to leave well enough alone?"

"Yes, for the time being. Everyone—Federation and Cardassian alike—has put a great deal of work into rebuilding Cardassian institutions, Admiral. Let's see how well they've done their job."

"Very well. And in the meantime—should I be concerned about what I hear about this new political party? Cardassia . . . What are they called?"

"Cardassia First."

"Cardassia First." Akaar sighed. *"Where do they find these names? Hardly subtle, is it? Should I be worrying?"*

"Not according to Fry."

"So clashes between rival groups of political activists on the streets of Cemet—"

"Are, according to Fry, a signal of the strength of Cardassian democracy, rather than the other way around."

"That wasn't the case under Meya Rejal."

Picard shook his head slowly. Meya Rejal had been the civilian leader of Cardassia after the collapse of the Obsidian Order. Fearing electoral defeat at the hands of her rival, the beloved Tekeny Ghemor, she had delayed elections so long that the Cardassian people took to the streets to demonstrate their disapproval. When Rejal tasked Skrain Dukat to deal with the demonstrators, the result had been a massacre. "Cardassia is a different place now, Admiral. I can't see any leader opening fire on civilians."

"Are you quite sure?"

"Not Rakena Garan."

"But someone else might?" Akaar frowned. *"Evek Temet, is that who you're thinking of?"*

"Certainly Evek Temet stirs up people's passions. And the trouble for the castellan is that all this unrest undermines people's belief that she is in control. This suits Temet's purpose. The more clashes there are between these extreme groups, the more people will lose confidence in the castellan as a leader who brings stability. And it's stability that the Cardassian people want—understandably."

"Stability, of course, is not the same as democracy. Look at the Tzenkethi."

"No, although ideally the two are aligned."

There was a pause. Eventually, Akaar said, *"We don't want Temet as castellan."*

"We most certainly do not. He's not said it in as many words as yet, but he's surely anti-Alliance."

The admiral was instantly alert. *"Pro-Pact?"*

"It's hard to tell. He might simply be an isolationist. Nationalists of his type often are."

"Isolationist or pro-Pact, he's not who we want."

Ultimately, however, it was not their choice. It was the choice of the Cardassian people, and both men knew this.

"My strong sense is that it won't come to that. Temet has enjoyed plenty of publicity while the castellan has been away, and he'll enjoy more until she returns, particularly if the castellan's spin doctors continue to fail to control the fallout from this leak.

But the castellan will be home shortly, and then President Bacco will be here. Nothing makes a politician look more serious than standing next to a colleague from another power. Temet will sound provincial by comparison."

"*Let's hope that's the case. Give my regards to the ambassador when you see him.*"

"I will. He's invited us to dinner. And he gave me a book."

"*Dinner and a book?*" Akaar began to laugh. "*Garak must be thinking of you as a friend, Jean-Luc. Watch your back. Akaar out.*"

Lieutenant Aleyni Cam had been quartered in the residential blocks that formed most of the eastern part of the HARF compound. Parking her skimmer, Mhevet saw a handful of children playing in a nearby yard. *Family quarters.* She sighed. Speaking to the widow was bad enough. She hadn't thought there might be children. . . .

She knocked at the door of Aleyni's small, single-story house. After a few moments, the door was opened by a young Cardassian woman who looked as if she hadn't slept for a while.

"Aleyni Zeya?" Mhevet said, uncertainly.

When the woman nodded, Mhevet had to conceal her surprise. She'd assumed that Aleyni would be married to a Bajoran or, at least, would have chosen a partner from one of the diverse species that made up the Federation. But a Cardassian wife? That, sadly, only supported Mhevet's instinct that the murder was racially motivated. An ugly crime; amongst the ugliest. Hateful and irrational. Such a waste.

At the woman's invitation, Mhevet stepped inside. The narrow hallway was lined with *perek* flowers, traditional after a death, and their perfume took Mhevet back at once to the small funeral service she had performed for her parents after the war. She'd found a single flower somehow, crushing its petals over the rubble that had been her childhood home, cutting into her hand to let the blood drop upon them, chanting the names of her dead all the while. Her fingers had held the heavy scent of the flower for days afterward, and her hand still bore the scar.

Aleyni Zeya led her to a small room that served as both kitchen and living quarters. She made red leaf tea. "I'm not what you were expecting, am I?"

Mhevet breathed in the pungent steam. "I have to admit that you aren't."

"Your expression . . ." Zeya gave a wan smile. "That's how everyone always looks. They try to cover it, but they're never quick enough."

"I'm sorry. Rude of me."

"It's all right. I know it's a surprise. A Cardassian and a Bajoran. People still aren't quite ready for it. Do you think that's why he died?"

"I don't know. I don't know much yet."

That was true enough. Mhevet had been trying to track Aleyni's last movements. She knew his shift had ended late afternoon, and that shortly after leaving the HARF compound, he had taken a tram down into Torr. After that he slipped off the sensors until his reappearance the next day, dead, in a broken-down warehouse in the Munda'ar sector. Mhevet had put in a request for surveillance footage before leaving the department, but coverage was patchy, and the form filling complicated. The Federation (who had, after all, put in the infrastructure) didn't like to see it used routinely to monitor their personnel, or even Cardassian citizens, but Mhevet had a friend in the CIB who came in handy for this kind of thing.

"I was always afraid this would happen," Zeya said. "That I would be the reason that he died. He didn't think it was a risk, but I wasn't so sure. It hasn't been a problem. Not here on the compound. Not really." Her tea stood by, completely forgotten. Mhevet hoped she was not forgetting to eat. She remembered this period of vagueness, of numbness, when nothing seemed safe to concentrate on for too long. All Cardassians knew and recognized this state.

"What about your family?" Mhevet asked. Perhaps somebody there had not liked to see her marry a Bajoran.

"Family?" said Zeya. "There's nobody."

"And his?"

"His family on Bajor knows nothing about me."

"Really?"

"His mother is a prominent vedek. Very traditional. I think she may have been active in the resistance as a young woman." Zeya pointed to a picture on a far wall: a family group, all Bajoran, with a stern woman at the center. "That's her. Scary, isn't she? She's getting old now. Cam never said, but I think it would have killed her if she'd known he married a Cardassian. You know, the Occupation." She sighed. "It never seems to end, does it? They kill us and we kill them, and for good measure, we kill each other."

"It's not as bad as it was."

"No? I'm not so sure. Sometimes I think there's something wrong with us. Something wrong with the Cardassian soul. There's something cruel about us. We nearly destroyed ourselves once. I think it will happen again. Maybe not in my lifetime, but one day."

"I don't believe that," Mhevet said, gently. "I don't believe our nature is fixed in that way. I believe that we can choose to change."

Zeya didn't reply. Instead, opening the drawer on the table, she drew out a stack of papers. Mhevet looked through these with increasing disgust: a pile of graphic and violent images depicting what might happen to a Bajoran man and a Cardassian woman that got too close.

"Any idea who might have sent these?"

Zeya shook her head.

"Do you mind if I take them?"

Zeya shrugged.

Mhevet took a swig of tea. "Did you notice any changes in Cam's behavior recently?"

"Well, he was worried. We both were."

"Worried?"

"About the withdrawal. About where he would be sent next. I couldn't go to Bajor . . ."

No, Mhevet thought, *that wouldn't work.* "Have you eaten anything today?"

Zeya hadn't. Mhevet poked around the kitchen and found some flatbreads and some cold *terik* stew. She warmed this up and sat watching Zeya, murmuring encouragingly each time the young woman put a forkful in her mouth.

"I have to ask about his job," she said, once Zeya had eaten most of the bowl of stew. "Cultural outreach? What did that involve?"

"He went into schools! He went round schools and explained what HARF did, why they were here, how they were trying to help. He organized exchange programs between students at our universities and universities across the Federation. The last time we spoke, he was excited because he had thought he had persuaded a Klingon medical student to come and work on a study into children's health . . ."

Zeya began to cry. Mhevet took her hand. "Cam wanted children," Zeya said. "But I'm glad we didn't. We should never have married. This was only ever going to end in grief."

Mhevet stayed with her until the crying stopped, then helped clear away the plates. Offering her condolences, she left and made her way back to her skimmer. She was relieved to get away from this sad, broken home. Back in her skimmer, she saw a message from her friend Erelya Fhret at the CIB. It contained the footage she was after, and a short message: *You still owe me lunch.*

She watched Aleyni Cam board the tram. She watched him sit motionless for the time it took him to get to North Torr. She watched him leave the tram and disappear into the warrens of that explosive district. A Bajoran, walking around North Torr, as the day ended. Insanity. What had Aleyni been thinking? What had he expected would happen to him there?

Doctor Beverly Crusher was an old hand at diplomacy and familiar with the residences (official and private) of a large number of dignitaries across the quadrant. So the modesty of the home of the Cardassian ambassador to the Federation surprised her. But then most private homes on Cardassia Prime must be this way, she reflected, with resources rightly poured into public housing, as well as hospitals, schools, and roads.

Garak's home was jury-rigged from a combination of Federation materials and whatever rubble had been left behind by the Jem'Hadar. The building consequently had a ramshackle feel, but the area in front was surprisingly beautiful. Here, a series of small monuments had been built, piles of dry stone formations, none of them higher than shoulder height. Around these, a garden had been planted: small, but surprisingly verdant, and very well tended. Crusher wondered who took care of this, given how much time the ambassador spent away from his homeworld. Inside, the rooms, although small, had been arranged cunningly to suggest space, and with considerable taste. There were not many possessions: chiefly books and a few pieces of art. Presumably most of the ambassador's possessions were back on Earth. Or perhaps this was all that had survived.

Garak had invited along another Cardassian, a man of about his age whom he had called "my very good friend, Kelas Parmak." Crusher, learning that Parmak too was a doctor, quickly fell into conversation with him about various health-care projects under way across the Union. Public health, always a problem on a world where water was in such short supply, had been a priority for each administration since the end of the Dominion War. Crusher was impressed by Parmak's grasp of policy, and was relieved to hear that the Cardassians were now treating the health of all the members of their Union as a matter of general importance. Beyond this topic, conversation ranged from the vagaries of the water supply (a Cardassian obsession to match other cultures' preoccupation with sports or the weather), to the problems of introducing Earth fauna into the Cardassian climate (Garak had been drawing on the experience of Keiko O'Brien), to Garak's forthcoming public debate with Temet (the promise of which Parmak, at least, found hilarious).

Supper was plain and simple, but good—rationing was all but over within the Union, apart from a few luxuries and the ever-scarce water, and the ambassador could cook. After, the four of them sat outside in the garden. The air was perfumed by unknown herbs and late-blossoming flowers. Garak strolled around the space lighting yellow lamps. The monuments cast long shadows. A dry wind had passed through the city, clearing some of the dust, and it was a relatively clear night. Crusher saw a few white stars twinkling through the haze.

When the lamps were lit, Garak sat down, and they all looked past the stones to the lights of the city beyond. Crusher heard Garak sigh quietly to himself. His expression, watching over his city, was a curious mixture of love, pain, and desire.

"I finished the book you gave me," Picard said.

Garak's expression became one of uncomplicated delight. "Really? What did you think of it?"

"What book did you give him?" asked Parmak.

"*Meditations on a Crimson Shadow.*"

Parmak laughed out loud. "Elim, you're extraordinary! Was this intended in the spirit of friendship?"

Garak looked put out. "Of course. Why wouldn't it be?"

"Only you, Elim, could give someone a book describing the destruction of their civilization, and expect it to be taken as a gift."

"It did make for difficult reading at various points," Picard acknowledged, with a smile. "Particularly toward the end."

"No wonder," said Parmak. "A repulsive book."

He kept one eye on his friend as he spoke. "A fantasy of eternal and permanent Cardassian conquest—"

"That's unfair," Garak protested.

"You think so? An abject Bajor, defeated and obedient? The obliteration of the entire Klingon people? What about the whole final act—the loving, meticulous description of the fall of the Federation? Culminating in the triple flag of the Union flying above a ruined Paris? Are you sure I'm being unfair?"

"I admit that I agreed with you, once upon a time," Garak said, "and certainly that must be the reason the book was licensed for publication, but when I read it again . . ." He looked around the space where his father's house had once stood. "I read it almost on this spot, in fact, but down in the cellar, while all around me the Jem'Hadar were bringing this city low, and I couldn't read it the way I always had. At every possible point, Preloc allows her non-Cardassian characters to express contrary viewpoints—"

"Only for them to be destroyed," Parmak said.

"Not all of them," Garak said. "Not the doctor."

"A book in which the doctor survives?" Crusher said. "I like it already." They all laughed, and Parmak conceded that this was a point in the novel's favor. "But I'm intrigued to hear you say that you read the book differently," Crusher said. "What changed?"

"To read it while my own world was being destroyed? How could I not see it as comment upon our crimes, rather than exhortation to greater crimes? Preloc's imagination was *vast*. We know this from her other works. I'm prepared to accept that this was her intent—even if that does mean she got a seditious text past the Order's licensing committee."

Picard laughed. "Point to Preloc."

"Game to Preloc," Garak replied. "And gladly conceded."

"Even so, Elim," Parmak said, a fond expression on his face, "perhaps it was you that changed."

"Then the book changed with me."

"What happened to her?" Crusher asked, suddenly, not entirely sure she wanted to hear the answer. "To Preloc?"

The two Cardassians exchanged a look. "She died before the Central Command lost power," Parmak said. "She had a state funeral. You could call it a happy ending."

"Certainly happier than many that came after." Garak's eyes darkened as he surveyed the city. After a moment, he roused himself. "But Kelas and I have an argument along these lines every time I come home. You've not yet told me your opinion, Captain."

Picard rested his chin upon his hand. He, too, contemplated the city. "As I read," he said reflectively, "I became increasingly struck by the similarities with one of humanity's great dystopian novels, *Nineteen Eighty-four*—"

"Yes!" Garak said. "What an excellent comparison to make!"

"How have you read so much human literature?" asked Picard.

"At one point I had more time on my hands than I knew what to do with," Garak said. "Reading about home was too painful and, besides, given that I was surrounded by humans and looked likely to be in that calamitous condition for some time to come, I thought it best to learn something about you. Since hardly anyone would talk to me, I resorted to books—"

"What Elim is trying to say," Parmak said, "is that he's besotted with your culture."

Garak frowned at his friend. "'Besotted' isn't right. . . ."

"You prefer 'enamored'?"

"I'd prefer . . . *'intrigued.'*"

Parmak smiled. "Whatever you say, Elim."

"Thank you." Garak turned to address Picard again. "But let us compare and contrast those books, Captain, because I believe you're onto something. At the end of Orwell's book, we are asked to picture a boot stamping on a human face forever."

"An image of permanent conquest and the total obliteration of freedom," Picard said. "Thus making it a very apt comparison with *Meditations on a Crimson Shadow*—"

"But that's not how Preloc's book ends," Garak said. "This is exactly my point! How does Preloc's book end? It ends with the human doctor finding the rose in the ruined chapel. Orwell's book concerns the will to power—the lust in some of us always to dominate, always to try to extinguish dissenting voices.

Preloc's book does this too, yes, but she insists on the survival of an opposing dynamic. The desire for freedom, the irrepressible urge within each one of us to live according to our own lights. No boot in the face forever. Instead we have a rose among the ruins."

Picard laughed and drained his glass. "That's a very persuasive argument!"

"Yes, well, I'm a very persuasive man."

"Don't encourage him, Captain," Parmak said. "He's wrong on every count about Preloc, and the sooner he admits that, the better. He's reading what he wants to find in that book, not what's actually in it. How could Eleta Preloc, the darling of Central Command, have produced the book he thinks she wrote?"

"I can see it," said Crusher slowly. "A book about surviving the end of the world with one's spirit intact? What could be more Cardassian?"

Garak was smiling at her. "Thank you, Doctor Crusher. You have understood my point. Kelas, admit defeat."

"You're not all-conquering yet," said Parmak. "But I'm content to leave the last word on the subject to the human doctor."

Crusher raised her glass. "I'll drink to that."

After the captain and the doctor departed, Elim Garak and Kelas Parmak remained outside for a long while, amongst the memorials and the long shadows cast by the lamplight, and they were comfortable enough together not to talk. Garak pottered around peacefully, pulling a few weeds and deadheading some wilted flowers with the ruthlessness of the experienced gardener who knows that they will bloom again.

"I remember us rebuilding these, Elim," Parmak said, at last, gesturing to the nearest of the memorials. "After Mondrig's men kicked them down. It was dawn when we finished. You and I and Alon Ghemor stood here together and watched the sun rise. I was exhausted, but I remember feeling more hopeful than I'd ever been before in my life." He rubbed his eyeridge. "Poor Alon."

Garak did not reply. Savagely, he dealt with some longweed that was winding its way around the *mekla*. Despite his offhand treatment of the subject over dinner, tomorrow's debate was preying on his mind.

"Are you worried about Temet?" Parmak asked, watching him.

"I'm always worried about those who demonstrate lust for power. Always."

"So what are you doing about it?"

"Besides tomorrow's foolishness? What makes you think I'm doing anything else?"

"Elim . . ."

"What can I do, other than what I'm doing already, and what I've already done? I've spent my life in service to Cardassia, and I've done my best, in recent years, to atone for what I did in the past. I've tried to secure peace for our people. If those people now want to throw away all that hard work and elect a man like Evek Temet, then they're welcome to him."

Parmak smiled and shook his head. "You're not going to let Evek Temet take power."

"Well, fortunately for me, and as she is always keen to make clear to me, that is the castellan's affair. My chief business is to ensure that relations between the Union and the Federation remain as cordial as they possibly can."

"This is something I've never asked you about—why not an alliance with the Typhon Pact, Elim? Why the Khitomer Accords? I remember watching Klingon officers standing in the ruins of this city and laughing as they kicked their way through the dust. Why them, and not the Pact?"

Garak himself had pondered this when Bacco had made her offer of alliance. He too recalled scenes such as Parmak described, and they still rankled, deeply. But a Cardassian could look anywhere around the quadrant and see grudges and enemies. The difficulty was learning to look around and see friends.

"I like Nan Bacco," he said.

"Forgive me, Elim, but that's hardly grounds for an alliance—"

"No? What better grounds are there? If I like Nan Bacco—which I do—and she likes me—which I venture to suggest she might—then from that basic affinity grows friendship, and from that friendship grows trust. Isn't this exactly what organizations such as HARF and our own reconstruction committees have hoped to achieve? To put former enemies along-side each other, and have them work together con-structively, and from that to let friendship emerge? Don't underestimate the importance of respect and friendship in diplomacy, Kelas. You can't do deals with someone you don't respect."

"But the *Klingons*, Elim . . ."

"What's that old saying? 'My friends' friends are not necessarily my enemies—'"

"That's not an old saying; you just made it up."

Garak smiled.

"Don't be coy, Elim. Tell me what you're think-ing."

Garak sat down and wiped the soil from his hands. Parmak, who knew him, had guessed correctly: there was indeed another motive behind his desire for this alliance. Something that went much deeper than cal-culating the odds and deciding that the Accords were a better bet for his world than the Pact. Softly, he said, "What we choose to do at this point in our his-tory is critical for us, Kelas. I'm no longer willing to allow us to indulge our worst impulses. My intention is to remake the Cardassian soul."

Parmak looked at him fondly, and with great compassion. "Nothing *too* ambitious, then?"

Garak laughed. "Merely a small project to keep my mind ticking over as I approach old age. And I must thank you for your contribution to my diplo-matic efforts tonight, Kelas. I cannot think of anyone better to demonstrate to Captain Picard and Doctor

Crusher that decency is a universal quality, and that not all our people lust for power."

"So you do have Temet in mind." Parmak all but rubbed his hands together. "I cannot *wait* for tomorrow. What are you going to do to him?"

"I'm going to do exactly what Rakena Garan's aides tell me to do. Temet is unequivocally her business. She's the one that has to secure a consensus in the Assembly to defeat him and remain castellan." Garak looked longingly around his garden. "I've been thinking of retirement."

Parmak snorted. "You? Retire? Don't be ridiculous. You'll die with your boots on."

Garak shuddered. "Don't say things like that."

"This is why I don't believe you're not playing some game," Parmak said. "It doesn't sound like you, letting someone else run the show."

"I promise you, Kelas, I had no intention of finding myself exposed to such public scrutiny. I let my concentration slip for a moment, and the castellan volunteered me."

"What do you have in mind for him?"

Garak shifted uneasily. "I could, of course, do what I did in the past. Pursue Temet with impunity. Set out to destroy him, and have him destroyed. But if I've learned anything from our bitter and bloody history, it's that I cannot control everything, and that trying to do so only leads to murder. I'm not going to forget that. I'm never going to forget that."

Parmak stood up. He went over to his friend

and put his hand on his shoulder. "Good," he said. "Good."

They smiled at each other. Above them, a few faint stars twinkled in an obsidian sky.

"And so I have to trust our people," Garak said, "will not fall for the lies of a man like Temet. In my heart, I believe that most of our compatriots feel the same as we do—that each of us who lived through those years bears some responsibility, however slight, for the calamity that overcame us, and that denying this will only bring us full circle. Perhaps destroy us for good, next time. Therefore it is incumbent upon each of us to prevent it happening ever again."

"A lot of people suffered, Elim. It's easier to blame than to accept blame."

"I know. I also know that few have hands as bloody as mine. But in my heart, Kelas"—he tapped his chest—"I believe our people have become wise. They won't listen to a Dukat again."

"It's good to hear you sounding optimistic."

"Well, I wouldn't go that far. . . ." Garak shivered, suddenly. "It's getting colder. Shall we go inside? A game of *kotra* and *kanar* before bed?"

Parmak laughed. "But you always win, Elim!"

"And thus the time when you must win is surely close at hand."

They clasped hands, and Parmak pulled Garak to his feet. "I'm not convinced of the logic of that," Parmak said, but he accepted his inevitable fate, and they went inside, and closed the doors, and settled down opposite each other with the board in between. And, although the Cardassian ambassador to the Federation's preoccupation with what might occur the following day allowed his opponent numerous unexpected openings, Parmak's time did not, in fact, come. As the contest moved toward the endgame, Garak relaxed and secured a comfortable victory. But the board upon which he was accustomed to playing was set to change, irrevocably.

Next day the dust lay thick on the city, and Garak's spirits were low as he made his way to his encounter with Temet. The castellan's office had sent a skimmer for him and, as promised, the castellan also had sent one of her aides to brief Garak thoroughly. Garak looked out of the window at the fug. Watching the shadowy figures of the city dwellers, their faces hidden behind their masks, he could not find the heart to feign interest in what the young man was telling him. As the skimmer drew up outside the studios, the young man gave up.

"I know you're going to do whatever you want, but please, Ambassador, *please*—don't lose your temper."

"Lose my temper?"

"Just try to remember that there's an election coming."

"I believe," Garak said softly, "that I may have heard something about that."

"The surest way for this to backfire further on the castellan is if somebody as closely associated with her as you are loses his temper. It makes us look out of control."

"Be assured I'm perfectly in control."

For some reason, this didn't mollify his companion. Garak felt a twinge of conscience. He had no desire to make this young man's day more stressful than it must be already. But he was truly angry at Evek Temet's self-interested sabotage in what had constituted months of work on his own part. He was also, although he did not care to admit it, rather nervous. Garak looked out of the window of the skimmer and breathed in, slowly, as if to succor himself with the processed air of the skimmer.

"I promise to remain very calm," he said.

"In which case, we might just get through this unscathed," said his companion. "And I might still have a job by the end of today."

When, Garak wondered, as they got out of the skimmer, *had everyone become* so *rude?* Cardassia had always been such a courteous place. This was the downside to everyone being able to say exactly what was on his or her mind, he supposed. At the entrance, another youth who was surely barely old enough to vote met them and whisked them briskly past security and through the building. *A whole new industry,* he thought, as they went through open-plan spaces filled with researchers and journalists and editors. *Plenty to keep everyone busy. Perhaps we should have thought of this before.* He realized that his presence was attracting considerable (if discreet) attention:

heads turned as he passed, and lowered voices spread the news of who exactly this was. Garak's unease grew. He'd spent a lifetime avoiding exposure. Now every step was bringing him closer to the spotlight.

He entered the studio. Bright lights. Holo-cameras. Plenty of action. Three comfortable seats arranged easily around a table, looking not remotely like an inquisition room. And yet, and yet, all these *lights* . . .

Garak looked around covertly. He counted three potential exits out before Ista Nemeny appeared, looking like the holder of a winning ticket in the Union lottery. No wonder. Getting Ambassador Garak to appear on this sideshow was surely going to be one of the coups of her career. Most likely she would pick up a professional award; be feted by her colleagues; devote a substantial portion of her eventual memoirs to the event . . .

"A pleasure to meet you face-to-face, Ambassador," she said, offering her palm.

Garak lightly touched his palm against hers. "The pleasure is most surely mine."

"You're not nervous, are you?"

Garak laughed. She had the instincts of an interrogator. "It is on the whole more fun to be the one who is *asking* the questions."

Someone standing nearby gave a small, involuntary gasp. Nemeny grayed, but her smile remained gamely in place. *I must remember not to joke about the Obsidian Order in polite company,* Garak thought. *It's not as if we were a laughing matter.*

"This is a new world to me," he said gently. "Perhaps you might explain what happens?"

Collecting herself, Nemeny walked him around the studio, running through the procedure. She introduced him to the show's anchor, a stocky, white-haired man named Edek Mayrat who had a northern accent and who impressed Garak with his ability to look him fearlessly in the eye. Garak took his seat to Mayrat's right, and therefore was ideally placed to watch the arrival of Evek Temet and his entourage.

He'd seen Temet on many 'casts, of course. You couldn't get away from him these days. He was in his mid-thirties, and handsome, but in an obvious way that had never held much appeal for Garak. He had a clear speaking voice that sometimes shook (when he spoke about "our boys," for example), and there was an intriguing uncertainty over where and how he had served during the Dominion War. Temet insisted he'd been on the Romulan Front, but records from that conflict were of course very fragmentary, and there weren't many people left to confirm or deny his stories. A few months ago, a woman from a client world—a non-Cardassian—had claimed that she had been forced to serve the Cardassian unit stationed there as a comfort woman, and that Evek Temet had been one of her regular patrons. Unfortunately, the woman concerned had been exposed as ex-Maquis, and the furor that followed precipitated a breakdown that had necessitated her being hospitalized. The story had died a quiet death. There were many alive who did not want all of their actions during the dying days of Dominion rule to be subject to scrutiny. Still, a part of Garak yearned to have unfettered access to Evek Temet for a short while. Just for a *short* interview.

The young man, seeing Garak, smiled. "Ambassador," he said. "Nobody from the castellan's camp willing to come along?"

"You'd have to ask them," said Garak. "I'm here to talk about my work."

Brash music signaled the start of the 'cast. Garak didn't take his eyes off Temet. Beads of sweat appeared on the young man's brow. Perhaps it was the lights. Garak felt warm himself. Mayrat introduced them both (Garak appreciated the reference to his own impeccable war record alongside Damar) and then, as agreed, Mayrat turned to Temet first.

"Representative, your party has been at the forefront of criticizing the current administration's handling of Starfleet's withdrawal—"

"Indeed we have, and I have to say that it comes as no surprise to me that Rakena Garan has once again bowed to pressure and given her Federation allies unwarranted control over our affairs. It doesn't suit the Federation or Starfleet to have a powerful Union on its doorstep."

"Actually," said Garak, "it *does* suit them to have a powerful Union on its doorstep—as long as it's a free and democratic Union, and not some cut-rate version of our so-called glory days. Strong allies are good allies. Weak allies are a liability."

"That's beside the point," Temet said. "What concerns me here is not so much the meddling in our affairs, but the signal this sends to the Cardassian people. It's ten years now since the end of the Dominion War, and we have worked hard to rebuild our lives and our worlds after the devastation wrought upon us by the Jem'Hadar."

Not just the Jem'Hadar, Garak thought. "Let us not forget that entry into the Dominion was met with dancing on the streets in many of our cities—"

"Yes, yes, we hear this all the time," said Temet. "How long are we going to be punished for the crimes of those who went before us? When are we going to be allowed to move on from that whole sad affair?"

"A '*sad affair*'—?" Garak was speechless. Yes, he supposed, that was one way of characterizing the collapse of one's civilization and the cruel proof of its hollow moral core. Although, Garak had to acknowledge, if you *had* spent part of the war raping women, you might indeed want to somehow "move on" from the whole business.

"Rakena Garan does not speak for all of Cardassia," Temet said, gaining confidence from Garak's silence, "and she must listen to the voices that disagree with her. I'm therefore going to take the opportunity to announce that Cardassia First will be holding a rally outside the HARF compound in two days' time so that the people of this city can make their opinions known."

"A *rally*?" Mayrat was clearly taken by surprise.

Even the most cosmopolitan of us, Garak thought, *can't quite reconcile ourselves to the idea of people being permitted to stand outside and say whatever they like. The whole notion certainly fills me with terror.*

"Rakena Garan speaks from the past," Temet said. "Cardassia First speaks for the future. We're not paralyzed by a sense of guilt about what we did or didn't do more than ten years ago. We're optimistic about our Union's ability to be strong again—but we think we should be strong on our own terms, and not terms dictated by the Federation. We're going to have our say, and the castellan must listen."

Time to be heard.

"And you think stirring up riots is the best way to do that?" Garak asked.

"If you have any evidence that I've incited people to violence, Ambassador, I'd like to hear it. Besides, freedom of assembly is a democratic right these days. You of all people should be pleased to see people able to exercise that—"

"Oh, *please*!" Garak cut him off. "You have about as much interest in the democratic rights of the Cardassian people as I have in the hound-racing—"

"Liking democracy less than you thought you would, Ambassador?" Temet smirked. "Perhaps you're nostalgic for the old order."

Later, Garak would decide that it was the smirk that tipped him over. At the time, he was simply nothing short of astounded that Temet had chosen to allude to his past. It seemed so . . . *rude.*

Putting aside the lights, putting aside everything, Garak addressed himself directly to Temet. Eye to eye. Better men than Temet had broken under that gaze. "It has been my observation," Garak said, "that people who play with fire tend to get burned. Take care, Representative. I'd hate to see you . . ." He pondered the correct word. *"Combust."*

Temet produced a close facsimile of outrage. "Ambassador, was that a threat?"

Slowly, carefully, as mindful of the effect of how he moved as he had always been in these face-to-face encounters, Garak placed both hands in front of him and leaned forward.

"Young man," he said, holding Temet's eye and not blinking, "I am nothing more than a servant of the Union. What threat could I make that could *possibly* strike fear into your heart?"

A chill descended upon the studio. The specter of the old Order now loomed very large; a dark shadow over the arena of debate. Nobody spoke. From the corner of his eye, Garak saw Nemeny mouthing frantically at Mayrat: *Say something!* He seized the moment before it disappeared.

"Memories seem to be very short on Prime these days," Garak said. "So let me remind you"— he swept his hand outward—"let me remind *anyone* who happens to be watching, of the reasoning behind the treaty that we signed at the end of the Dominion War. What happened to our Union was a tragedy, but a tragedy substantially of our own mak-

ing. *Dukat . . ."* As he said the name, Garak realized
how rarely it was said this day, and how much like a
hammer blow it sounded. Still, it had to be said. People had to remember that name. Finding the holo-
camera, Garak addressed the Union. "Skrain Dukat
found fertile soil here for his lies. We let him loose,
and now we live with the consequences of the fire
he brought down upon us. Corat Damar and then
Alon Ghemor tried to bring us back from that. Now
Castellan Garan is doing the same. What has Representative Temet done other than encourage fire start-
ers? I knew Corat Damar. I knew Alon Ghemor." He
turned to face his enemy. "You are no Corat Damar.
You are no Alon Ghemor."

Garak stopped and let all the implications of
that statement seep through. Mayrat got there first.
"Are you implying that Temet has more in common
with . . . with another former leader? That's something of a comparison to make—"

"I stand by it," Garak said. Impatiently, he waved
his hand. "I have no time for these games. Either we
are serious in our attempt to remake ourselves, or we
are not. But I condemn in the strongest terms this
man's attempts to make his name at the expense of
our collective future. You're playing with fire, Temet.
Our Union deserves better."

Garak stopped. *I think I've said everything I wanted
to say.* At a signal from Nemeny, Mayrat began to wrap
up the show. When the cameras had stopped, Temet
rose from his seat and stalked out without a word.

Garak stood up more slowly. He looked around the silent studio, indisputably ruler of all he surveyed. Nobody spoke to him or met his eye. Eventually, Nemeny, after a short whispered conference with Mayrat, approached him.

"Well," she said. "That was . . . must-see broadcasting."

"We've gone through a great deal to achieve freedom of speech," Garak said, letting his voice carry around the room. "It seems a shame to waste it on telling lies to each other."

Unexpectedly, Nemeny smiled. "You're not hearing any complaint from me, Ambassador."

"Nor from me," said Mayrat, and he leaned forward to press his hand against Garak's. "I enjoyed that. I hope you'll come and speak to us again, Ambassador."

"With the greatest of respect, I'd rather be eviscerated."

Mayrat smiled. "I don't think that's likely to happen. Not on this channel."

Nemeny and Mayrat escorted him from the room like an honor guard. Outside, the castellan's aide was standing with one hand to his forehead. Garak, stopping in front of him, said, "Was that the kind of thing you had in mind?"

The aide didn't reply. Garak, hearing the soft buzz of the personal comm in his pocket, took it out and read a message from Parmak: *Dying with your boots on, Elim?*

Four

Dear Doctor,

I enclose the following holo-recording without further comment other than to note that I was press-ganged into performing this duty and did not request it.

EG

So far this new job had been easy money for Rakhat Blok. The man with the smile and the data card welcomed his call and invited him to come and meet him at the same *geleta* house before it opened for the evening.

The house was empty, with that musty air that lingers around all drinking holes when the clientele are not there to provide life and color. Two big men stood at the door, barring entrance. Seeing Blok, they let him in and without a word one of them took him to a small booth at the back of the house. Blok's new friend, who went by the name of Dekreny, was sitting there.

Dekreny was wearing an expensive suit and displaying on the table in front of him several state-of-the-art communication devices. Blok, instructed by the wave of a hand, sat down opposite. Two small glasses of *kanar* materialized, and then Blok was intensively grilled about his childhood on that remote client world (dull); his time as a foot soldier (dull with occasional moments of terror); his opinions on the Romulans (unkind), the Klingons (unspeakable), Starfleet (unprintable); and his hopes for the future (ill-defined).

Eventually, Dekreny stopped asking questions. He drained his glass and clicked his fingers. One of the big men appeared. "This is Leng," Dekreny said. "He'll show you around."

Blok stood up. Uncertainly, he said, "Does that mean I have a job?"

Dekreny smiled. "Of course you do, son. Just do what Leng tells you, and you won't be short of money again."

That had been slightly over a week ago. Since then, Blok hadn't done very much. With some money Leng gave him, and following specific instructions, he went and bought himself some smarter clothes. Then all he had to do, it seemed, was turn up at the *geleta* house at the same time every night and look big. The locals, the company he'd talked to that first night, jeered when they saw him in his new clothes, then cheered and bought him drinks. Now he was like a piece of the furniture, comfortable and familiar.

One night, just as Blok was about to head over to the house, Leng contacted him and instructed him to wait on the street corner instead. Blok waited for a while, worrying he'd got the wrong place, and then a big skimmer pulled up. Leng hopped out and told Blok to drive. He directed him out to the very southeast of Torr, a desolate area where ruined tenements backed onto the shells of unreconstructed industrial units. They stopped outside one of these, in better condition than the rest. Blok, at Leng's instruction, stayed in the skimmer, at the controls. Looking in the mirror, he saw two other men, both wearing dust masks, come out of the shadows to talk to Leng. He watched as they opened up the big sealed door on the nearest unit. Then he watched a group of females— maybe seven or eight of them; small, most of them, petite—shuffle out and into the back of the skimmer. Some were crying; some were simply shocked. He stopped looking before they were all inside.

Leng got back into the passenger seat, and they set off. They drove in silence for a while, along the empty nighttime perimeter route that looped around the south of the city. Eventually Leng said, "You all right with this?" and Blok said, "None of my business." They dropped their cargo off on the western edge of the city at a big building with a high wall around it and lots of security lights that came on suddenly and flooded the place with a harsh glare. Blok stayed in the skimmer throughout and this time put on music. Afterward, Leng dropped him off at his corner, and Blok went home and slept until mid-afternoon. Then he went to the *geleta* house, which he did the day after, and the day after that.

This evening, Dekreny sat at the back as usual. Blok and Leng stood around and did whatever he asked, which was mostly bring him drinks and clients. The mood of the company, however, was more fractious than on most nights. The big screen on the wall kept showing pieces of a debate that had happened earlier in the day between a politician called Temet and a man called Garak who wasn't a politician but who had obviously outclassed the other man. The company—who seemed to be big fans of Temet—was furious about the whole thing.

"Who does this Garak think he is anyway?" one of them asked. "Has anyone ever cast a vote for him? Evek Temet is a member of the Assembly—"

"I heard he's hardly been on Cardassia Prime the last twenty years," someone said. "He's been living with Bajorans and humans. What does he know about Cardassia?"

"To be fair," someone else pointed out, "he's got a good war record, or so they say. Didn't they say that at the start?"

"He said Temet was like Dukat as if it was a bad thing," someone at the back muttered. "It was Damar that got us into trouble with the Dominion."

Still, whatever their opinion, he'd certainly pummeled Temet in that debate. So much so that the representative had arranged for another interview, this one on the steps of the New Assembly, with the new big building behind him. He looked very serious and businesslike.

"What the ambassador doesn't understand," Temet was saying, *"is these constraints on our military spending are a double betrayal. Not only is there the implication—offensive, of course—that we can't be trusted simply to defend ourselves responsibly, but this has practical consequences for people's lives. The research, the development, the manufacturing—all of this could bring jobs to Prime and to other parts of the Union and help our economic reconstruction. It's as if the Federation—and the other Khitomer powers—don't want us strong and equal again. And these are supposed to be our allies! The ambassador seems to think that these people are our friends—and they might be his friends. But I say, with friends like this—"*

"Allies," someone said, and spat on the floor.

"I wonder how it got out about that spending limit," Blok said. A couple of people sitting next to him looked up. Blok didn't talk much; he stood there mostly. "You'd think they'd want to keep a lid on it."

"So let me remind the people of the city that Cardassia First will be holding a rally, in two days' time, outside the Headquarters of the Allied Reconstruction Force. And I say to everyone who's concerned about this agreement, everyone who's concerned what it means for their lives and jobs, and who doesn't want to see Cardassians as second-class partners in this or any alliance, that you're right to be concerned, and you should come out and let yourself be heard."

"What I mean is," Blok said, "you'd think they'd want to be extra careful. So I wonder how it got out."

One of the people next to him, the man with the white scar, gave him a cold smile. "Don't you know? Because we're everywhere. People like us—we're everywhere. The constabularies, the civil service, the CIB." He laughed. "A hundred people could have leaked that document. A thousand." He looked at Temet, looked at him hungrily. "They can't stop us. We'll be in charge soon. Rakena Garan's a dead woman walking."

Blok turned back to the screen. A woman was speaking now, a woman with flashing eyes and a fierce way of talking.

"If Evek Temet wants people to show how they feel, then we'll show him. We showed him and his thugs in Cemet, and we'll show him in the capital. He can claim he talks for the people, but the people will show him what they really think. We won't be lied to by men like Evek Temet ever again, and we won't let men like Evek Temet take charge again."

"Bring it on, gorgeous," said the man with the white scar. "We're ready for you."

A rumble of agreement passed around the room. Blok, looking around, suddenly realized how much they loved this. How much they reveled in it. How they were spoiling for a fight.

From behind him, he heard the snap of Dekreny's fingers. Obediently, he went back. Dekreny smiled at his prompt arrival.

"Blok," he said. "I've got a job for you tonight.

Let's see if you're up to it. Leng will go with you, show you the ropes." He looked past Blok's shoulder. "And because it's such an important job, I'm sending Colak with you too."

Blok looked behind him. Colak, it turned out, was the man with the white scar, the one who thought the castellan was a dead woman walking.

"Just to make sure that everything goes smoothly," said Dekreny. "Do you understand, Blok?"

And Rakhat Blok thought that he was indeed beginning to understand, very well.

Arati Mhevet sat at her desk in the darkening office. A file of statements from HARF personnel about their last sightings of Aleyni Cam lingered unread on the padd before her, and she had not followed up the analysis into the images Aleyni Zeya had given her. She was breaking her own rules and listening to a newscast. A woman who called herself "a representative of an East Torr residents' organizing committee" was being interviewed about her opinions of the rally promised by Cardassia First.

"It's a disgrace," she said. *"Starfleet has done more to put the Union back on its feet than most of the representatives in the Assembly combined. Where was Evek Temet during the first days of the reconstruction? Nobody has ever answered that question. But Starfleet was here. They had no reason to help us but they did, and they kept helping even during the Borg crisis when they surely could have made better use of their resources—"*

As Mhevet listened, her heart sank lower and lower. She agreed with everything the woman was saying, but the tone of it—angry, hostile—increasingly disturbed her. As she brooded over this, a shadow fell across her desk. She looked up to see Tret Fereny, bearing two cups of red leaf tea.

"You're looking glum," he said. "Trouble?"

"Cardassia First can send as many people as it likes to harass our friends in the Federation. But we'll be there to show our support. They won't win. Never again—"

Mhevet reached out and switched off the 'cast. "Not yet. But there might be."

Fereny eased himself into the chair opposite. "There's always trouble in Torr, or about to be trouble. That's the nature of the place."

"Mmm." It hadn't always been like that though. Once upon a time it had been a proud place, full of hardworking people who helped each other. But they'd gotten into a habit of mistrust, letting what kept them apart from the rest of Cardassia run so deep that they expressed themselves in violence. "There are some deep divisions in Torr, I agree. But people there have more in common than they like to admit. I wish they'd realize that."

"I don't see that the people of North Torr and East Torr have much in common, Ari. Different aspirations, different politics—"

"They all suffered the same at the hands of the Jem'Hadar."

"I'm sure you know the place better than I do."

Fereny's eye fell on the padds. "How's the Aleyni case going?"

"Oh, you know . . ."

"Do you need me to handle anything for you?"

"I'll cope," she said. "It's routine."

"I wouldn't know," he said, and sighed. "Still not been let loose on a murder case. Still, I suppose it makes sense to have you handle it, given your links with HARF. The whole case must be even more sensitive now. Sounds like things are more strained than ever between the government and the Federation."

Mhevet idly examined the first file. "I think it will take more than the death of a lieutenant to destroy an alliance."

"You think so? You sure it's not a sign that there's a deeper problem?"

Mhevet scrolled the file up and down. Words whizzed past, empty of meaning. "What do you mean, Tret?"

"Come on, Ari. I know you. Nothing gets past you. You must know which way the wind is blowing around here."

"I'm still not with you."

"Ari, they've stopped serving human coffee in the canteen. There was a directive about it from on high. A directive. About the coffee. The *human* coffee."

She blinked at him. *Go on.*

"It just seems to me that people who are considered friendly with the Federation might find themselves suddenly on the outside once they've gone." He nodded back down the corridor. Toward Kalanis's office. "Nobody wants to find themselves out in the cold," he said, and gave her a meaningful look.

Mhevet closed the file and switched off the padd. "If you did know me," she said, and stood up, "you'd know I never discuss politics at work. Directive 964. None of us should." Harsh, perhaps, since the directive was increasingly honored more in the breach than in the observance, but she wasn't going to break it herself.

The young man looked mortified. "Ari, I'm sorry, I didn't mean to offend you. I just wanted to hear what you thought—"

"Don't worry. Thanks for the tea, Tret," she said, and left.

She drove around aimlessly for a while, through the dusty evening, pondering what Fereny had said, and wondering too whether friendship between the Federation and the Union was indeed an impossible dream. Mhevet did not like to think that this might be the case. She had worked well with many Starfleet personnel over the years. Was that all over now? Was that friendship coming to an end? Had it only ever been temporary? Why did so many of her compatriots hate these people who had only come to help, and who had not, on the whole, blamed ordinary Cardassians for the calamity that they had brought upon themselves?

At the next junction, Mhevet swung the skimmer around and headed toward the north end of Torr. She passed through the once-familiar streets, remembering old times here when her family had been intact, and she stopped at last outside a small *geleta* house. She sat for a while in the skimmer, contemplating her next move, and watching a few familiar faces go in. At last, she got out of the skimmer and went inside.

Conversation stopped immediately. The company glared at her, united in their hatred. "Well, well, well," someone said from the back, "look who's come to visit."

"You've got some nerve coming here, Arati Mhevet."

"It's a long time since you've dared to show your face here, Ari. What's brought you here tonight?"

"What are you after, Ari? Dinner? Dancing? Treachery?"

Mhevet ignored them all. She said to the house owner, "Is he in the back?"

The house owner nodded. Mhevet strode through. Sure enough, there was Dekreny, with his usual posse. A new one Mhevet hadn't seen before. She filed that away for later.

"Hello, Ari," Dekreny said. "How's the family?"

She ignored the jibe. "I have a dead Bajoran on my hands."

Dekreny smiled. "Good."

"I wonder why this made me think of you."

"I bet I'm never far from your thoughts."

His gang laughed. Mhevet leaned forward. "I know what you are, Dekreny. Known for years.

You're like a tumor. Not even the Jem'Hadar could destroy you. But I know all about you. You won't win this city."

"The *city*?" Dekreny burst out laughing. "Oh, Ari, you're *way* behind the times!"

"Nobody gets away with murder," she said. "Not on my watch." Mhevat turned and strode back through the house, his laughter still ringing in her ears. *I should be watching these people,* she thought, furiously, *not stuck with a murder case.* Fereny could handle that: wanted to handle it. She should be here. This was where she belonged. This was what she worked for.

"Reta," she muttered, as she fired up the skimmer, "I hope you know what you're doing. I hope you've got this all under control."

"Cardassians," said Margaret Fry, "never fail to surprise."

Šmrhová watched Worf refrain from commenting. But would it be any surprise if the Cardassian people decided, in the very last days of Federation presence on their world, to send them off with a demonstration complaining about the evils the Federation had wrought upon their world? "They're certainly contradictory," she offered.

"Contradictory or not," said Picard, speaking from his ready room on the *Enterprise, "we now have to take these threats seriously. What happened in Cemet last week could easily translate to the capital, could it*

not? In which case the HARF compound could find itself a focus for violence. Any thoughts on how to proceed?"

"Would a show of strength be in order?" Šmrhová suggested. "Anyone approaching a HARF installation with the intent to commit acts of vandalism or violence should be clear in their minds that these compounds are defended not only by the current personnel, but by the presence of the *Enterprise.*"

"No," Fry said, shaking her head. "That would send entirely the wrong message. We have to let the city constabularies come to the fore here. Anything else will undermine years of work reestablishing the legitimacy of the police across Cardassia Prime. I know that this is not how we hoped this withdrawal would happen, but for the Federation, in its last days on Cardassia Prime, to signal that the democrats are only in power because of our support will be disastrous. The Cardassians *have* to police this wave of unrest themselves."

"Commander, what if they cannot?"

"I believe they can."

"But if they cannot?"

There was a silence.

"Then the will is not there," said Fry. "And all our work has been for nothing."

"Captain," Worf said, "I think for the moment we should stay calm. When we looked outside earlier, there were no more than twenty or thirty people gathered there. That is hardly the makings of a riot."

That was fair enough, Šmrhová admitted to herself.

And everyone she had seen looked pretty young—there'd even been a few kids. A lot of banners were being waved—and there was some shouting when they'd shown their faces—but certainly no attacks.

"I take your point, Number One. But my understanding is that the opponents of these people intend to make their presence felt, and that is what is likely to mean an escalation toward violence."

"Yes, sir, that's possible. However, it is their hard-won right to come and say what they think, and Commander Fry is correct when she says that the constabulary should be left to handle all this."

Šmrhová slowly nodded her agreement. "I take back what I said about a show of strength. Right now it would be provocative. We're leaving. The Cardassians are saying good-bye to us by shouting at each other, making a few speeches, perhaps throwing a few stones. We should let them get on with it, and leave as and when we said we would."

The security officer saw that the captain was nodding. *"Let's hope that stones and speeches are all we get, Lieutenant."*

"It's true that this could go either way," Worf admitted. "But it is not our business, sir, and the Cardassians should be the ones to handle it. Anything else will add fuel to the fire that Cardassia First is stoking."

"What matters is that the Cardassian people don't start to become afraid," Fry urged softly. "This kind of violence depends on people feeling that the world around them is becoming unstable. What ordinary people on this world fear most is a return to chaos. The best thing that we can do is signal our absolute trust in the Cardassian constabularies to handle this situation."

"Do they have the resources to do so?" asked Worf. "Not to mention the will?"

"I can only hope so," said Fry. "Soon we're not going to be here. The withdrawal is happening, Commander. Soon it will be out of our hands."

"Very well," said Picard. *"Put everyone here and on HARF installations across Cardassia Prime on alert. Take all sensible precautions. But under no circumstances is any Starfleet officer or Federation citizen to get involved. This is Cardassian business, and the Cardassians must deal with it themselves."*

Despite his speechifying in the *geleta* house, Colak once in the skimmer was a model of taciturnity. Even Leng was more talkative. Colak sat in the back, one finger running lightly along his scar, and he didn't say a word until the skimmer turned off the main throughway and into a scruffy district well inside North Torr. The street lamps were low and sporadic and didn't do much against the dust anyway. Blok saw shadows hurrying along the walkways and in and out of dark doorways. They reached a small square surrounded by low, squat buildings made from emergency plasticrete.

"Stop here," said Colak, "on that corner."

Blok did what he was told and the three of them got out of the skimmer. The building they were outside was some kind of shop. A harsh bright rectangle of artificial light marked the entrance; the windows were barred and covered in cheaply printed posters offering cheaply produced goods. Blok looked around. Music was thumping out of an open window across the square. Nearby, two sickly *tiatha* trees were struggling to stay alive, black branches clawing upward. A few figures, flitting past, saw the men and hurried on.

"Put your masks on," said Colak, and Leng and Blok obeyed. Colak, reaching into the skimmer, brought out two large bats for playing *kitik*. He handed one to Leng and the other to Blok. "Go on," said Colak. "Get it done. We don't want to be hanging around here all night."

Leng didn't need to be told twice. He squared his shoulders and went inside. Blok, hesitating, glanced past Colak. A few people had gathered. Not too close; but close enough to watch. From inside the shop, there was a scream, suddenly cut off, and the sound of something smashing.

"You waiting for something?" Colak said.

"No—"

"Then get on with it. Or do you have a problem? Something I need to take back to the boss?"

So this was a test, Blok realized, to see how far he'd go. To see how loyal he was. "I don't have a problem," he said, and went inside.

Leng had been hard at work. The place was a shambles: glass and food and drink all mixed up. As Blok walked in, Leng took another swing at a couple of densely packed shelves, and their contents came tumbling down. The shelving followed. The shop's proprietor, a small man, cried out, begging Leng to stop.

"Shut up!" Leng yelled. He nodded at Blok. "Get him outside. Our man wants a word with him."

Blok strode over to him, his footsteps crunching. He hauled the man up and dragged him outside. Behind him, he heard Leng yell as he took another swing.

There were a lot more people outside now. They were wearing masks too, but flimsier, little bits and pieces of cloth. One or two simply had a hand over their mouths. Some of them were whispering and muttering, but this all stopped when Blok and the shopkeeper came out. Colak, standing to one side with his arms folded, said, "Well, look what we've got here. Tried to go independent, did we?"

"I didn't!"

"We don't like that."

"I swear I didn't!"

"We particularly don't like it when it's the Federation you go into business with."

There was a pause. "I swear I didn't," the man said.

"Shut up," said Colak and then, to Blok, "Hit him."

"What?"

"Are you stupid? Hit him!"

Blok stepped forward. But before he could do anything, someone pushed his way through the crowd. "You lay one finger on him and you won't be the only one hurt here tonight!" a young man, hair aggressively short, fists clenched by his sides, said. "You leave him alone!"

Colak turned his attention on him. "Who are you?"

"I live here," he said. "And you can't come here and attack people like this. We're sick of it! We're sick of you! You won't get away with this!"

"You reckon?" asked Colak. He turned to Blok. "Go on," he said.

"What?" asked Blok.

"He's said his piece. And he's free to do so. So show him the consequences of free speech."

Blok did what he was told. He took a deep breath and half closed his eyes, lifted his bat, and hit and hit and hit over and over. When he opened his eyes again, the young man was lying on the ground at Blok's feet.

"Nice job," said Leng. "Very nice."

Colak stepped forward and addressed their audience. He had a gleam in his eye. *He loves this,* thought Blok. *He loves all this.*

"People like this," said Colak. "They're not right. They love humans. They love Bajorans. They think we can all be friends. But we can't. Starfleet wants us under its thumb. And when we're down on our knees again, the Bajorans will come to Cardassia and they'll do what they always do. They'll murder our children. And people like this"—he tapped the toe of his boot against the young man on the ground—"that's what they want for you. But we won't let that happen."

Colak's voice was getting louder. *Nobody around here would miss this,* Blok thought, whether they were standing right here, or sitting at home with the windows shut and the sound up on the screen.

"You know who we are!" Colak yelled. "And you need to understand—all of you—that it's not Starfleet that runs things around here any longer, and it's not those traitors at the constabulary. There's only one power around here, there's only one law— and that's us. Remember that. You can lead happy lives and you can lead safe lives—but only if you understand who lets you do that. And that's us. You get that?" He reached down and pulled the young man's head up by his hair to show his bloodied face. "There's no place in North Torr for people like this. And soon there'll be no place on Prime for people like this. So each of you, go on home and decide—whose side are you on? Ours? Or his?" And with that, he let the man's head fall back against the ground.

There was silence. The music across the square had long since stopped. "Get in the skimmer," Colak ordered, and Blok and Leng did what they were told.

They drove off. In the distance, Blok could hear a siren, but he couldn't tell whether it was coming closer or going away. His sight went fuzzy. He shook his head and tried to concentrate, but it was no good. He pulled over to the side of the road, got out of the skimmer, and threw up, violently.

When he was done, he felt Leng's hand upon his back. "Don't worry," Leng said quietly. "You'll get used to it."

They got back into the skimmer and drove on. After a little while, Colak spoke. "Dekreny will be pleased with you," he said. Blok, glancing up into the mirror, saw that the man's eyes were shining. "You've not seen anything yet, Blok," he said. "Wait for the rally. That's going to be a good night out, believe me. We're going to have some fun."

The skimmer was now heading straight into the heart of North Torr.

"It's all going our way," said Colak. "There's nothing we can't do. There's nobody we can't touch."

If you walked out of the city that night, out north beyond the ruined mansions of Coranum, past the home and the garden that Elim Garak had raised over his father's ruined house, and on out into the hills, you would come in time to a point where you could stop and look back and see the whole city below you. Watching the lights, and distanced from the clamor, you might persuade yourself that this was a city at peace. Cities don't sleep, but in their night hours they can convey a sense of ease, of a place running on automatic until morning arrives.

But this is not a city at ease, and our players do not have the luxury of rising above the city tonight. They are embedded in it: embedded in its passions, its hopes and histories, its rivalries, its long-held grievances. Arati Mhevet lies unsleeping in bed, listening to sirens, and pondering her case. Pondering who might murder a man whose work in life was to bring greater understanding between enemies so that they might be friends. Pondering what that work might be, who might take an interest in it, and why it might take him into North Torr late one evening. And when she finally admits to herself that nobody is that simple, and that Aleyni Cam must be something other than he appeared, she gets out of bed, because she knows that sleep is impossible, but there is nothing to be done until the morning.

Aneta Šmrhová is not sleeping tonight either. She has taken herself up to the third story of HARF's central administrative block, the highest building on the compound, and she is watching lights gathering outside. She is reminded of those ancient movies, where the villagers come with torches and pitchforks. No wonder she is not sleeping. In the early hours of the morning, she is joined by her superior officer, a grim-faced Worf, who says nothing, but hands her a padd and informs her that these gatherings are happening across Cardassia Prime. As night falls, groups of people are coming out under cover of darkness and dust masks to stand outside the Federation compounds and signal their disapproval. Oddly, this information comforts Šmrhová. It tells her that she is not alone. It tells her that nobody at HARF will be sleeping tonight.

Elim Garak is awake too, but then one might hope that a man such as Elim Garak does not sleep easily. Indeed, one might consider the punishment light, when weighed against the crimes he has committed: murder, torture, aiding and abetting tyrants. Those deeds are, of course, all in the past—but still one might consider it suitable penance that tonight Elim Garak cannot sleep for fear that murderers and torturers and those who would aid and abet tyrants are coming ever closer to taking control of his beloved home. He in turn might take consolation from the knowledge that his castellan has not slept either. He is not alone in his fears, although the night is very dark, and the shadows of his blood-soaked past are very close.

But some people are sleeping tonight. In North Torr, a little girl has nodded off in front of the holoscreen in her tenement flat, and she will sleep until her father gets home in the early hours, fresh from some trouble with his friends. Kelas Parmak is sleeping too, with a clear conscience. And Jean-Luc Picard is sleeping well tonight, high above this world in his quarters on the *Enterprise*. Picard knows that on the hard, bare world below, good people have matters in hand, and that a man in his position with any sense sleeps when he can, storing up reserves for unforeseen crises. Picard is a wise man. Because far in the distance, sirens are wailing, as if not only Cardassia Prime but a whole quadrant is suddenly on high alert. And in the very early hours of the morning, ship-time, Jean-Luc Picard will be woken by the insistent chime of a communicator, and he will be confronted by a shocked and ashen Leonard Akaar, bringing the news that Nanietta Bacco, the president of the United Federation of Planets, is dead.

Part Two

The Response

"Qo'noS is the enemy. Brute force will be overcome by other force."

—Preloc,
Meditations on a Crimson Shadow,
Vol. II (Qo'noS), 6, xii

Five

My dear Julian,

What can I write? What can I say? What can any of us say? I was with Bacco, in her office, not three weeks ago. We went through the final terms of the agreement, shook hands, and then she tore apart Torlak's anthology. (She was not harsh enough.) How at ease we were in each other's company! We both knew how close our civilizations were to a true and lasting friendship. We were proud of how far we had come and what we were about to achieve.

What did a leader of yours once famously say, when asked what a politician most fears? *Events, dear boy, events.* Events have indeed overtaken us, in the most tragic and shocking way. But events are not random. Events have instigators. We will find the instigators of this crime, and we will bring them into the light, and we will punish them. Our peoples have been cheated of our chance to come together in celebration. So let us be united in our grief, and in our desire for justice.

I find I cannot write more.
Elim Garak

Jean-Luc Picard sat and watched as his senior staff filed silently into his ready room and took their places around the table. Geordi La Forge; Beverly Crusher; Hegol Den, the ship's Bajoran counselor; and Rennan Konya, the deputy security chief. Worf and Šmrhová remained on Cardassia Prime, liaising with the Starfleet personnel at HARF. Quickly Picard sketched for his team what Akaar had told him: that during the formal ceremony to mark the opening of the new station, President Bacco was assassinated, and that a Bajoran was under arrest.

"A Bajoran?" Konya said. "For what reason?"

"It seems that the individual concerned did not approve of the president's growing friendship with the Union, and particularly the Cardassian admittance to the Khitomer Accords."

Hegol Den covered his eyes with his hand. "The Occupation casts a long shadow," he said. "How terrible if Nan Bacco was the latest casualty."

"Now perhaps you understand why I've asked Commander Worf and Lieutenant Šmrhová to remain on Cardassia Prime. I want to send a very clear message that the friendship between us is not in any doubt. This is a critical moment for the alliance." He looked around the table. "We must not let the shadow of grief darken our hearts and poison our actions toward others."

He watched as his senior staff agreed.

"What happens next?" Crusher prompted gently.

"What happens next is that a president pro tem will be appointed," Picard said. "After sixty days there'll be elections."

"And what about the *Enterprise,* Captain?" asked La Forge. "We were here . . . well, we were here to take Bacco home, weren't we?"

"I'll be speaking to the president pro tem later. No doubt there'll be new orders. My guess is that the flagship will be wanted back home." Picard looked with compassion around his team. "In the meantime—speak to your staff. Support them, and let them support each other. This is a time of deep sorrow for all of us. We're all grieving; we're all in shock. I'll be making great demands on each one of you over the coming weeks. On us falls the burden of the grief of others. We were expecting to welcome our president here to Cardassia Prime and to escort her home after an act intended to further the cause of peace across the quadrant. Instead we find ourselves bereaved. We must honor her memory by doing our duty. Speak to the people in your care. Speak to each of them, face-to-face. I shall address the whole crew later today. And after that . . . a ceremony to remember her, for anyone who wishes to attend. Although I doubt any of us will ever forget Nanietta Bacco."

*   *   *

Dim morning light filtered feebly through a clouded window. The last dust storm of the year had rolled in from the plains. All through the night the dust had been silently gathering in the cover of darkness. The sleepers of the city woke early, coughing and gasping at a dark morning without a sunrise.

In a quiet antechamber in the castellan's wing of the new Cardassian Assembly, Elim Garak sat with his hands folded in front of him, waiting to be called into his meeting. Grief, he knew, did strange things and this, he supposed, explained his current state of mind. For Garak was blisteringly angry with himself.

He had not seen this coming. Something this huge, this terrible—and he had missed the warning signs. This terrified him. Yes, of course there were people with other agendas, of course there were people who wished to steer Cardassia onto a different course. Garak spent his days second-guessing his opponents and what they might do, laying careful plans that looked well beyond the next day into the future. And still he had not seen this coming. All his careful calculations, his patient work, slowly moving his beloved Union toward a state of greater safety— all for nothing. All bets were off now. Yesterday's squabbles over the fine print of the agreement seemed petty and pointless. Someone had struck to the very heart of the alliance—and he had not seen it coming.

Garak studied his hands. There were faint scars all over them from his numerous previous trades.

Soldier, murderer, torturer. The fine-tuned weapon of empire. But also he had been a tailor. And a gardener.

What am I? What use am I?

Garak stood abruptly and walked over to the window. Outside, the world seemed still, as if uncertain how to respond to this news. Dust crept even into this well-protected place. Garak breathed on the window and then, with one fingertip, drew a shape in the mist: a long stalk and petals on the top, a *perek* flower. His fingertip was now red from the dust.

What did I miss? What did I not see?

Nan Bacco, I am so sorry. . . .

The door opened behind him. Garak wiped his hands with a quick movement. One of the castellan's aides approached him: a youngish man with a tired air about him. "She's ready for you now."

Garak nodded and went through into the castellan's office. Rakena Garan was sitting behind her desk. She too looked exhausted, and they didn't bother with pleasantries, instead sitting in silence while the aide poured out ettaberry tea: pale green, sweetly scented, a balm to sandpaper-dry mouths, scoured throats, and sore eyes. Garak drank eagerly from his cup, and the castellan too sighed in relief as she picked up her tea.

"What do we know about the new president pro tem?" the castellan asked, as soon as they were alone.

"He's Bajoran." Garak left it at that.

The castellan put her hand to her forehead. "This is appalling. Bacco and I were speaking only a matter of days ago. We discussed what we would do while she was here. . . ."

"I understand completely," Garak said.

"Have you met him? The new man?"

"I've been in the same room as him on several occasions. On at least two of those occasions we were participants in the same conversation. I would not say that we have talked, exactly." Garak was conscious, suddenly, of how much his usefulness to this woman had depended on his friendship with Bacco.

The castellan stared into her cup, as if that might contain advice or answers. "I'm speaking to him later this morning. I'll be telling him that we are declaring a Union-wide day of mourning and that I personally will be leading a public commemoration event on the day that she was due to arrive here on Prime."

"I would sincerely hope that Ishan Anjar would hear the genuine sorrow behind all of that," Garak said.

She eyed him. "That's what you hope? And how do you *think* it will be heard?"

Garak drank the last of his tea. "It's important at this point that we make no statements that can be misconstrued. We should limit ourselves to communicating our deep sense of loss at Nan Bacco's death and our desire to comfort and support our allies at this time."

"But will he *hear* that?"

"Rakena, if you're asking me whether a man who was brought up under the Occupation is likely to be well disposed toward the Cardassian Union, my answer is 'no.' If you're asking whether I think that Ishan Anjar will set the tone for Cardassian-Federation relations from here on out, my answer is 'I have absolutely no idea.' But we should bear two things in mind: Firstly, this is a temporary appointment. There will be elections in sixty days. Who knows who the president will be then? Secondly, while the Federation is of course currently on high alert, my sense is that right now our allies want to know who their friends are. You and I . . ." *For all our differences,* he silently added, and then he paused until she looked at him, in the hope that she would hear all that he was trying to say. "You and I are friends of the Federation. We are devastated by this news. If we remain constant now, we will do more to secure this alliance than anything else we have done throughout the entirety of our careers."

She played with the handle of her cup. "I know that I'm not what you wanted as castellan," she said, after a while.

Garak, startled, thought: *This is new. . . .* He said: "I have absolutely no idea what you mean by that—"

"I am not Corat Damar. I am not Alon Ghemor," the castellan went on, with a slight smile. Of course she would have watched the 'cast too. "And I know that this is a source of great disappointment for you. But I have always tried to do my best for the Cardassian people."

Garak felt ashamed. He didn't think he'd been so transparent. "I don't doubt that, ma'am," he said quietly. "I've never doubted that. It's true that I regret the deaths of both those men deeply. Rakena, they were my *friends. . . ."*

And they were both murdered. Garak looked down at his hands again. There was still a faint red stain on his fingertip from before. He rubbed urgently with his thumb and took a deep breath. "You should be proud of what you have done during your time as castellan. The Union is not an easy ship to steer. I know that! You've done exceptionally well keeping us afloat so long, and keeping us steady. I hope you'll be rewarded for this at the election." He added, "You'll have my vote."

That wasn't a lie. And it seemed to help.

"Thank you," she said. "Thank you." The castellan cleared her throat. "I understand what a wrench it must be for you each time you leave Cardassia. I am grateful for all you do for my administration. You're tireless, Garak."

"I love Cardassia." His voice came out thick. From the dust? From the dust. "All I have ever wanted to do is to serve her people to the best of my ability."

"I understand," she said. "You do. You have."

"I try," he said.

"Will you make a public statement too? I think it would be for the best. I know you prefer to keep a low profile, but a response from someone else who knew Bacco well and who is not a politician would be helpful—"

"It will be no sacrifice for me to speak about Nan Bacco," Garak said softly. "And I shall do so in the warmest of terms."

She nodded. He rose from his chair, and she did the same. They pressed palms, and he headed for the door. Stopping there for a moment, he said, "If the architects of the alliance are now targets, Rakena . . ."

"I'll speak to Crell. You should too."

Garak left. What a great shame, he thought, that it had needed this to make them try to be friends. He walked out into the dark red day, his security detail filing into place alongside him. With his hands across his mouth and nose, he dashed toward his skimmer, sitting back in relief once he was inside the covered space. He began a missive to Crell: *Utmost urgency . . . Situation has changed . . . Know how you must be on high alert . . . But straight from the castellan . . .*

As he crafted this message, one arrived from Parmak:

This is not your doing. This is not your fault.

Struggling from her home in East Torr to Constabulary Headquarters in a skimmer with air filters that had long since been taxed beyond capacity, Mhevet choked her way through the morning traffic and abandoned all plans to speak to Starfleet Intelligence about Lieutenant Aleyni. She doubted she would be able to raise her contacts at HARF, and she would have been embarrassed to try. Assassination of their leaders was something the Cardassian people had been grimly accustomed to at one time, but there had been a sense, under Rakena Garan, that those days were passing. For it to happen

to an ally, and one who had always been a model—
the model—for stability, was horrible.

Everyone in the department was somber today,
whether they harbored friendly feelings toward the
Federation or otherwise. There was little in the way of
idle chatter. The large office was filled by the whirr of
the filtration system and occasional bouts of coughing from colleagues. The general mood—already
poor—soured when it was discovered that the bot-
tled water—a lifesaver on days like this—hadn't been
cooling overnight and was warm. On reflection, it
was only a matter of time before someone lost his
temper.

Mhevet sent a few messages of consolation to
people at HARF with whom she'd worked, and then,
listlessly, looked around the office. Work seemed to
have been abandoned for the morning. Everyone was
standing and watching the speeches in front of the
big screen at the far end of the room. There were a lot
of speeches. The most reliably Cardassian response to
unexpected events was to stop and make a speech.
Not that this was guaranteed to make them any happier. The castellan, for example, looked, to Mhevet's
eyes, shattered underneath her careful presentation.
Evek Temet too was shocked and grief-stricken: at
least, he was saying repeatedly how shocked he was
by this news, how grievous it was . . .

"Here it comes," said Istek. One of the older
members of the department, born and brought up
in East Torr, he had bitter memories of the massacre

that had happened there under the orders of Skrain Dukat. He had little time for Cardassia First. He was a reasonable choice to take over Mhevet's operations in North Torr, but he was driven too easily by anger. You needed to keep cool. You needed to keep your head. "The political point scoring will start any moment now. . . ."

"Of course," said Temet, *"if what we're hearing now is true, that a Bajoran is responsible for this obscene crime, it will be necessary for the castellan to look very closely at our relationship with the Federation. We understand the Federation's charity in bringing Bajor under its wing. This was of course what Cardassia once tried to do. Perhaps the Federation is now discovering what we have already learned, that there exists within Bajoran society a violent element that cannot live in harmony with other peoples—"*

"But why do you think this means reevaluating the alliance, Representative?"

"It's not for me to comment—"

"'But'?" Istek prompted.

"—but if I were in the castellan's position, I'd be thinking very carefully about whether the Federation is stable. First the Andorian secession, and now it seems the Bajorans are making their displeasure with the Federation system known, and in the most shocking way. Are we wise to be close to such a volatile power? There's a danger that Cardassian lives will be put at risk. The castellan should take this opportunity to rethink our involvement in this alliance, and she

won't be serving the Cardassian people well if she does not—"

Istek made a noise like a buzzer sounding. Some of the people gathered around laughed; others didn't. Mhevet, moving closer to the screen, perched on the side of a desk and watched her colleagues rather than the screen. She wondered if she should remind them of Directive 964, the bar on political discussions. But they were adult enough to know that they were in violation and, besides, she wasn't in violation. She was sitting here drinking warm water.

"Watch what's coming next," said Istek. "You'll be glad to hear you can get your requests for leave back in. He's about to cancel his rally. Stupid idea in the first place."

"I'd also like to take this opportunity—"

"And you're all about taking opportunities, aren't you, you unscrupulous bastard," Istek said cheerfully.

"Now hold on a minute," someone said, while others tried to hush both sides.

"—to cancel the rally that was due to be held to protest the terms of the withdrawal agreement. Under these circumstances, that would hardly be appropriate. But while we are prepared, out of respect, to forgo the opportunity to speak, I hope the castellan realizes how deeply people feel about this issue, and how many of us think that our concerns are going unheard. I commend the castellan's decision to hold a ceremony of commemoration, and I look forward to speaking on behalf of Cardassia First at that event."

"And we'll look forward to switching over when your smug, lying face comes on-screen," Istek called.

Some people were getting angry. Mhevet glanced over at Fereny who was standing to one side and looking anxious. He looked at her, and she shook her head. *Don't get involved.* Another man came on-screen: the ambassador who had given Evek Temet that dressing-down the other day. He was standing in front of some stone memorials in a small garden. He was serious and suave. Mhevet's father wouldn't have liked him, she suspected. This kind of urbanity had always struck him as un-Cardassian.

"Ah!" said Istek. "Now we'll hear some sense!"

"You're out of your mind, Istek—"

"This is devastating news," the man said. He clearly meant it. *"My heart goes out to all who knew and loved Nan Bacco. My deepest condolences to the people of the United Federation of Planets. It has been my privilege as ambassador to the Federation to know Nan Bacco and to have been able to work with her. I cannot think of a better friend to our Union—"*

"Yes, a tragic loss," said the interviewer. *"Do you have any sense of what this might mean for our alliance with the Federation, Ambassador?"*

"This is not a time to be thinking about politics or alliances or to make any response other than to grieve alongside our friends in the Federation—"

"But Nan Bacco was one of the driving forces behind the Union's entry into the Accords. You must be aware that many voices are now being raised suggesting that

our continued association with such an unstable power should now be open to debate once again—"

The ambassador's polish took on a steely glint. *"I would suggest in turn that such people showed a little compassion, and a little restraint. For pity's sake—a good and courageous woman has been murdered! Let us take the time to honor her life and her achievements before scoring a few points off each other."*

"Who is this man?" asked Dhrok, one of the junior investigators. "He seems everywhere at the moment."

Istek laughed. "Do you really not know who that is?"

"If I did, I wouldn't be asking, would I?"

"That's only Elim Garak."

"I'm still none the wiser."

"Ambassador to the Federation—"

"Yes, I got that."

"Adviser to Alon Ghemor. Corat Damar's right-hand man during the Dominion Occupation. And . . ."

Mhevet listened with interest. Would he say it all?

"And . . . a man with an interesting past."

No, not even Istek, who wasn't averse to the sound of his own voice, would go so far as to mention the Obsidian Order by name. It was as if everyone was afraid that the Order might hear and crawl out of its grave to torment Cardassia once again.

"Oh," said Dhrok, plainly none the wiser, "*that* Elim Garak. And why exactly should I care what he has to say about all this?"

"Because he's seen more of political life on this world that most of us have had measures of *kanar*," said Istek. "And I drink a lot of *kanar*."

Patrak, another of the junior investigators, was quivering with anger. "The man was a cold-blooded killer!"

"Listen, son," said Istek, "I don't think you're old enough to remember how things were before the Jem'Hadar got here. It was a different world. None of us are proud of the world that was—"

"Not everyone worked for Enabran Tain. Which he did happily, by all accounts—"

"I'd rather a man who understands that what he did in the past was wrong," said Istek, "than someone like Temet who goes to some lengths to cover over what he's done!"

Mhevet drew in a breath. Oh, yes, that hazy period in Temet's past, back during the Dominion War . . . Mhevet, looking around the room, was suddenly sure who amongst her colleagues would very soon be voting for Cardassia First. There were some low and angry murmurs, rising steadily—and then suddenly everything went dead quiet. Glancing over her shoulder, Mhevet saw Kalanis, her arms folded, a cold expression on her face.

"Patrak," she said. "I'm surprised at you. Istek, I'm not surprised, but I'm still furious." She looked around. "The rest of you—you know the regulations. You keep this for the *geleta* house." She glanced at Mhevet. "A word, please."

Mhevet followed her superior down the corridor.

"What exactly was that all about?" Kalanis asked.

"Just some steam being let off—"

"In contravention of 964. There's a reason that regulation exists, and it's to stop scenes like that. You were the senior person present. Why didn't you enforce it?"

Because nobody really obeyed it any longer. "It got out of hand more quickly than I expected—"

"What do you expect these days? You might have spared a thought for Fereny—his mother's brother was murdered by the Order."

Mhevet frowned. "I'd forgotten that."

"You seem to be forgetting a great deal these days, Ari. How's the Aleyni case coming along?"

"Stalled."

"Stalled?"

"I want to speak to Starfleet Intelligence—"

Kalanis looked at her sharply. "Why?"

"I think Aleyni might have been more than simply a cultural liaison officer."

"Why? What evidence do you have?"

"It's a hunch. . . . I mean, Reta, come on—'cultural liaison'? That's a euphemism for 'spy' if ever there was one."

Kalanis was thin-lipped with anger. "This is a murder case, nothing more. It's tragic, but there's nothing suspicious about it. Stop trying to dig up secrets, and start finding your murderer. In case you've been meticulously following 964 and avoiding the 'casts, you might not have grasped that there's a Bajoran at the top of the Federation now. And if the city constabulary can't be bothered to solve the murder of a Bajoran, we are going to have a great deal of explaining to do, at the highest levels."

"I'm sorry, ma'am—"

"I know you think I've moved you away from important work, but this is important too. So get busy, Investigator, and don't get distracted because you think this job is beneath you." Kalanis began to head off down the corridor but turned back and raised her voice so that it carried into the office beyond, where Mhevet's silent colleagues were now making a show of being hard at work.

"As long as I am here," Kalanis said, "Directive 964 and all it stands for are at the heart of this constabulary. We are not enemies. We serve a common purpose to protect the people of this city. That is who we are and what we do." And quietly, to Mhevet, she said, "And I expect you—you, of all people—to be making sure of this."

Six

Dear Julian,

Did I ever tell you about the funeral ceremony I performed not long after coming home? I don't mean the burials, not those . . . I don't wish to recall those, nor do I wish to make you think of them. . . . I mean for my own dead, here in what is now the garden.

I had no *perek* flowers, which was another grief. You want to feel you have done your best, but there were no flowers to be found in the city. Still, I had my knife, and I had my voice, so I cut across my hand and let the blood drip onto the ground, and I chanted all their names: Tolan, Tain, Ziyal, Mila, Damar. Does it surprise you that Tain's name was on the list? It might surprise you even more that I added Dukat.

I chanted his name because nobody else would. Somebody has to remember him. Otherwise we'll forget.

Garak

—not sent—

*   *   *

The president pro tem of the United Federation of Planets, Ishan Anjar, was an intense, understandably humorless, and plainly very weary man. Given his age, he must, Picard thought, have been brought up under the Cardassian Occupation. For the moment, the focus that President Ishan brought to the task at hand impressed itself upon Picard, as did the man's grasp of even the smallest details of what was happening on Cardassia Prime. This was not someone who gave the impression of being thrown by the situation in which he had found himself; this was someone who thoroughly grasped the gravity of the situation. Surely, Picard thought, this was to the good.

Present also in the discussion were Admiral Akaar, speaking from San Francisco, and Ishan's newly appointed chief of staff, a Tellarite named Galif jav Velk, who was with the president in Paris. When the introductions, handled briskly and without ceremony by Ishan, were completed, Picard spoke.

"I regret that we must speak for the first time under such tragic circumstances," Picard said. "May I offer my deep sympathies to you on the death of President Bacco? You must have known her well, and the situation in which you have found yourself is surely a uniquely painful and difficult one—"

Ishan waved a hand to cut him off. *"I've neither the time nor the energy to waste on self-indulgence, Captain. Let's save our strength for the crisis at hand."* He lifted up a handful of padds. *"You'll forgive me for having only read your briefings very rapidly. The past few days have necessarily involved a steep learning curve."*

"I quite understand, Mister President. Let me assure you that all Starfleet personnel stationed here on Cardassia Prime are on full alert. The *Enterprise* is of course ready to leave on your instruction—"

"Enterprise *will remain where you are for the time being,"* Ishan said. *"These reports about demonstrations outside HARF installations are very alarming. I want to make sure we have a presence in Cardassian space to remind the castellan that we take such threats very seriously."*

Velk was nodding his approval. Picard glanced over at Akaar, who was impassive.

"I'm meeting the castellan later today," Picard said. "This is surely a grave loss to her too, both personally and politically. I imagine she also takes seriously any threat to an ally of her government—"

"Yes, I'm aware that meeting is scheduled. You can inform the castellan when you see her that the withdrawal of our personnel from the Cardassian Union is now naturally on a new timetable."

"I'm sure she's expecting that. President Bacco's visit here was to sign that agreement. To continue with any such ceremony would be entirely inappropriate."

Ishan looked back with cool eyes. *"You misunderstand me, Captain. I'm not talking about shifting the date forward. The Federation's withdrawal from Cardassia is under review, and our forces will remain—"*

Akaar was plainly startled, as he broke protocol and interrupted the president. *"This is a radical shift in policy—"*

"Perhaps so, Admiral," Ishan replied. *"Nonetheless, while Nanietta Bacco may have been satisfied that our interests in Cardassian space are secure, I am not."*

"While I understand this perspective, sir," Picard said carefully, "I must say that any such change in policy is risky. This withdrawal agreement is the culmination of many months' work. There is a consensus on both sides that Starfleet is no longer required on Cardassia Prime. Our continued presence here will, in effect, be an occupying force of a friendly power—"

Velk intervened. *"The Federation is under threat. Surely you take that seriously?"*

"Of course I do—"

"The responsibility has fallen upon me," said Ishan, *"to ensure that we are protected."*

"From our enemies, yes," Picard replied. "But not, surely, from our friends?"

Velk shook his head impatiently, as if Picard was not keeping up with something that was patently obvious to him. *"We can no longer assume that our friends are indeed true friends,"* he said. *"Your own briefings tell of significant anti-Federation sentiment on Cardassia Prime."*

"Yes." Picard nodded. "There is some ill will. There is never going to be perfect consensus. I imagine we could find many in the Federation who would not speak well of Cardassians—"

The moment it was out, he could have bitten off his tongue. Ishan's eyes hardened.

"Quite," he said. *"And they might well be speaking from experience."*

"All that we are saying," Velk said, *"is that we must not be complacent. We must be sure, even of our friends. If, as you say, the castellan is so well disposed toward us, she will surely understand."*

"One can only hope that she will," Picard said.

"Tell me how this murder investigation is proceeding," Ishan said.

"I have no further information on that—"

Ishan frowned. *"I wish I could feel that the Cardassian constabularies were taking the death of a Bajoran seriously."*

"I'm sure that everything that can be done is being done. The investigating officer is known to Commander Fry. I'm sure that she can give you further assurances—"

"I'm speaking to Commander Fry next," Ishan said. *"She'll be instructed to order all Starfleet personnel to remain on HARF installations for the foreseeable future."*

Picard thought of the briefings he had received from Šmrhová and Worf on the set-up at HARF, and the integration policy at the heart of all their operations. "That might be difficult to achieve if we want HARF to remain functioning—"

Admiral Akaar looked like he had swallowed something sour.

"Commander Fry," Velk said, *"must make sure all Starfleet personnel across the Union are safely inside our installations. I'll be instructing our embassy to advise all non-military Federation citizens to do the same. I'm not going to have any of our people—who have, after all, gone to Cardassia with the purpose of giving aid—be harassed or threatened."*

Picard addressed Ishan directly. "Mister President, you'd be wise to listen to Commander Fry's advice on this, sir. She has more experience with the Cardassians than any of us—" Again, he stopped himself.

"I can assure you that I have plenty of experience to draw on," Ishan said. *"Captain, you have your orders. Convey my cordial respects to the castellan, and inform her that Starfleet's withdrawal is under review. I'll be giving Commander Fry her new orders myself. And may the Prophets guide us through these difficult days."*

The channel to the president's office closed. *"'Cordial respects,' is it?"* Akaar asked. *"Garan is going to hit the roof. . . ."*

"Admiral, this is an appalling decision. I cannot think how this can be presented to the castellan as anything other than an insult. We are, in effect, signaling that we no longer trust the Cardassian government. A suspicious mind—and we need look no further than Ambassador Garak—might even draw the conclusion that the Federation thinks the Cardassians are implicated in the assassination." Picard frowned. "I assume Starfleet Intelligence is not pursuing that as a possible explanation?"

"Not that I've been told. I think you're reading too much into this. President Ishan has found himself unexpectedly thrust into the limelight in the most shocking of circumstances. I can't blame him for wanting to show his strength at every available opportunity—"

"But the long-term cost of that might be considerably greater than any temporary gain—"

"You have to consider the mood at home."

Picard pressed his fingers against his brow. "I can't even bear to think—"

"Jean-Luc, it's worse. The president is taking the correct approach. People here want to feel protected." Akaar rubbed his tired eyes. *"This is a temporary appointment. In sixty days there will be an election. I suggest we keep him happy for as long as he's here."*

"Very well, sir," said Picard, although not without misgivings. "But we run the risk of throwing away a great deal of hard work and a great deal of goodwill."

"I have every faith that you can make both the castellan and the ambassador understand. Good luck, Jean-Luc."

Aneta Šmrhová, standing in the square outside the main Starfleet building at HARF, was watching an uncharacteristically stressed Commander Fry trying to placate a young and very angry Bolian doctor.

"I know how hard this is. But it's straight from the top. I promise it won't be for long—"

"Maggie, I've got a shift starting at a free clinic in East Torr in"—the young man checked the time—

"twenty-five minutes. What am I supposed to say? 'Sorry, I can't come'?"

"That's exactly what you have to say."

"And how am I supposed to explain it to my colleagues? We're understaffed as it is—"

The security officer went back inside the building. She took off her mask and brushed the dust from her hair. Turning to Worf, who had been watching the scene from inside, she said, "I don't think this is a good idea, sir."

"It is clearly difficult. But we have our orders. We are all distressed by the news of Bacco's death. And we have seen signs already that many Cardassians are not well-disposed toward us."

"It's not the Cardassians' fault the president is dead."

Worf narrowed his eyes.

"I know that there's some pretty ugly history between the Empire and the Union, sir," Šmrhová said, "and the same is true between the Union and the Federation. That's not a reason to turn on them. It's not their *fault*."

"Our responsibility is to protect Starfleet personnel and Federation citizens here on Cardassia, Lieutenant."

"Protect them from what exactly? A few civilians who turn up and wave some banners and call us some names? We don't need to cower behind walls. They're civilians. Half of them were kids!" She kicked the floor with the heel of her boot in frustration. "If I didn't know better, sir—"

"Tread very carefully, Lieutenant."

Šmrhová subsided. "My apologies, sir."

"These orders are from the office of the president, Lieutenant. Ignoring them will only add to the confusion. Not to mention to the captain's burden. If I know Ambassador Garak at all, he will not be happy with this turn of events."

"But it's as if we're painting all the Cardassians with the same brush. It's wrong. We've both served alongside Cardassians, sir. Think of Dygan!"

Worf nodded. "Ravel Dygan is an excellent officer and an honorable man."

"I just think this is an overreaction. Are we going to put up force fields next? Point weapons outward? This place wasn't meant to be a fortress! It was meant to be where both sides could work together! If I was a Cardassian bringing my kids for their appointment at the clinic today, only to learn that my doctor is barred from walking around my city because his superiors think I'm going to attack him, I'd be insulted!"

"I remind you that a Starfleet officer was murdered in this city less than a week ago, Lieutenant."

"Yes, sir. Who knows what he was doing? Maybe he didn't pay his bar bill. Maybe he got drunk and went up to someone and called him a spoonhead. Maybe he was the attacker—"

"Whatever he was doing, Lieutenant, your fellow officer did not deserve to be beaten to death," Worf shot back. "This is not a permanent situation. A few days at most, and the city will surely have settled down, and all our people can resume their duties."

"But in the meantime, sir, won't the damage be done?" Right down at the lowest level, where the trust had been so painstakingly nurtured, over so long. *This was like seeing a few weeds,* she thought, *and bombing them from orbit.* The weeds wouldn't survive. But neither would anything else.

Worf sighed. "We can only hope not."

Sitting on a bench inside a quiet stone garden, Mhevet peered through the dim day, watching for her friend's arrival. Erelya Fhret was at the Cardassian Intelligence Bureau. Mhevet had worked with her often during the early days of the reconstruction of both the constabularies and the intelligence services. The peculiar demands of that time, what they had required from the people who had been there and willing to push through the necessary changes, had formed a bond that cut across organizations. Mhevet and Fhret probably had more in common than many of the newer people they worked alongside now.

Fhret had agreed to meet on condition it was somewhere private. Mhevet had suggested a tiny eatery near the department building that they used many times before, but Fhret had suggested this place instead and hinted that she couldn't stay long. So Mhevet had grabbed a makeshift lunch of *feyt* and warm flatbreads. The flatbreads were cooling. Fhret was late.

The dust was thick in the air. Mhevet was suffering behind her mask. She was about to give up, when she saw a figure emerge from the gloom. Masked. She raised her hand, tentatively, and then with more confidence when she saw the smart clothes and elegant hairstyle. Yes, this was Fhret. Mhevet moved along the bench to let her friend sit down.

"What have you got there?" Erelya's voice was muffled behind her mask.

"Nothing special."

"Anything's fine. I'm starving. Working us like hounds at the moment. You know, big scare on."

Mhevet split the breads between them. They dug into the *feyt*, expert at eating in a way that meant their food didn't get coated with the red grit. Between mouthfuls, Mhevet explained that she wanted to check out her suspicion that Aleyni was connected to Starfleet Intelligence. "His assignment would take him to North Torr—but during the day, during school hours. What would take him there at night? A Bajoran, in North Torr, at night? It must have been important. And, really—'cultural liaison officer'? I'm not stupid. I bet that's your info too."

"Actually, mine says information analyst." Fhret munched on her bread. "You realize you're not going to get anywhere near Starfleet Intelligence now?"

"I know."

"Have you got any water?"

Mhevet handed over a bottle. "I thought you might be able to help."

Fhret drank deeply. When she was done, she passed the bottle back to Mhevet and put her mask back on. "Sorry, Ari. This time I can't."

"But I'm stuck—"

"You're going to have to resort to good old-fashioned donkey work, I'm afraid."

Mhevet looked closely at her friend. She seemed tense, taut. "Is there something going on over at your place, Erelya?"

Fhret looked at her sharply: two bright stars of eyes glinting from an otherwise hidden face. "Why? Is there something going on over at yours?"

"Well, you can't get coffee there any longer."

"*Coffee?*" Fhret gave a dry laugh, like something was scraping along the back of her throat. "I bet you're going mad."

"Kalanis is behaving strangely—"

"Withdrawal. You two are basically junkies—"

"She took me out of North Torr. Put me on this murder case."

"Oh, I see! So that's why you're hoping there's another angle."

"No, it's not that . . ."

"What, then?"

Mhevet rubbed her eyes. "You must feel it too." She lowered her voice, although there was nobody around. "They're going. The Federation. And people are getting ready to make a move."

"People?"

"I don't know. Just people. It's like . . . any day

now all bets are off. People are maneuvering. Getting ready."

"People." Fhret brushed some crumbs from her beautiful smart dark suit. "Thanks for lunch, Ari. Sorry I can't help."

"Is that it?"

"I said I couldn't help this time. But . . ." She glanced around. "I'm getting out, Ari."

"What?"

"I won't be there soon. I don't want to be pushed, so I'll jump first. Maybe you should think about doing the same. Hey, we could go into partnership. Fhret and Mhevet, Private Investigators."

"Mhevet and Fhret. Why would I leave?"

Fhret shrugged. "You're Fed-friendly too, aren't you? Take care of yourself, Ari. Keep your head down. Who knows—being stuck on a routine murder case might be the safest place you could find yourself right now. I'll be in touch. I'll bring you a contract. Make you an offer you can't refuse." She stood and faded away into the haze.

The captain of the Federation flagship sat in the castellan's office, accepting the offer of ettaberry tea, though he had a guilty conscience. He drank a little, welcoming the soothing effect upon his mouth, and then cleared his throat and began to relay President Ishan's new policy. His audience of two, listening to what he had to say, was reacting in very different ways. The castellan was staring at him in undisguised horror. The ambassador, however, had acquired a blank expression that was doing very little to allay Picard's concerns.

Rakena Garan collected herself. "Does President Ishan understand the position that this puts me in? I've staked my political reputation on this alliance. I've put all my weight behind this agreement, permitting terms about which I had some misgivings, about which both Ambassador Garak and I had misgivings." She turned to Garak, perhaps hoping for some support, but he was sitting perfectly still. "And now the Federation wishes to renege on this?"

"Not renege," Picard said firmly, hoping this was true. "Simply to delay for a while. I sympathize entirely with your position." And he did. What was meant to be a diplomatic triumph for the castellan was rapidly turning instead into a political nightmare. "Castellan, as far as I'm concerned, nothing about our alliance has changed. This is a delay, nothing more. But do, please, understand the president's position. We have been attacked, and we have no idea who has committed this terrible crime against us—"

"A Bajoran is being held, yes?" asked the castellan. "Does this not suggest that this is an internal matter, some grievance over their world's admittance into the Federation?"

"Castellan, the investigation has barely begun—"

"A delay in the formal signing of the withdrawal agreement I could understand. It would hardly be appropriate to go ahead, given that Nan Bacco was meant to be in attendance. But from what you seem to be saying, this is intended to be a prelude to a review of the whole agreement."

Picard glanced across at Garak, still motionless and expressionless in his chair, hearing everything, giving away nothing.

"Am I correct?"

"Yes, ma'am," said Picard.

"Captain Picard," the castellan said, "is this the first step to ending the alliance between our civilizations?"

Garak jerked forward. Firmly, Picard replied, "That would be a great shame, Castellan, when we have hardly had the chance to get to know each other."

"Yet you don't seem prepared to deny it!"

Finally, Garak spoke. "Moving back from the withdrawal. Pulling your people into your installations. You're treating us like criminals, Captain," he said quietly. "And yet we're guilty of nothing." The castellan choked back a short cry of distress. Picard noted that Garak had his hand upon hers. "Rakena," he continued softly. "Remember how it was when Alon Ghemor died. Remember how distressing a time that was for us, and how we looked to our own defenses. Our friends within the Federation are surely experiencing something very similar now. I do not believe," he said, his blue eyes fixed upon Picard, "that this signals a return to the old hostilities. Let us be patient with one another, while the shock passes.

Let us not say anything rash, or do anything rash. Nan Bacco deserves better."

He had known her too, Picard thought, looking down into his cup. *Worked with her, dealt with her. They both did. This is not only our grief.*

The castellan pushed Garak's hand away and sat back with one hand covering her face. Garak watched her for a while and then turned to look out of the window. Eventually, the castellan collected herself.

"Very well," she said. "Cardassia will wait. Captain Picard, you must make your superiors understand—the longer this continues, the greater the damage will be done to me. I am your friend, the best you have here on Cardassia. If I go, people less friendly toward you may gain power. The Federation might not like what replaces me. I hope you can make President Ishan understand this."

Dismissed, the captain offered, "Castellan, I shall endeavor to do so."

Garak followed Picard out, and they stood together in the small room beyond the castellan's office.

"Captain," Garak said, in a low voice. "Please allow me to express my shock and grief at this news."

"Thank you."

"I understand the shock waves that are passing among you now. Your beautiful Federation. Its generous, hospitable people. Unbearable!" Garak shook his head. "Captain, I am committed to Cardassia's role as a full partner in this alliance—no, not simply a partner, a *friend*. I know your world very well. I've long understood what we can learn from the Federation."

"You understand that my hands are tied?" Picard asked quietly. "I must follow my orders."

"I understand. But I also understand that castellans and presidents do not last forever and that we are players in a longer game." Garak reached out, tentatively, and touched Picard upon the shoulder: a surprisingly consoling gesture. "We'll get through this. But you must trust me," urged Cardassia's most accomplished liar. "After all, I'm trusting you."

After Picard returned to the *Enterprise,* Garak stood for a while outside the castellan's office, deep in thought. *Things fall apart,* he thought.

"I think I may have spent too much time reading human literature," he told the wall.

"I'm sorry, sir?"

Garak suppressed his reflex to jump. Behind him, one of the castellan's aides was waiting to go past into the castellan's office. He had an apologetic air about him, as if embarrassed that he had gotten so close without the ambassador noticing. Once upon a time, Garak thought, that would not have happened. *I'm getting old. I'm losing my grip. The center cannot hold.*

"Can I get you anything, sir?"

"Not unless you can turn time back by thirty years."

"I'm afraid that's not within my skill set."

"Twenty years would do."

"Still sorry to have to disappoint you, sir."

"Then . . . may I have a brief period of time undisturbed with the castellan?"

The aide glanced down at the padd in his hand, looking, presumably, at the castellan's agenda. He jerked his head toward the door. "Don't say who let you through."

Garak nodded. He knocked three times on the door in rapid succession and went straight inside. The castellan was entering something into a padd. Garak closed the door behind him and leaned back against the wall, folding his arms and waiting. When the castellan was done, she put the padd aside and sat back in her chair, looking at him thoughtfully. "Who," she said, "will rid me of this turbulent priest?"

Pushing himself off the wall, Garak approached her desk. "I'll not inquire how you've become so well informed about human literature—"

"I spend a great deal of time listening to you." The castellan gestured at the chair Picard had lately vacated. "I assume that you and Captain Picard assured each other of your undying friendship?"

"There was a brief exchange along those lines, yes."

She picked up another padd and began to read. "Your advice is to sit this out, isn't it?"

"Ishan will be gone soon."

"But the damage will be done by then."

"It might."

She continued reading. Garak leaned forward in

his seat, clasping his hands before him. "I'm going to say something now that you won't like hearing, Rakena."

Her head shot up. "What do you mean?"

"I mean about Evek Temet."

She jerked her head, as if confused by this sudden change of subject. "Temet? What about him?"

"He wants to speak at Bacco's commemoration ceremony."

She drew in a breath and returned to her reading. "He's deluding himself."

"It's imperative that he speaks."

"No."

"He'll have something planned, Rakena. Don't let him sabotage the occasion—"

"Are you listening, Garak? No."

"If Ishan is concerned that popular opinion is shifting toward Cardassia First, then we need to demonstrate that we have Temet under control. That we don't fear him—"

"No!" The castellan threw down her padd with a clatter. "I've had enough of Evek Temet! At every turn, that man has tried to make political capital out of this tragedy. Well, no more! Only a few days ago, he was saying that Nan Bacco was the reckless leader of an unstable nation on the verge of collapse. And now he wants to eulogize her? He can forget it!"

Garak's alarm had been growing throughout this outburst. This was not the caution and moderation that he knew. This was unexpected, and not entirely explicable. "What's the matter? Is there something going on that I need to know about?"

"Is there something going on?" The castellan stared at him across her desk. "The leader of our closest ally has been assassinated, our alliance is teetering on the brink, and my political reputation is hanging in the balance—"

"I know all this. It's not grounds to panic. You have not been elected to this position to panic—"

"I am not panicking!"

"Very well." *You could have fooled me.* "But you must see that preventing Evek Temet from speaking at the ceremony is playing right into his hands? I can see the headlines now—'Silenced by the Castellan'—"

"*Garak!*" The castellan slammed her hand flat on her desk.

Garak, shocked, subsided.

"I must remind you," she said, "that you are the ambassador to the Federation, not one of my advisers. When I want advice, I'll turn to one of the many people who I employ in that capacity and not someone who left the political scene years ago!"

Garak looked at her in surprise. *Well,* he thought, *I believe I have just been reprimanded.*

"There is no reason for Evek Temet to expect that he can speak at the ceremony," the castellan continued, "and his assumption that he will speak is typical of his opportunism. His party isn't even one of the largest in the Assembly!"

"Not yet," Garak said.

A chill descended across the room. The castellan picked up her padd and began to read. Garak blinked. *Am I being dismissed?*

"Temet's welcome to attend in a private capacity," the castellan said, coldly. "For him to speak would break with protocol and, frankly, would be an offense to the memory of Nan Bacco."

"Do as you think best, Rakena," Garak said. "But think it through before making a final decision. You don't want to be the castellan who wouldn't let her opponents speak for fear of losing the argument. You don't have to look too far back in our history to see how badly that's turned out for those leaders."

The castellan grayed, and Garak wondered whether drawing a comparison with the late Meya Rejal was going too far. Rakena Garan was unlikely to end her political career shot in a military coup. At least, one hoped not. Garak sighed. "I wish you would trust me," he said. "I wish you would listen to me."

"Why?" she shot back. "What reason have you given me to trust you? At every opportunity, you have conveyed to me your regret that I am neither Corat Damar nor Alon Ghemor. No, I'm neither of those men. But I am the castellan of the Cardassian Union. And I'll make my own decisions."

That brief moment of friendship, born of grief, they'd shared only the day before now seemed an age away. Wounded, Garak struck back. "You might not be in the position to make decisions for much longer."

"But I'll have done what I thought best, and I'll have done it for the good of the Cardassian people. You're not the only one who loves this world, you know. You don't know best." She gestured toward the door. "Thank you for your time, Ambassador. When I require your help—*if* I require your help—I'll contact you."

There was no further good-bye. Garak rose from his chair and left. The aide, seeing his face, looked alarmed.

"Don't worry," Garak said. "You're not the one in trouble."

He went out into the stifling morning. One of his security detail took him around to his skimmer. He sat in the back, confused, and more than a little hurt. He had believed that their antagonism was over and that, if nothing else, the death of Nanietta Bacco might have taught them that friends were not to be squandered. He didn't mind when people reacted this way to something he had done. It was all he deserved. But this seemed unjust. . . .

A message arrived from Parmak: *What's going on?*

Under his breath, Garak said, "I wish I knew."

Elim Garak was not the only servant of the Union to find himself at odds with a superior that morning. Arati Mhevet, arriving at the department, found instructions on her desk to report to Director Kalanis as soon as she arrived. She looked around hastily for tribute, but there was nothing, so she armed herself with two cups of the canteen's red leaf tea. The moment she went through the door, she knew that Reta wasn't going to be satisfied with this or any other offering.

"Sit down, Investigator."

Mhevet sat down. She put the cups onto the desk and pushed one forward.

Kalanis ignored it. "Tell me what you were doing in North Torr the other night."

"I was . . . going home."

"Unless you've moved houses and not notified the department—which is a minor infraction punishable by a verbal warning—the Blind Moon *geleta* house is only on your way home if you're taking the scenic route. Given that Torr is the least scenic part of our city, if not our Union, tell me why you were there."

There was no point lying. She probably knew already. "I went to see Velok Dekreny."

"I see. And how does this relate to the murder of Aleyni Cam? I assume Dekreny didn't confess on the spot?"

"No, he didn't."

"No, I didn't think he had, given he's not in custody. So you went to see him. Why?"

"Just a little verbal warning."

"Not provocative at all. And why did you go and see your friend from the CIB?"

Mhevet looked at the other woman in shock. "Reta, are you having me followed?"

"It's my business to know what every single member of this department is up to. And when I tell one of my investigators to investigate a murder, I expect her to do just that. Not pop into every *geleta* house in North Torr and hassle the patrons—"

"Velok Dekreny is more than that, and we all know it—"

"Nor do I expect her to have lunch with a friend in the spying business."

"What is this? The Obsidian Order? Am I going to be given a list of approved acquaintances next—?"

"Don't push your luck, Investigator."

Mhevet swallowed. "My apologies, ma'am."

Kalanis picked up her tea. She swilled the liquid around in her mouth, as if to clear away the taste of something unpleasant. "The Aleyni case is being talked about at the highest level. Ari, are you watching the 'casts?"

Reta knew how she hated watching the 'casts. "A little . . ."

"The president of the Federation has been assassinated."

"Yes, I know."

"Good. You might also want to be aware that diplomatic signals from the Federation to the Union have changed overnight from cloyingly congratulatory to barely cordial. Meanwhile, this department appears blithely untroubled about the unresolved murder of a Federation officer. I was very clear to you at the outset, Ari—*this* is your case. Not policing North Torr, not talking to the CIB—solving a murder."

"Someone else should be doing this! Everything's

heating up in Torr, and you're wasting me on this! Fereny is desperate for his first murder case."

"I don't want Fereny on this! I want you on this! Ari, I didn't think I'd ever have to say this to you, but you will take me step-by-step through all that you've done on the Aleyni case."

As she ran through it, Mhevet could see how it was embarrassingly little. She'd tracked his movements, but still there was the gap between entering North Torr and turning up dead in Munda'ar. She showed Kalanis the messages he and Zeya had received, but she had to confess that she had gotten no further tracing them back to their source. Mhevet explained that she believed his job would be worth exploring more for any hint that he might have been involved in intelligence work, but that she was unlikely to get close to anyone at Starfleet Intelligence right now.

"This is hardly anything, Ari," Kalanis said, when she finished.

"I know. I'm sorry."

"What about the kids?"

"What kids? Cam didn't have any kids—"

"Ari! The kids who found the body! You've not spoken to them?" Kalanis shook her head. "Will you see to that as soon as possible? And please, Ari! Understand how important this is. I'm relying on you, more than ever."

"Yes, ma'am." Mhevet stood up. "I really am sorry, Reta."

Kalanis relented slightly. "All right. Get on with it. Thanks for the tea."

"You're welcome."

"But for the love of the Union, will you find a source of coffee in this city?"

"I'll do my best."

Fereny was hovering outside. "Trouble?"

"Nothing I can't cope with," Mhevet said.

"Anything I can do to help?"

Mhevet headed for the door. "Don't let her get her hands on any coffee."

Seven

Julian,

Have you ever wondered how you will be remembered? I've told you how, as a boy, I helped my father-uncle Tolan tend the memorial grounds to our great and good. How I longed that one day a great statue would be built in my memory, to honor me, and to be a physical symbol of all that I had achieved on Cardassia's account. Latterly, I believed that the alliance might be that. In many ways, I'm still that same boy at heart.

But my reason tells me that none of us are remembered in the end. All our labors are ultimately fruitless. In the end, we're all ashes and dust.

Garak

—*not sent*—

A warm wind, blowing up from the coast and through the city, had cleared away some of the haze, and the sky, bright yellow and startling, could now be seen. But anyone who had spent some time living in the Cardassian capital could have told you what this meant. From Elim Garak to Arati Mhevet, from Commander Margaret Fry up to the castellan herself—they all knew what the last warm wind of the year foretold. Later today the thunder would start: low, dry rumbles without rain. The night would be stifling, horribly hot, and so would most of the day after. Then the rain would come: relentless and red.

But for the moment, you could loosen your mask, and breathe, and be outside. It was a timely respite, allowing the people of the city to make their way toward the place where, once, the old memorial grounds had stood at the heart of the Tarlak sector. Nothing remained of these old triumphal markers that Elim Garak had tended as a boy: great towering monoliths commemorating the long line of guls and legates whose ambitions had brought Cardassia to her knees. Now there was only a single tall stone there, black as obsidian, pointing upward toward the sky like a finger lifted in censure or warning.

"Is this a monument to the particular memory of anyone?" Picard asked Fry, in a low voice.

They were sitting together on a small dais that had been raised near the stone. On Picard's left side sat Garak and, beyond him, was the castellan. Various other dignitaries sat in the rows behind them: senior Federation figures from HARF and the embassy; other Starfleet personnel; not to mention members of the Cardassian Assembly and numerous other local officials. Picard had not failed to spot Evek Temet, sitting near the back. Altogether, about fifty people were seated here, but in the open ground beyond the black stone, many more thousands had gathered to pay their respects to the dead president of another civilization.

"No," said Fry. "There's a separate monument to Corat Damar over by what was once the Veteran's Bridge, and there's a stone garden to remember Alon Ghemor over by the new Assembly. But I don't think that this obelisk was dedicated to a particular figure."

"It is intended as a cenotaph in the truest sense, Captain," Garak said. "An empty tomb remembering the dead who are buried elsewhere or who could not be found to be buried. Eight hundred million, give or take. Our reminder to ourselves of where we brought Cardassia." The ambassador studied the gathering crowd. "I saw another in a city on Earth that I visited with Benjamin Sisko. I've seen others too. . . ." He sighed. "Do all civilizations create memorials like this? Empty tombs for the uncounted dead? If I thought about that too much, it could depress me."

"Yes, indeed," said Picard softly.

"We are not, on the whole, a religious people, Captain," Garak said. "But we remember very well. And we understand this particular grief all too well."

The memorial had a restraint that Picard had not expected from Cardassians who were presented with the opportunity to make speeches. There were a few speeches early on from city spokespeople who had been due to meet Bacco on her arrival: community organizers from Torr; a teacher from a free school; the director of an inoculation program in a rural district to the north. But these speeches were short and heartfelt. Perhaps Cardassians had come to feel that funerals were not to be lingered over. Perhaps they had become too experienced at conveying their grief succinctly.

After these speeches, there was a short procession. Ten of the people sitting on the dais, Picard included, carried scarlet flowers to put at the base of the black pillar. Garak had explained the significance of the particular flowers to him earlier; they were *perek* flowers, traditional for funeral services. As they performed the task, a chant rose up: Nanietta Bacco's name, said nine times nine. It started at the dais, but spread quickly around the whole gathering, her name picked up and lifted by thousands of people to fill the hard yellow sky. When the chanting finished, silence fell and it seemed to Picard that Bacco's name echoed for some time after. When all was quiet again, the castellan stepped forward to make her own speech.

Then it happened. Picard didn't notice at first. He had been deeply moved by the chant, and his head was down. The castellan, in a clear and dignified voice, began to address the gathering. "Friends," she said. And then Picard heard Fry gasp, and Garak hissed under his breath and whispered, "I'll *destroy* you for this!"

Turning his head to see what was happening, Picard saw Evek Temet and two young men on either side of him covering their mouths with black cloth. At first, Picard thought that they were putting on dust masks. And then he grasped what the gesture was supposed to symbolize: *We have been silenced. We have not been permitted to speak.*

"Did you hear what happened over at the black pillar?" Fereny could hardly contain himself. *No,* Mhevet thought. *Because I try not to listen to the 'casts. Because our boss told us to obey Directive 964.* "Why don't you bring me up to speed?"

"During the speeches, the representatives from Cardassia First took out gags and put them on. You know, because the castellan wouldn't let them speak."

"I think I get the symbolism."

"Preposterous behavior," said Istek, whose instincts always led him toward any potential fight. "There were people there from Starfleet and the Federation. People who've been here for years, helping out. It's a national disgrace—"

Patrak, coming over, was more than willing to give Istek what he was looking for. *They're welcome to tear each other apart,* Mhevet thought, *only I wish they wouldn't do it on top of my desk.*

"Temet was only trying to say what many people are thinking," Patrak said. "The terms of the withdrawal are unfair! So much for free speech when the castellan won't let you speak—"

"A commemoration ceremony for somebody who's been murdered is hardly the place to make a political point—"

"Where else can he make it? The castellan won't debate with him. She didn't even send anyone from her administration to debate with him. She sent that ambassador. . . . What's his name again?"

"Garak," said Fereny.

Istek smiled happily. "And didn't he wipe the floor with your precious leader? Cardassia First!" He laughed. "I'd pay good *leks* to see Elim Garak take on Evek Temet again."

Mhevet stood up and picked up her bag. "I suggest you all get back to work, gentlemen," she said. "Kalanis wouldn't like this." They wandered off and settled down, but she knew that once she was out of the door it would start again. Fereny, watching her get ready to leave, said, "Anything I can do, Ari?"

"No, all fine."

Which it most certainly wasn't, Mhevet thought, as she drove out to Torr. A low roll of thunder accompanied her as she turned onto the road that led into the east part of the district. Temet's latest gesture was sure to rouse passions beyond the offices of the city constabulary, and Mhevet was starting to get a bad feeling about how this day might end. It was getting hotter, not cooler, and heat had always been part of what triggered violence on Cardassia Prime. People who couldn't sleep went outside and got angry with one another.

Mhevet took the skimmer along a wide street of busy shops, passing an open-air food market and pulling up outside one of the apartment blocks that made up the district. She stopped briefly at the market to pick out some *leya* fruit to take as a gift. Heading back over to the tenement, she rang the buzzer for a loft on the top floor. While Mhevet waited, she looked down the street. She had lived near here for a while after quitting the constabulary, and she had become immersed in the district's busy life. Eventually she'd moved on. The area was a shadow of its old, vibrant self, but the people who had survived, and those who had returned, were doing their best to put something of that old spirit back into the place.

The buzzer sounded to let her inside the building. Entering, Mhevet strode up the stairs to the loft. She hammered on the door and a Cardassian female opened up.

"Ari," she said, in surprise. "What brings you here?"

"Just passing. How are you doing, Irian?"

The woman glanced back worriedly over her shoulder. "I'm fine. How are you?"

"The usual." Mhevet looked past Irian into the loft. "Is she about?"

"Yes, but I don't think she'll be pleased to see you."

"I only want a quick word."

With a sigh, Irian opened the door wider and let Mhevet enter. The loft was small, but it was overflow-

ing with books and pamphlets and some gorgeous
artwork: weavings from the north continent; Feder-
ation-style batik; an Oralian Way mask. Gifts from
friends; part of the informal economy that had always
operated in this part of town. There was a comforting smell of homemade *aytlik* soup. Mhevet felt a
pang of nostalgia for the time she had spent here. But
those days were gone, and she'd chosen to leave them
behind and would have to live with the consequences
of that decision.

At the kitchen table, another Cardassian female
was sitting hunched over a battered old personal
comm, bashing away at what Mhevet assumed was
her latest article. Probably about what had just happened at the black pillar.

The woman looked up from her writing. Her
face darkened at the sight of Mhevet. "What are you
doing here?"

Mhevet held her hand. "Hi, Coranis."

"You've got a nerve coming here—"

"Sit down, Ari," said Irian. "I'll get you some ettaberry tea. Iced?"

"Great, yes," Mhevet said, wiping her brow and sitting at the table. Irian kept up a steady stream of calm
small talk about the heat, the inevitable forthcoming
storm, and the astonishing fact of ice for the tea. When
the tea arrived, Mhevet brought out her own token
of friendship, the bag of fruit from the market. Irian
took one of the *leya* fruit and bit into it with evident
pleasure. Coranis had been glowering the whole time.

"So," Mhevet said. "Plans this evening?"

The two women glanced at each other. "Are you here on official business?" asked Irian.

Technically, of course, Mhevet was no longer overseeing operations monitoring extremist and radical activity across Torr, so she couldn't be here on official business even if she wanted. But these two didn't need to know that. "I'm here as a friend."

"A friend?" Coranis gave a bitter laugh. "Nobody who wears the badge you do is a friend of ours."

"Nonsense," said Mhevet, firmly. She'd heard this many times before. "But anyone who intends, for example, to take advantage of a hot night and go and make the streets of Torr a little less safe will be pushing at the limits of my patience."

"Make Torr less *safe*?" Coranis was openmouthed. "How can you come here and say that to us? Do you know what's going on in the north end—?"

"Of course I know—"

"People are being attacked. Their businesses are being destroyed. Where are you and your people when that's happening, Ari? Why are you turning a blind eye? Are your friends in the constabulary earning a little on the side from all that?"

Mhevet took a long, slow sip of cooling tea. "That's a serious accusation, Coranis. If you have any evidence of connections between organized crime in North Torr and the city constabulary, I suggest you tell me—"

"Evidence?"

"Don't scoff. You've no idea the amount of hard work and effort that goes into what we do. If I tried to lock someone up without proof, you'd be the first one screaming abuse of power—"

"If you want evidence, you just have to spend an evening in North Torr with your eyes open," Coranis shot back. "But I guess that's too dangerous for you and your brave colleagues over at the department. You leave the place to gangsters, and then you have the nerve to come around here and tell us not to cause trouble. The trouble's already happening. Why aren't you stopping it?"

"Why do you think confronting these people is the best way to stop the trouble from escalating?"

"Somebody's got to make it clear to these bastards that they can't get away with what they're doing. These people are *dirt,* Ari. They're trying to rule by force. Somebody's got to do something about it—"

"That's what the constabulary is for—"

"But will you stop them?"

"Of course we will."

"Are you sure? Are you sure which side your people are on? I remember when the constabularies shot people in East Torr for walking down the street together and saying what they thought—"

"Not this constabulary," Mhevet said firmly. "That was years ago, Coranis. We're different people now."

"You're still there."

"I *quit* because of what happened then!"

"But how do we know who else has survived from those days?" Irian said softly. "We might be able to trust you, but who else is still there?"

Mhevet ran her finger around the rim of her glass. "We wouldn't have let anyone back in who was involved with that. Nobody who took an order that originated from Skrain Dukat serves in the constabulary—"

"Skrain Dukat's long dead," said Coranis. "That battle's over. It's the people listening to Evek Temet who we're worried about."

Irian picked up the jug of tea and refilled Mhevet's glass. Quietly, she said, "Can you really tell us that you don't have colleagues who think Evek Temet is the best thing to happen to Cardassia in a decade? I bet they're all younger too. I bet they don't remember much before the Dominion. Life's always been a struggle for them, and they're sick of it. They're sick of hearing about atoning for crimes that they didn't commit, and they want to feel good about themselves."

Mhevet rubbed her cheek.

"See what we mean?" asked Coranis. "You can't expect us to rely on the constabularies. We made that mistake once, and we'll never make it again. Yes, yes—perhaps we do trust you to do the right thing, and perhaps even some of your colleagues, but we're not going to fool ourselves that people like you will always be in charge. There are others there—there are always others there—waiting to crawl out from under their stones. They stole our Union from us once before, and they brought us to the Fire. That's not going to happen again. We won't let it happen again."

Mhevet put down her glass. "You know I have some sympathy with what you're saying," she said. "But all this . . ." She gestured around the room, taking in the posters, the books, the pamphlets, Coranis's latest half-written call to arms. "You're keeping the Fire burning. This won't bring stability."

"Cardassia was stable for a long time under the Obsidian Order, Ari," Irian pointed out quietly. "But at what price?"

"You should have stuck with us," said Coranis. "You shouldn't have gone back to the other side. Have you ever considered maybe that's why we don't trust you? We thought you were one of us, and then you crossed over to the other side."

"I'm not the other side! Why can't you understand that? We're not the same constabulary that existed under the Dominion, and we're not the same one that was let loose in East Torr! Don't you understand that's *why* I went back? To make sure that the constabularies would never fail like that again? I've worked very hard to make sure of that. It's not made me popular, but it was the right thing to do."

"And are you? Sure of it?"

Obscurely, Mhevet found herself thinking about coffee. "Of course I am! How could I be part of it otherwise? We're here to serve and protect *you*."

Coranis shook her head. "Police forces serve whoever is in power."

"The people are in power now on Cardassia," Mhevet said.

"You think so?" Irian sighed. "I suppose that explains why you did what you did."

"You'll see," said Coranis. "The constabularies will look after the people as long as the people agree with whoever is in power. The moment that changes . . ." She snapped her fingers. "They'll come and shoot at us all over again. If you won't do anything to stop Evek Temet and his gangsters taking control of North Torr," said Coranis, "then why shouldn't we think that you want them to take control? We'll have to stop them ourselves." She turned back to her comm and started writing again.

"Thanks for the fruit, Ari," Irian said, as she took her to the door.

"Please be careful," Mhevet said. "Don't put yourselves in harm's way."

Irian smiled. "We're old hands at this. You take care too, out there among the enemy."

Back at the department, Mhevet sat listening to the thunder build throughout the afternoon. At last, she went and knocked on the door of Kalanis's office. Closing the door behind her, she launched straight in.

"Don't be angry with me, but I happened to pass through East Torr today—"

"Just happened, did it, Ari?"

"And there's going to be trouble tonight."

Kalanis sighed. "What did I say to you about this?"

Quickly, Mhevet pressed on, "I know you told me to stay away. I know I'm supposed to be solving a murder case—but this is serious, Reta. All the signs are there. There'll be trouble tonight and I don't think it will be limited to Torr."

Kalanis drummed her fingers against her desk. "Well," she said, "in that case, I suppose we'd better be prepared. Overtime for everyone."

Mhevet sat down, pulled out her personal comm, and began to sketch out operations. "My guess is there'll be two flashpoints," she said, "at the tramlines and at HARF. I'll speak to Commander Fry."

There was indeed trouble and of exactly the kind that Mhevet feared: bitter and divisive. "You'll get abuse from both sides," she told her people as they put on armor and collected batons. "Don't listen. If we kick off first, they've got their excuse to go in. Keep your visor down but your badge visible. Knowing you can be identified is what will stop you from doing anything stupid."

At the tramlines that marked the unofficial border between North and East Torr, the two sides gathered. It began as chanting on one side and singing on the other. The people from the constabulary formed a double line between them: shields up. The sun began to set, and the chants got angrier and the songs more accusatory. Mhevet watched the last rays of sunlight sink behind the tenements. Then both sides surged forward.

Over at HARF, Šmrhová stood at the window of Fry's office and watched what was happening outside. Darkness had descended, but the compound was lit up like a bonfire under bright security lights. Beyond the perimeter fencing, she could see the orange lights of the constabulary units and, beyond that, dark figures moving. Here and there, she caught the occasional red flash of disruptor fire.

Worf came to stand beside her. "Hard to watch," he said.

"I hate not being part of the action," Šmrhová said. "I hate not knowing what's happening. I don't know whether everything's going as it should be."

"We have our orders," said Fry. "Nobody goes out, and nobody comes in."

"Assuming the line holds," Worf said. "Otherwise, they'll all be coming in."

"The line will hold," said Fry, calmly. "The constabularies know what they're doing."

"Be ready anyway, Commander." Worf turned to Šmrhová saying, "You may be called upon to defend this installation, if the constabularies can't hold back that crowd."

Double bind, thought Šmrhová, peering out again into the gloom, trying to grasp what was happening. *If they do get through, we'll be brought forward. And that's exactly what these agitators want: Starfleet officers*

*pointing weapons at Cardassian civilians. It will be on
every 'cast seconds later.*

The line held, this time. Later, it would come to be
known as the Battle for the Heartland: the worst
violence seen on the streets of this turbulent city for
years. Later, there would be holodramas about it,
showing the plucky constabularies holding the line
against two implacable forces set on tearing the capital apart. Mhevet would start watching one of these
holodramas one night: at Year's Turn, when most
people were out on the streets, partying rather than
rioting. She didn't get very far through. It tried to
make sense of the events. But there wasn't that kind
of sense, in Mhevet's experience. Quite the contrary.
There had been confusion and terror, and mistakes
were made in the heat of the moment. There had
been too much alcohol or other stimulants flying
around; a gang of people (some in uniform) gorging
on the violence; and another set of people (almost all
in uniform) who were not being paid enough to try
to stem the tide.

Arati Mhevet had been there before in the cha-
otic days that followed the war and the crisis after
Ghemor's assassination, and, before all that, she had
been out there when the Jem'Hadar went on their
rampage. This time, like all the other times, she
strode in and was patient, careful, and focused, and
as dawn began to rise over Cardassia's beaten capital,
something like order began to take hold. Under the

rays of the red sun, Mhevet shoved one more young man into the back of the big skimmer.

He grabbed her hand.

"Take that off me, Sunshine," she rasped, "or I'll break your wrist."

He let go, quickly. "Please," he said, voice low. "I need to talk to you."

She looked at him. He had gray eyes. Intelligent eyes. She put her hand against his head and pushed him into the van with the rest of them. If he was really so smart, he wouldn't be here. "Don't worry," she said wearily, "I'll be talking to everyone here soon enough. Your turn will come."

Eight

Late. The air thick and the stars blinded. On a night like this, I can believe that nothing else exists beyond this poor battered world. I can believe there is no chance of escape from its clutch. Perhaps you are wise not to visit Cardassia Prime. She only breaks the heart.

EG

—not sent—

A long night, made longer by the threat of the long, hot day that was bound to follow. By mid-morning Mhevet had conducted fifteen interviews, nowhere near half the number of the people arrested the previous night. Nationalists and radicals alike. Mhevet didn't discriminate.

Taking a break to stand outside the interview room where her latest rioter was waiting, Mhevet gratefully received a water bottle from Dhrok, who had been assisting her in the interviews. "Who do we have now?"

Dhrok checked her padd. "Rakhat Blok. Mean anything to you?"

Blok . . . Mhevet shook her head. "Nothing."

Not that the chief instigators were likely to give their real names or, indeed, to have been anywhere near the riot when it happened. Having lit the fire, they'd have been well away before the explosion. Maybe even as far away as the Assembly itself.

Splashing some water on her hands, Mhevet pressed her palms against cheeks, forehead, throat, the back of her neck. "I suppose we should hear this one's story before we charge him."

Wearily, she went inside, Dhrok following behind. The whole process was fairly predictable. People tended to make one of two defenses. There were those who said they were out shopping or seeing a mate or maybe simply going for a walk when they'd turned a corner and ran straight into the trouble. Bad luck, they said. Wrong place at the wrong time. The others at least admitted that they'd gone out on purpose, but only to see what was going on—they had nothing to do with any of it. Mhevet wondered which Blok would turn out to be. It would all be sorted out by the holo-recordings from the cams on the officers' visors, but that would take time.

Something about Blok seemed familiar. Mhevet had seen too many faces in the past few hours to be able to place him, but she knew she'd get there in the end.

"Oh, at last," he said, as Mhevet and Dhrok took

their seats. "I've been asking all night if I could speak to someone."

That was who he was: the young man she'd arrested and unceremoniously bundled into the back of the skimmer. "You're speaking to me now," Mhevet said. "So, which is it? Were you in the wrong place at the wrong time, or had you gone out for a look and found yourself mixed up in things?"

"No, no . . . This is important. Do you have a padd?"

Dhrok pushed her padd forward. Blok took it and started entering numbers. "This is a code number for a secure line that will get you through to a friend of mine. It's very important that you contact him at once—"

Mhevet cut him off. "You do realize you're under arrest?"

"I know. Please, you have to contact this person. It's incredibly important—"

Dhrok leaned over to speak quietly into Mhevet's ear. "Just to remind you that he does have the right to contact somebody. We ought to let him if we don't want to run into trouble later at the arraignment."

Good point. It would slow down things for now; it would speed things up later. "All right. Dhrok, pass him your comm."

As the young man placed his call, Mhevet studied him. He was powerfully built and in excellent physical condition. Her instincts told her that this was not somebody born and brought up in Torr. He would have been smaller, less healthy. Children of the old service grades usually were. So who was he? A rich kid playing at militant? He looked a little too old for that, even with the brutal haircut and the army-style clothes. Still, Mhevet would put *leks* on this call being to an expensive lawyer, paid for by a wealthy parent. . . .

"We need to talk, sir," Blok said. "What? No, no . . . Look, I've been arrested. What? Well, how do you *think*—? I'm at—" He glanced up questioningly at Mhevet.

"Constabulary HQ."

"Constabulary HQ. Ask for . . ." Another querying look.

"Senior Investigator Mhevet."

"Senior Investigator Mhevet. What? All right, yes, that's fine, yes, I'll do that. Yes, I completely understand; I'll make sure of that. Of course, sir. Thank you, sir."

He ended the communication and passed the padd back.

"Care to explain?" Mhevet asked.

"What?" Blok rubbed his eyes. "Look, I know you must have had an appalling night, and this must be an exhausting morning, and I'm sorry that I'm taking up so much of your time. But this really is important, and he won't be long."

"He? Who are you talking about?" Mhevet leaned forward on the table, imposing herself onto the space between them. "If you think your connections can get you out of here, you're fooling yourself—"

Blok shook his head. "It's not like that—"

"Then who is 'he'?"

"He said not to say. . . . He also said that only you should be here, Investigator." Blok looked apologetically at Dhrok. "Sorry."

"I don't believe this. . . ."

"He's coming to the back door. He said to meet him there, Investigator."

"You really are something, aren't you?" asked Dhrok.

"I'm sorry about this. But it's very important."

"And what we do isn't?"

Blok ran his hand through his short hair. "I think," he said, "you'll find out that we're in much the same business."

Mhevet picked up her water bottle. She took a swig and rolled the liquid slowly around her mouth. "All right," she said. "Dhrok, off you go."

"What?" she said.

"Go and have breakfast." She fished in her pocket and pulled out her card for the canteen. "My treat."

"Ari, there always has to be two of us—"

"That's fine," said Blok quickly. "Really, that's fine."

"How often," said Mhevet, "do I bend the rules?"

Dhrok sighed and stood up. "All right," she said. "But if there's any flak for this, Ari . . ."

"I'll take any flak."

She left, taking Mhevet's canteen card with her.

"Back door?" said Mhevet to Blok.

"Back door. He won't be long."

He wasn't. Soon enough, a sleek, well-maintained skimmer pulled up at the end of the alley. Two men—one look told Mhevet they were bodyguards—got out, and then another man, smaller and trimmer, emerged. Mhevet felt a faint prickle of unease. Who had she arrested when she'd brought in Blok? Surely, from that skimmer, this was someone of influence. Was she finally finding the connections between the organizers of the street violence and the powerful of the city?

The man moved toward her quickly with speed and grace. He was wearing a mask, although the dust wasn't too bad this morning. Blue eyes observed her sharply.

"Investigator Mhevet?"

"Yes."

"Thank you for this. I'm sure you have a great deal to do. Your assistance in this matter is appreciated."

"That's fine. . . ." She was sure she'd heard that voice somewhere. "Do you want to step inside?"

He nodded at his two bodyguards, who withdrew. "Let's speak out here for a moment," he said. "My experience of interview rooms tells me that they're usually equipped with recording devices."

"All right. . . . What's going on?"

"Firstly, let me clarify who you're holding. Rakhat Blok, yes?"

"Yes."

"Good. In fact, his name is Glinn Ravel Dygan."

"*Glinn* Dygan?" Mhevet asked.

"Yes, a very highly regarded officer, both here and on the *Enterprise*—across Starfleet in general, in fact. He's been investigating on my behalf amongst the more . . . *excitable* residents of the Torr sector."

"Investigating? What kind of investigating?"

He looked at her coldly over the edge of his mask. "What kind do you think?"

Mhevet decided she'd had enough of all this intrigue. She rested her hand upon her baton. He followed the movement with amusement in his eyes. "Who are you, exactly?" she asked.

"Who am *I*?" The man smiled genially and tilted his head. "It's something of a relief to know that I can still pass unrecognized in some quarters. My name, Investigator, is Elim Garak. I'm the Cardassian ambassador to the United Federation of Planets. May I speak to Glinn Dygan, please?"

At the ambassador's request, she brought Blok out into the alleyway to speak to him. She tried not to think about how many regulations she was breaking. She watched from inside as they conducted a hurried conversation. Eventually Blok put his head around the door.

"He'd like a word."

Blok—Dygan—took her place inside, by the door, leaving her alone with the ambassador. He still had his mask on, but when he looked at her, she saw that his bright blue eyes were no longer sparkling with amusement. They were dulled, anxious, like those of a careworn old man. "All you all right?" she asked. "Here, have some water."

He took her water bottle and, expertly, pushed it under his mask, drinking without revealing much more of his face. When he handed the bottle back, she could feel from the weight that he had drained it dry. But he looked less likely to collapse in the heat.

"Another alleyway," he said, looking around. "Makes a change from a small room, I suppose. There's a universe of wonders out there, Investigator, and yet I seem to have spent my life in little rooms and seedy alleyways."

"I know what you mean," she muttered.

"My apologies for drinking all your water."

"I'd rather that than a case of heat stroke on my hands. How do you know Blok? Dygan, whatever his name is."

"He's been serving with Starfleet. I'm professionally interested in relations between Cardassian and Starfleet military personnel. Well, I'm professionally interested in relations between Cardassia and the Federation in general, but the military in particular have been doing some interesting work. I've been monitoring Dygan's career for a while and he's impressed me. So when I decided I wanted more information on these ultra-nationalists that have been so plaguing our major cities, he seemed the person for the job."

Mhevet stared at him. "You've had a man undercover in North Torr? I didn't know about this—"

"No, I'm sorry about that."

"And neither, I'm sure, does the CIB."

"I sincerely hope not." The ambassador's eyes went stern. "That was the whole point of having Dygan as an independent observer. I don't believe anything coming out of the CIB these days. Do you?"

Her conversation with Fhret came back to her. Slowly, she said, "I know that there have been some changes there recently—"

"Crell is not in favor of the alliance with the Federation—or, more particularly, any alliance with the Klingon Empire." Garak frowned. "I have to say that given the choice, I wouldn't go near the Klingon Empire either, but then Starfleet is a considerable buffer, and I'd rather the Klingons than the Romulans. But Crell does not agree, and I fear this may have opened him up to influence from some rather unsavory people." His eyes were sharp above the mask. "I think you know what I mean."

People. People in the shadows waiting for the Federation to leave. "If you didn't trust the CIB, you could have trusted us—" *Trusted me.* "Trusted the constabularies."

"If one institution has been compromised, why would I assume that another hasn't?"

"Because we're the new constabulary, sir," Mhevet said, with hot pride. "We're not the people used by Skrain Dukat to murder our fellow citizens. We've built an organization that serves the Cardassian people as a whole and is not in the pay or power of any elite—"

"Oh, yes?" Garak looked at her piercingly. "Tell me, Investigator—where do you get your human coffee these days?"

"What? That's beside the point—"

"Of course it's not beside the point. Details, Investigator. Pay attention to the details, scattered around you like the dust that coats this poor beleaguered city!" He swept his hand around, theatrically. "Directives from the top, instructing that any trace of Federation culture or influence within the constabularies should be removed? Think about the signals that's sending to the old guard. *Starfleet is leaving, gentlemen. It's safe to come out.*"

"Sir, this is entirely beside the point. My question is, do you in fact have *any* authority to place an undercover agent in North Torr?"

"Authority?" Garak's eyes twinkled. "Of course not! I asked Glinn Dygan's commanding officer to release him to me for unspecified services to Cardassia. He had the good sense to comply and ask no more. If Dygan then chose to come to Cardassia Prime and embroil himself with some of the less pleasant residents of the capital . . ." He held up his hands. "Has he broken any laws? Have I?"

"That's a fine line you're treading—"

"Yes, well, it usually is. Anyway, much as I'd like to chat all day, I have some very pressing business to attend to. So, if you could release Dygan, I can get back to that business, and Dygan can get back to being Blok."

"I'm sorry, sir, I've no intention of releasing Dygan."

"No?"

"Not unless you can assure me he has no intention of going back undercover in North Torr."

Garak breathed out impatiently beneath his mask. "Well, of course he's going back to North Torr. Where else do you think he's going?"

The idea of a random element in Torr horrified her. And these two men had no authority to do what they were doing. She shook her head firmly. "I can't allow that—"

"I rather think you can. I rather think you must." He placed his hand upon the wall next to her and leaned toward her. "On Cardassia Prime there are forces at work now intent on destroying all that people such as you and I have struggled to achieve since the Fire." He moved closer, lowered his voice. "You know who I mean, don't you, Arati? The shadow people."

She started. His eyes narrowed.

"Yes, you know," he said. "The people of the night. The ones who loathe our new Cardassia and wish to return us to the old ways. All the work you and I have done—it's hanging in the balance now. They're waiting for Starfleet to leave, and then they'll come out. Only in the past few days, they have done some terrible harm, for which the Cardassian people may yet be terribly punished. I'm doing all that I can—but I need Ravel Dygan. Please—let him go."

He was very persuasive. But that was what you

had to resist, wasn't it? Being pulled away from your purpose to serve someone else's. Mhevet took a deep breath. "There are numerous police investigations under way in North Torr at the moment," she said doggedly. "Glinn Dygan adds an unpredictable element to the mix. His presence could put several constabulary people at risk."

"I see." Garak pulled away from her, pressing his hand against his face. His shoulders sagged. For a brief moment, she again had the impression of an old man with the weight of the entire world upon him. Then he snapped back into control.

"All right," he said. "Let's deal. If you release Dygan to continue his work in North Torr, I'll instruct him to gain as much information as he can about the murder of Aleyni Cam."

Cold fury passed through Mhevet. The nerve of the man . . . Surely he didn't think that his position put him above the law? Those days on Cardassia were long over and would remain so as long as she had breath in her body.

"Sir," she replied coldly, "if you know anything about the death of Aleyni Cam, you will tell me now. I'm sure you know that withholding information about a murder is a criminal offense and that if I suspected you of that, I would have to arrest you."

She realized that Garak's eyes were looking at her in approval, like a proud father might look at a clever child. "That," he said, "was an *excellent* response. I'm glad to learn that at least part of the constabulary remains incorruptible." He took a deep breath. "Before you make your reputation by locking me up, you might want to listen for a while. I have a tale to tell. And when I'm finished, you'll understand. You'll give me Dygan, and you'll send us both on our way with your blessing."

Mhevet blinked. He was mesmeric. It was frightening. She wouldn't let herself be corrupted. She stood and faced him squarely, head on, arms folded. "Oh, yes? And what makes you think that?"

"Why? Because you loathe these people, of course. As well you might. They did, after all, drive you and your family from your home."

Mhevet swallowed. She felt her arms and legs begin to tremble. Thickly, she said, "How do you know that?"

Garak's eyes were very kind. "You don't think I walked in here blind, do you? I've been playing this game a very long time. Do you think I wouldn't have found out all that I could about Investigator Arati Mhevet?"

"There's nothing to find out—"

"No? Formerly a resident of North Torr, but since just prior to the age of emergence, a resident of East Torr? That is unusual, I thought. People don't leave North Torr. Northerners stick together. So I rummaged around a little more."

"Shut up," Mhevet said, harshly. She turned to leave, but Dygan was there, looking out, worriedly, blocking the entrance.

"Your uncle." His voice was like silk. "Ontek. He played with you, when you were little—"

"Shut *up*!"

"What a shame he made such bad friends. My . . . former colleagues didn't approve." He moved in again. His arm blocked any getaway down the alley, and Dygan was in place on the other side of the door. "I imagine it was terrifying when the Order came to visit. That was certainly the intention. Did your father instruct you to tell us everything you knew? Or was that your own idea?"

Mhevet's mouth was dry. "Father didn't tell me to do anything. I don't know to this day whether or not he forgave me. Ontek was his brother. . . ."

"Ontek was an unpleasant man. You were in an impossible position. You made a hard but practical decision. You certainly saved your father's life."

"I *ruined* his life. He was heartbroken. We all knew what would happen to Ontek—"

"I won't insult you by trying to claim that the Order was a force for good in old Cardassia, but on this occasion we were certainly the lesser of two evils." His eyes were full of compassion. "Did you ever discover that what you told our agent prevented a bombing in the Barvonok Sector?"

Mhevet licked her lips. "No. I didn't."

"Perhaps that might help."

She twisted away. Perhaps, if she'd known that at the time . . . But who would have passed on information like that, back in those days? It had been her duty to tell the Order all they wanted to know and to leave the rest to them. Why would they bother to tell her if her actions had, by chance, had good effect? All that Mhevet and her parents had seen had been the disaster, the fallout: being shunned by the rest of the family, ostracized by their community around them, and having to move away. One rule in North Torr: You didn't tell, you didn't inform. And if you did, you suffered the consequences. She'd known, at the time—known for certain—that what her uncle was doing was wrong. She'd known he had to be stopped. But the powers that had existed to stop him were pitiless, and the labor camp had killed him.

She looked at Garak; or, she looked at his eyes. He was, if all reports were true, a torturer, a murderer, a man with blood on his hands.

"I think it will help," he said. "In time." Garak sighed, and once again she had that impression of great weariness. "I'm going to trust you with a secret, Arati Mhevet. You've made difficult decisions before, and you've made them well. So I'm going to tell you what Dygan just told me, because I know that you'll understand, and I know that you'll help."

She must have given herself away, some imperceptible shift in stance, or perhaps she blinked. He was not the kind of man to miss a signal. He took off his mask. He was not smiling. Could someone like this really bring absolution?

"Listen carefully, Investigator. If Dygan's story is

true, then people like you and I and Dygan have got a fight on our hands. The fight of our lives."

Ravel Dygan watched wearily as Garak and Mhevet talked. He was exhausted. He'd been in the thick of the battle, and he hadn't slept well in the cells last night. He thought he might leave things to Garak for a moment. He leaned back against the wall and closed his eyes. The long weeks of pretending to be the kind of man Blok was—unaware of what his actions really meant, pleased only to have fallen in with powerful friends—were taking their toll.

There was a tap on the door. Dygan forced his eyes open. Garak was gesturing to him to come out and join them.

"Well," Dygan said, looking at them both. "Can I go?"

"You can go," said Mhevet.

Dygan glanced worriedly at Garak. "What's going on? What did you do?"

"To my surprise," Garak said, putting his mask back on, "all Investigator Mhevet wanted was the truth." The ambassador brushed away dust from the sleeves of his jacket. "So that's what I gave her."

"You *told* her?" Dygan looked at Mhevet in alarm. "Are you sure we can trust her?"

"Trust her?" Garak's eyes opened wide. "I trust her as much as I trust you."

"Am I going back in?"

"If you're happy to do that," Garak said.

Dygan ignored the churn of his stomach. "That's beside the point, isn't it? I have to—"

"We need evidence," said Mhevet. "We need proof."

"I don't know whether I can get it," Dygan said. "It's not as if they take minutes of their planning meetings."

"No," said Mhevet. "But they do talk."

"Will that be enough?"

Mhevet fished around in her pocket, brought out a small recording device, and handed it to him.

"Is this legal?" Dygan asked.

"*You're* not legal," Mhevet replied. "Shall we worry about that later?"

Garak studied Dygan carefully. "You could be in a great deal of danger now. We have no idea the extent to which the constabularies have been compromised."

"I suppose that's a risk we have to take," Dygan said.

"The risk is primarily yours," Garak pointed out.

"I'm prepared to take it."

The ambassador leaned back against the wall and looked up at the sky. There was a long, low roll of thunder. "*When* will it rain?" he asked, to nobody in particular.

"Later," Mhevet said, with confidence.

"Do you need some water, sir?" Dygan asked, looking at the older man with concern. The thunder had subsided, but the air remained quivering hot.

"I'll live, Dygan. But thank you." The ambassador looked at them both sadly. "Your generation," he said, with a sigh that came from the depths of his being. "What a hideous mess we bequeathed you! You'd be right to refuse anything we asked of you."

"Don't you see, sir?" Dygan asked. "You *ask*. That's the difference now. You don't order. You don't expect us to willingly sacrifice ourselves."

"A different contract now," Mhevet said softly. "A different world. We mustn't go back to the way we were."

"Well," said the ambassador, "far be it from me to get in the way of such dedication and desire to serve. Back to where you were, please, Dygan. But you must be very careful now." He nodded at Mhevet. "Get in touch with Investigator Mhevet, in extremis."

Mhevet gave Dygan the code for her personal comm. "What are you going to do now, Ambassador?" she asked.

"Me?" Garak sighed. "I have to speak to the castellan, of course. Tell her what Dygan has told me."

Dygan looked at him with pity. "I don't envy you that conversation."

"My job these days," Garak said, "consists almost entirely of having unpalatable conversations with heads of state and their representatives. Fortunately, I've always enjoyed a good chat." He checked the time. "I must be going. Take care, Dygan. The moment you notice them looking at you carefully—get out."

Dygan smiled. "Advice of an old hand?"

They pressed palms: a gesture of comradeship and respect. "An old hand who has, hitherto, outlived most of his enemies. You'd be wise to listen."

Mhevet walked the ambassador back down the alley to his skimmer. He had a quick word with one of his bodyguards, who had brought out three bottles full of water—a more than generous replacement for the rations Garak had drunk.

"Be careful, Investigator," he said. They pressed palms, and then he grasped her upper arm and squeezed. "There are dark forces gathering who will stop at nothing. I'd hate to see you become yet another casualty. Take care. Watch your back. Trust nobody."

"Nobody, sir? What about you?"

"Trust *me*?" He looked at her sadly. "Well, if you must."

Later, back inside, Mhevet found Dhrok sitting with Fereny in the canteen. Dhrok waved her card at her. "What happened with Blok?"

"Bailed," she said, looking her straight in the eye. "Famous mother. Expensive conservator."

"Typical," said Fereny. "Money always does the trick. Some people get away with murder."

In the back of his skimmer, Garak took a moment to cool down. Then he put a message through to the castellan's office requesting an immediate and urgent meeting. Her office tried to put him off until the next day, but he refused to get off the line, and eventually the aide capitulated. Garak was not easily deflected.

What am I supposed to do now? he wondered, as the skimmer sped on. His instinct, he realized, was to conceal all that was happening; to deny, to obfuscate—to lie. Already his mind was racing: assembling schemes and plans; laying trails that led elsewhere; spinning, spinning, spinning. . . . But how well, really, had that served as a strategy? He had ended up in exile, and his world had come to the edge of destruction.

I must find another way through this, Garak thought. *If any of us are to survive.* Outside, the city passed by: half-ruin, half-rebuild, entirely Cardassian. People were moving about slowly, struggling against the heat, trying to keep going until the rain brought relief. Garak watched them with increasing desperation.

Who can I turn to? Who are my friends in this?

They stopped in front of the New Assembly. Garak sat for a while longer in the back of the skimmer. His eye fell on the low walls of the stone garden that had been built to commemorate Alon Ghemor.

All my dead friends, Garak thought. *How do I honor you? How do I keep your memory alive? Why have the best of us died?*

He stepped out into the oppression of the Cardassian day. He paused for a moment by the garden, placing one hand lightly upon the stone of the wall.

Unaware of what he was doing, he began to remove some moss that was growing between the stones. He was thinking about the boy who cried wolf. *Honesty is the best policy*. Wasn't that the moral of the story, according to Julian Bashir? Or was it: *Never tell the same lie twice*.

He went into the cool interior of the building. The castellan wasn't pleased to see him. "I know that this is a delicate time diplomatically," she said. "But you're proving an exceptionally demanding colleague at the moment. Alon Ghemor was right to send you to Earth."

So she was still on maneuvers. "Rakena," he said quietly. "Please. I've not come here to quarrel."

She looked at him sharply and then gestured with her padd that he should sit down. *Wolf!* he thought as he took his seat. "Have you ever heard of an organization called the True Way?"

The castellan examined her padd. "Garak, are you here as ambassador to the Federation, or are you assigning yourself a different office of state today?"

He didn't strike back. "Have you heard of the True Way?"

"Of course I have," she said impatiently. "You may recall that I have an entire Intelligence Bureau at my service—"

"Who are, no doubt, keeping you *spectacularly* well-informed. Yes, I can imagine how Crell is here every morning, sipping ettaberry tea and sharing a joke—"

"If you're done, Garak, you can leave."

"Rakena, this is serious. The True Way is an extremist organization of the most unpleasant kind. I . . . I know them of old. I know the kind of people that they were and the methods they used. And if they're even remotely similar to that old organization, I have no doubt that they'll be using Cardassia First to infiltrate and undermine our institutions. The police, the government, who knows where their people are—"

"Yet again," she said firmly, cutting him off, "I find myself having to remind you of the limits of your authority. These are internal affairs. Do you think I'm not kept informed about such things? Do you think my intelligence service is not telling me what I need to know about threats to the state—?"

"No," he said. "I think they might not."

Slowly, she leaned back. "What makes you say that?"

"Because I've just learned that someone whom I suspect is a member of the True Way has been boasting about the murder of a prominent human." Garak lowered his voice. "Rakena, I think they mean Nan Bacco."

The castellan didn't reply. She lifted her hand to her face and pinched her nose between her forefingers.

"Do you understand what I'm saying?" Garak asked. "Bacco wasn't murdered by a Bajoran. She was murdered by a Cardassian."

"There's no evidence," she said.

"That's only a matter of time. Do you think the Federation is going to leave any stone unturned in their hunt for the killer? With a Bajoran in charge? Rakena, we can't conceal this! Trust me, I know about cover-ups, and this one is too big. Someone on the streets of Torr is already boasting about the murder, and that's going to get back to Starfleet Intelligence at some point. They'll look into it, because they will look into everything. We can't delay. We have to tell them. Captain Picard will listen with an open mind—"

"Garak, of all the strategies that you have used to grab my attention, this has to be the most ludicrous—"

Garak slammed his hand against her desk. "Why won't you *listen* to me?"

She stood up. "If you don't leave now," she said, "I'm going to ask security to escort you from the building—"

"Rakena, please. We can't run the risk of Starfleet hearing this from anyone else. Who knows—maybe they've heard already." Pieces began to fall into place. "Maybe that's why the withdrawal has been postponed. Maybe that's why their personnel have been brought back into their installations. . . ." Garak rubbed at his forehead. He could feel his chest tightening, as if something was closing in on him, and he struggled to compose himself. "I know internal affairs are no longer my business, and I accept that. But the Federation has been my business for a long time now, and I know that they are able to distinguish between friends who *are* friends and friends who are enemies. If you delay in telling them this and they find out by themselves— that will *finish* this alliance! We'll be on our own again; the pariahs of the quadrant, again. Please, get Captain Picard here, right now. We can speak to him together, right now, we can sort this out, right now—"

"No—"

"Rakena, please—*listen* to me!"

"Ambassador, you're out of control!"

That came like a splash of cold water across his face, or a punch. Garak subsided. *Perhaps I am,* he thought, listening as if from a distance to his own breathing. Perhaps he was out of control.

The castellan pressed both hands firmly against her desk. "Consider how sensitive this is," she said. "You said it yourself. This could finish the alliance you've worked so hard to maintain. There's a great deal of grief and anger amongst the Federation right now—and who can blame them? How do you think they'll react to this news?"

Garak felt himself trembling. He heard Parmak's voice in his head. *Deep breaths, Elim. That's it, deep, slow breaths.*

"All I'm asking for is a little time." She sat down again in her chair. "Do you need some water?"

"No, thank you."

"Then . . . thank you for your concern, Ambassador. Now I must get back to work."

Garak stood up. Pieces were still shifting around in his mind. Slowly, he said, "I'm not bringing you news, am I?"

The castellan lifted her chin and looked him directly in the eye. "What makes you say that?"

"When I told you just now," he said, "your first reaction wasn't shock, or horror, or anything remotely like that. You said, 'There's no evidence.' When did you know?"

She didn't reply.

"Did you know when we met Picard?" Garak's eyes widened. "You did, didn't you? Oh Rakena, you *fool*!" He put his hands to his head. "This has gone far enough. I won't be part of this—"

He headed for the exit. He heard her quick footsteps behind him.

"Garak," she said, "I'm warning you—"

He swung around to face her. "*Warning* me? What do you mean by that?"

"If you inform Starfleet or the Federation of your suspicions I'll . . . I'll consider it treason and I'll act accordingly."

"*Treason?*" Garak burst out laughing. "Oh, *please*!"

"If this leaks, I'll know where it's come from. I'll know it's you. I'll have you arrested."

"That's the second time today somebody has threatened me with arrest," Garak said. "I wasn't particularly frightened the first time either."

She came to stand in front of him. She was so small. But she was still the castellan of the Cardassian

Union. "I mean it," she said. "You spent a long time in exile. It would be a shame to end your life there."

"Exile me? From Cardassia?" Garak turned his back on her and continued toward the door. "You'll have to kill me first."

"I mean it," she said. "I'll ruin you."

"It won't be the first time I've been ruined," Garak replied. "Yet somehow I'm still here."

He strode out of her office and made his way outside. He stood for a moment in the hot afternoon, breathing deeply to steady himself.

We are our own worst enemy.

His skimmer pulled up. He got inside and fell back into his seat, grief-stricken and afraid. His hands were shaking. Garak clutched the arms of his seat and took the slow, deep breaths his doctor prescribed, and then he committed himself fully to whatever was going to happen next.

"Computer, open a secure channel to the *Enterprise*. I have an urgent message for Captain Jean-Luc Picard."

The message was sent. About fifteen heartbeats later, Garak's skimmer exploded. That afternoon the rains came, violent and red as blood.

Julian, I'm frightened. All careening out of control. No, worse: all moving according to a plan. Somebody *intends* this. Somebody has their eye upon us.

Has their eye upon *me*?

—*later*—

Is this paranoia?
Can you make a diagnosis from that distance?
Or would that break some ethical code or other
of yours?

Is it paranoia if they're really trying to kill you?
Any medical reason it can't be both paranoia and
happening?

> *I cannot send this*
> *why am I writing this*
> *why am I even thinking this*

Get a grip, Garak
Deep breaths
Deep, slow breaths

> *I think I am in a hole*

—*not sent*—

—*deleted*—

Part Three

The Shadow

"Cardassia is everything. Hers is the hand that guides and punishes. Hers is the hand that will absolve."

—Preloc,
Meditations on a Crimson Shadow,
Vol. I (Cardassia), 1, ii

Nine

My dearest Kelas,

This is it, I'm afraid. This is the letter that comes
in the event of . . .

For what it's worth, I'm sorry. First of all, for
whatever it was I was doing at the time. It was
probably excessive, unwise, and unkind. These
have, sadly, been characteristics of most of my
actions throughout the course of my life. I'm sorry
about that. Most of all, I'm sorry that I've not had
the chance to prove that I could become a better
man. Despite everything, I believe that could still
have happened. I suppose it's too late now.

Your friendship, in these last few years, has
been not only a source of great pleasure to me,
but has also been a source of moral strength.
Kelas, as I have tried to become a better man,
you have been the necessary counterweight to
my tendency toward excess. More than that, you
have been my conscience.

Once, at my very lowest ebb, I asked a man to
forgive me. He had, at the time, no real idea of all

I had done. But he forgave me nonetheless—for whatever it was I'd done.

You, Kelas, in contrast, have much to forgive me. And now, despite all your gifts of loyalty and trust, I believe I may have added something else to the tally.

So—for all that I've done, and for whatever it was that I was doing now:

I'm sorry. Forgive me.

Please look after the garden.

Elim

Word spread around his city like fire. Suddenly, his story was everywhere: his time in the Obsidian Order, his exile, his return to fight the Dominion with Corat Damar, his friendship with Alon Ghemor, his service to Cardassia on Earth. As his life became public knowledge, people began to realize that with his death, something uniquely Cardassian had been lost. The city and the Union of which it was the heart realized that it was in mourning.

Grief, however, is often masked by anger. Questions started to be asked: How could this happen? Here, in the capital, how could this be permitted? Where was his security? Where was his protection? Are the old days coming back again? Is anybody safe? As these questions coalesced, one man became their mouthpiece: Evek Temet, speaking on as many 'casts that could be fitted into a single day:

"*Of course I had some robust public exchanges with the ambassador; everyone knows that. But that was a sign of my respect for him. Look how this remarkable man served us: a dedicated defender of the principles of the Union as a young man, later a hero during our war of liberation from the Dominion, most recently a fine ambassador for our people to the Federation. And, I understand, a close personal friend of our two lost great leaders, Corat Damar and Alon Ghemor. It's a tragedy that a man like this could not move safely around our capital. More than a tragedy—an outrage. What was being done to protect him? How could his death be allowed to happen? The city constabularies, and perhaps the castellan herself, have some questions to answer. . . .*"

Later, on another 'cast, Temet's target became much clearer: "*It's a sign of how far the current administration has lost its grip. Were there no warnings? The castellan keeps saying that Cardassia is safe in her hands—but, honestly, ask yourselves—what evidence do you see of that? An alliance with a fragile and wounded power. Riots on the streets of the capital. And now the death of a much-loved public figure. Is this a Union under control? It seems to me that we're sliding backward, back into the chaos we suffered after the Dominion occupation. And the people of Cardassia should be asking themselves—is this what we deserve?*"

The rain was lashing down: huge drops of rain red with dust. Already the streets were flooding. Arati Mhevet was doing her best not to get washed away.

From the cover of her desk, she watched as numerous high-ranking officials swept along the corridor toward Kalanis's office, and for the first time since she had been handed the Aleyni case, she was glad to be able to hide herself in its minutiae. Everyone in the room kept their heads down all morning. Mhevet was trying to think of a way of contacting Dygan, to see if he had any idea what they should do now that the ambassador was dead, but he had not given her a means of getting in touch with him. She set up her personal comm to allow calls from him only. She hoped that he was safe and had not been already targeted. In the meantime, she sat and sweated and tried not to think that her turn must be coming.

In the early afternoon, Reta Kalanis was escorted out of the building. Tret Fereny was over at Mhevet's desk almost straightaway. "She's been suspended," he said, in a low voice. "Over security failures in the city over the past few days."

What failures? We held the line. Are they really going to try to pin the ambassador's murder on her?

"Ari," he said, "I don't think she's coming back."

Mhevet said nothing. She was conscious of people watching her and aware that she did not know who was friendly and who was hostile. She pushed the secret that the late ambassador had shared with her into the very farthest corner of her mind. Calmly, she closed down her companel and stood up. All her colleagues were watching her.

"Ari," Fereny said, "what are you going to do?"

"Right now? I'm going to get some lunch."

"Everyone knows you were her protégée—"

"Fortunately for me," Mhevet said in a carrying voice, "I was ordered off operations in Torr and put on a murder case. And whatever else is happening, I still need lunch."

Fereny stepped aside to let her pass. Mhevet knew that he was bewildered by her reply, but what else was she supposed to say? Now was the time to keep quiet. At some point, Kalanis's enemies—who were, therefore, *her* enemies—would make their move, and their people would start to shift into position at the constabulary. No doubt then she would be called for an interview and asked to account for herself and all her decisions in the past few months. Mhevet knew the drill. Only a few years ago she had been the one asking those kinds of questions. In the meantime, there was nothing she could do, and the murderer of Aleyni Cam was still walking freely around the capital.

She went down into the garage where the skimmers were parked and sat with her head down and her hands on the controls. Yes, she would eat lunch, and she would focus on her case. And if she could only be sure that nobody around her could see how very frightened she was, she might get through the next few weeks, and she might be able to get out of here and take Fhret up on her offer. Easing the skimmer up and out into the deluge, she thanked Kalanis for putting her on this case, and she cursed the late ambassador for the terrible burden of knowledge.

"So now two architects of the alliance between Cardassia and the Federation are dead," said Akaar. *"This is surely a concerted attack on us. You've heard the latest from DS9?"*

"They've let the Bajoran go," said Picard.

"It looks like a Tzenkethi may have been behind this." The admiral shook his head. *"So now we are looking at the Typhon Pact. Presumably the CIB will be looking that way to find the ambassador's assassin. I can't help remembering that the assassination of the Romulan Senator Vreenak ended in the Romulan Empire going to war. Where's this all going to end?"*

Picard rested his hand gently upon the book that Garak had given him. "I wouldn't dare to conjecture, sir."

"What's the situation like there?"

"Tense. We're seeing ramifications already—one of the city's most senior police officers has been suspended pending an investigation into security failings in the city. She was an associate of the castellan—appointed by Garan, in fact, and a significant figure in the postwar reconstruction. Cardassia First is making a great deal of it, of course. More evidence, they're saying, that the castellan's judgment is flawed."

"Poor Garan. The noose does seem to be tightening around her neck. . . ."

"It seems that way," Picard said, his hand still upon the book. "But I wouldn't lose hope yet. Certainly this is a volatile time. But I still have reason to be hopeful. It's important that we keep calm and continue to send friendly signals to the Cardassians."

"In which case, you're not going to like what I have to say next. Orders direct from the president's office. I think you'll have a hard time making this signal seem friendly."

Captain Picard plainly did not want to have to pass on whatever Admiral Akaar's message was, Šmrhová thought.

"I'm delighted to be able to welcome you here, Captain," Commander Fry said. "I hope this means everything is in order. Any progress with the withdrawal agreement?"

"I'm afraid not," Picard replied. "You're not going to like what I have to say next."

Šmrhová went on alert. Fry, who had been about to sit down at her desk, stopped and rested one hand on a pile of books that were getting ready to be packed away. "Go on, sir," she said, with a sigh.

"The president," Picard said, "has issued instructions that HARF installations are now to be open only to Federation citizens."

"That . . . is a strong signal to be sending the Cardassians," said Worf.

"I'm aware of that, Number One."

"Perhaps too strong, sir?" Šmrhová suggested.

The commander was struggling to remain calm. "Given the trouble we experienced the other night," she said, "I'm prepared to accept that the decision to withdraw all Federation citizens and Starfleet personnel within the compound was a prescient one. But to require all Cardassian citizens to leave? Captain, not even when Ghemor was killed and this world was the closest it had been to civil war did we do that—"

"Nevertheless, Commander," Picard said, "those are our orders. You've already said how there's been considerable anti-Federation sentiment expressed over the past few days—"

"But from specific groups and most certainly not from people who work with us . . . sir." Fry's composure was slipping, Šmrhová thought. Understandable, perhaps, from a woman seeing a decade's care and labor destroyed in less than a week. "This is not simply a matter of asking Cardassian citizens not to come to work. In some cases, we'll be asking families to split. What, for example, do you suggest I say to the widow of Lieutenant Aleyni Cam? She's Cardassian born. A Cardassian citizen. Am I required to tell her that her presence in her own home is now considered a security risk?"

"In such cases, Commander, as in others," Picard said, "I believe we can—and should—exercise discretion."

"It's always the small people who suffer, isn't it, Captain?" Fry stood up straight. "Well," she said, "if

I have to go and tell some of the most loyal and hard-working people on Cardassia Prime that they have to leave their homes in the middle of the autumn storm, I suppose I should get on with it." She stopped at the door. "This order, and this order alone, will do more damage to the work we've done on Cardassia than anything else in the last ten years. Still, if it's an order straight from the *president* . . ." She strode from the room.

Šmrhová whistled softly under her breath. "Sorry, sir."

"I know what you're thinking, Number One," Picard said.

"As I said," Worf replied, "it is a strong signal."

"And I regret it," Picard said. "But to the best of our ability, and within the bounds of reason and compassion, we must implement this order. HARF installations within the Union are now closed to all non-Starfleet and non-Federation personnel."

Šmrhová watched as the *Enterprise*'s first officer looked his captain straight in the eye. "All, sir?"

Picard looked straight back. "Within the bounds of reason and compassion."

Lunch finished, Mhevet decided she had better go and interview the two girls who had found the body. The fewer gaps there were in her investigation when the new guard arrived, the better. She might be able to leave on her own terms, rather than be shoved unceremoniously out of the door.

Her first stop was a tidy tenement block near the Federation hospital on the northwest side of Torr. The woman who opened the door looked at her with distaste. "I was wondering when we were going to see you again," said the girl's mother. "Esla's been in a state since that day. We should sue."

"I'm not entirely sure who you would sue, ma'am, but don't let that stop you."

The interview was quickly over. The girl hadn't seen anything but the body, and thinking about that reduced her to tears and incoherence. As Mhevet left, Esla's mother said, "Are you going to see the other one now?"

"I guess so."

"Because if you're planning to interview her with a parent present, I doubt you'll be in luck."

"What do you mean?"

"Go and see. They built that part of town from rubbish, and rubbish moved in."

And it was indeed a run-down part of Torr, cobbled together from Federation supplies that were only ever intended to be temporary and should have been replaced years ago. She found the girl sitting on the step outside a tenement building, and she was eating from a bag of something sugary.

Mhevet stood in front of her and folded her arms. "Is your dad inside?"

The girl, sticky-mouthed and sticky-fingered, gave her a look that said: *What do you think?*

"Where is he, then?"

"Why do you want to know?" She was dark-eyed and tired, as if she had been up all night.

"Because I have to talk to you and I can't do that without your mom or your dad there."

"My mom's gone and my dad's been at the *geleta* house all morning."

It was afternoon now. Chances were he was long since drunk and wouldn't be much assistance in this interview anyway.

"I'm not gonna tell you anything anyway," the girl added, in a lackluster voice, more for form's sake than anything else, it seemed. "Police scum."

"Police *scum*?" Mhevet rolled her eyes. There was something to be said for the old days when holodramas had to be licensed: that had at least set some standards for content. She nodded at the bag, which the girl promptly scrunched up and threw on the ground in front of her feet. Mhevet bit her tongue. "What if I buy you some more of those?" she asked. "Better still, what if I buy you some proper food?"

The girl looked thoughtful. "Does my dad have to be there?"

"Would you rather he wasn't?"

The girl shrugged.

"Then let's make it just you, me, and some hot *terik* stew and *canka* nuts from that canteen up the street."

The girl kicked the bag with a grimy shoe. "And some of that?"

"If you pick up the bag."

The girl tutted, as if this was a flagrant violation of her rights, and picked up the bag. "All right," she said. "Deal."

At the canteen, the girl fell ravenously on her nuts and stew. Mhevet picked at her own plate and watched her. Poor thing. She was smart, but what chance did she have? No mother, useless father—it would fall like a shadow over her life, and she'd probably never get out of this place. She thought fleetingly of something the ambassador had said: *There's a universe of wonders out there, and yet I seem to have spent my life in little rooms and seedy alleyways.* He could have added "and bad canteens" to the list.

Dessert arrived. The girl dug in with gusto. "All right," Mhevet said. "Payment time. Tell me everything you saw that day."

"Just that day?" the girl asked, her voice muffled by the spoon shoved into her mouth.

"What do you mean? Was there another day?"

"Ye-ah! I saw that Bajoran down there loads. I used to go down there all the time. Not now. Esla's mother won't let her go around with me now, and it's not as much fun. Stupid." She blinked a couple of times. "Anyway, he was down there all the time."

Well away from any surveillance. So this was where he'd been going to—exactly where they'd found him. Mhevet sighed. Kalanis had told her to interview the girls. And why had she resisted? Because she'd been offended to be stuck with a case she'd thought was taking her away from her real work.

"All right," she said. "What was he doing there?"

"Meeting people. You know. Talking to them."

"Did you hear what they were talking about?"

"No. I used to hide. I could see them, but I couldn't hear. There was one time they argued, though. I think they were arguing about the Bajoran's wife."

"How many people were with him, usually? Just one other person?"

"Sometimes. Sometimes he was there too."

"Who? Who do you mean?"

"Your friend," the girl said, shoving another spoonful into her mouth and not realizing that she was in the process of kicking over Mhevet's already fairly flimsy world.

"My friend?" asked Mhevet softly.

"You know. The one who was there that time you came to look at the body." She looked at Mhevet. "The one who took us home."

Fumbling slightly as she reached into her pocket, Mhevet brought out her personal padd. She scrolled quickly through a series of images before finding the one she needed. From last Year's Turn. They'd had a great party.

"Yes," said the girl. "That's him!"

"I see." Mhevet put her padd away. "Did Esla ever see him?"

"No, I don't think so. Does it matter?"

"Yes."

She thought for a while. "No. She only came there

with me a couple of times. She knew she'd be in trouble with her mom."

"Is that the truth?"

The girl looked up at her angrily. "I'm not a liar!"

"I didn't say you were."

"Yes, it's the truth!"

"Good." One thing she didn't have to worry about. "Stay here," said Mhevet. "I need to make a call."

The girl ran her spoon around the sugary-sweet mess in her dish. "There's still loads left in here," she said. "I'm not going anywhere."

Mhevet went over to the public comm. "*Come on, come on . . .*" she muttered, as the call was put through. Then: "Hi, Erelya."

Erelya Fhret looked past her. *"Where on Prime are you now? Honestly, Ari, you find some real dumps to hang out in—"*

"Mm, well, comes with the territory. You fancy some lunch?"

"Not there—"

"Oh, but it's great," Mhevet trilled. "You'd love it. Best *scattel* fish in Torr."

Erelya's eyes narrowed. She was allergic to *scattel* fish and knew Mhevet was unlikely to forget. The effects were memorable.

"Maybe I will," she said. *"Everything good at your end?"*

"Oh, you know, the usual. People."

"People?" Fhret frowned.

Please, thought Mhevet, *get it. Please get it. And then please don't let me down. . . .*

"Okay, Ari," Fhret said. *"I'll be with you soon. How can I refuse?"*

The comm ended. Mhevet paid for lunch, in coins, and went back to the table. "Eat up," she said. "We're going."

"I've still got all this—"

"Bring it with you."

They went back outside and dashed through the rain over to the skimmer. "Are we going for a ride?" the girl asked, as they climbed inside.

"No," said Mhevet. "Not in this, anyway."

The girl was disappointed. "Really?"

"Really," said Mhevet, because it was a department skimmer, and it would be a matter of a moment's work for Tret Fereny to trace them, the same way he could trace her if she used her personal comm. "Don't worry, you'll get to go in my friend's. It's much nicer anyway."

It was, too, as the girl made clear when Erelya Fhret pulled up in her very flashy skimmer. Mhevet pushed the girl quickly into the back and climbed into the front.

"So," said Fhret, as she pulled out into the rain. "Where to?"

Mhevet tried to think of somewhere safe. "East," she said, at last.

The little girl kept up a constant stream of chatter and wisecracks all the way to East Torr, and she didn't seem to notice that the two women in the front were grimly silent.

"Left here," murmured Mhevet, and Fhret turned into a wide street. The market was closed today. The rain was pooling in the canopies over the stalls, which hung heavily and precariously as a result. "That building there."

Silently, Fhret eased the skimmer to a stop, aligning it perfectly to the building's main door. "So you don't get wet," she said.

"I can't thank you enough—"

"Shut up, and get on with whatever you have to do. But you owe me a lifetime of lunches for this, Ari."

Mhevet leaned over to kiss her friend quickly on the cheek, and she felt Erelya's hand upon her arm. "*Take care of yourself,*" the other woman whispered.

"*You too,*" Mhevet replied.

At Mhevet's barked instruction, the little girl hopped out of the back and dashed over to the tenement entrance. The skimmer pulled off as Mhevet rang the bell.

"She was nice," said the girl.

"Glad you approve," Mhevet said. "You won't like Coranis."

At first, Coranis seemed set on proving this: she wouldn't let them in until Irian intervened. "The kid looks worn out. Let's give them a drink, see if the rain eases up, and then send them on their way."

"The rain," Coranis grumbled, as she moved aside to let them in, "won't ease up for hours."

Irian made them red leaf tea. She must have slipped something into it because, thankfully, the little girl curled upon the couch and fell straight asleep. Irian covered her with a blanket. "Why have you come here, Ari?" she asked.

"I need to be off the radar for a while," Mhevet replied.

"Don't you have colleagues who can take care of you?" Coranis, seeing Mhevet's expression, burst out laughing. "So they've turned out to be not so reliable after all?"

"Some of them are reliable. But they're not in the ascendant right now. Coranis, this is important."

"What we do is important," Coranis said. "And first you opted out, and now you've brought trouble here—"

"Please. I need to be somewhere safe while I work out what to do next." She nodded at the girl who was asleep on the couch. "I need to keep her safe. Not to mention dry. . . ."

Irian touched her mate's arm. "She's a child. . . ."

Coranis sighed. "Oh, all right! But you can't stay here indefinitely. We don't want trouble."

Mhevet nodded her thanks. "Can I use the comm?"

Coranis and Irian glanced at each other.

"Nobody will know it's me using it," Mhevet said.

"Ari knows what she's talking about," said Irian.

"Oh, go ahead," Coranis said ungraciously.

But it was difficult to know who to contact. Kalanis, obviously, would have been her first choice, but Kalanis was almost certainly under observation.

Fhret had done as much as she dared, if not more so, given the way the CIB was going. She couldn't approach anyone at work, because she didn't know who was involved. *Never never never would I have guessed Fereny.* And she didn't want to put anyone not involved in danger. The ambassador, her single friend in a high place, was dead.

She had run out of Cardassian friends. What about Federation friends?

This is one big favor I'm asking for, Mhevet thought, as she started keying in Commander Margaret Fry's code, *but, then, I guess they're going soon. . . .*

She was only partway through the code when her own personal comm chimed.

"Are you going to answer that?" asked Coranis.

Mhevet hesitated. If she answered, she would certainly be traced. Then someone began to speak: *"It's Blok. Get in touch when you get this."*

She was hugely relieved to hear his voice. So there were still two of them. Quickly, reading from the screen on her comm, Mhevet keyed the code he had used into Coranis and Irian's comm. "It's me," she said. "What do you want?"

"We should talk. I have information for you."

"It's pretty awkward right now—"

"Tell me about it. . . . Where are you?"

"With friends."

He frowned. She saw realization dawn on his face. *"Like that, is it?"*

"Yes. And more besides."

"Can you say where?"

Coranis grabbed her hand. "Who are you bringing here now?" she hissed.

Mhevet shook her off and rattled off the address. *"All right,"* said Dygan. *"I'll get over straightaway."* He cut the comm.

"How *dare* you!" Coranis said. "You turn up out of the blue expecting us to help you, and now you invite someone over without even asking!"

"I'm sorry," Mhevet said. "I'm a bad person. I've got no excuse. But he's still coming around. When he's here, we'll leave. We'll go somewhere else. I promise."

Not that she had much choice in the matter. When the bell chimed, Coranis took one look at the man standing on her doorstep and exploded. "Who *is* this, Ari? Look at him!"

Mhevet could have kicked herself. She'd forgotten that Dygan was dressed for his role: hair cut brutally short and all in brown. He looked exactly like the thug he was pretending to be.

"He's undercover. . . . Look, it's better if you don't know anything about this."

"He's not coming in here!"

Mhevet glanced at the little girl, still asleep on the sofa, and said to Irian, "Look after her. Really, I can't stress how important this is. There are some bad people after her, and we have to look after her."

"Tell him to go around the back," Irian said. "And don't worry—we're old hands at this, Ari."

And they were, of course. They'd been radicals

in the old days, when Central Command and the Obsidian Order had an iron grip on Cardassia; and then they had lived through Meya Rejal's clampdowns and the Dominion purges. They were survivors, and they were good people.

Mhevet sent Dygan around the back and dashed out to join him. He'd folded his big, solid frame under the fire escape steps, and it wasn't keeping him particularly dry. Rainwater was running in little rivers down his face, and his brown jacket was soaked through. "Sorry," she said, pulling her jacket over her head and joining him under the steps. "They saw you and panicked."

"That's all right. I'd cross the street to avoid me. Listen, have you heard about the ambassador?"

She nearly sobbed. Couldn't stop herself. Dygan looked at her with concern. Strange from someone with his appearance. "Hey, it'll be all right."

"Oh, yeah? It's all blown up at the constabulary," she said. "My boss has been suspended. There are new people in there, and I don't think they're our kind of people. On top of that, I've discovered who killed Aleyni Cam. One of my colleagues."

Dygan swore.

"A little girl found the body. I went to see her. She recognized him."

"A *girl*? Where is she now?"

"Up in the apartment with my friends—"

He glanced up the steps nervously. "Can you trust them?"

"I can trust them to be suspicious of authority and to put themselves between her and anyone who comes knocking at the door. Look, can you help? I don't know where to go. I can't take her back to the department. I don't know what's going on there. I don't know how high up this goes."

"No. No, you can't go back there. . . . It's only you and me now, you realize?"

"I know."

"The ambassador wasn't stupid," Dygan said. "I think he knew that once he found out, he'd become a target. The thing is . . ." Dygan wiped rain from his face, smearing red across his cheeks and brow. "The other thing is . . . after the ambassador was killed, I overheard a couple of people talking. They said that the word was that the ambassador had just come out of a meeting with the castellan. . . ."

Mhevet looked at him in terror. "You think the *castellan* knew?"

"Well, obviously she knew by the time the ambassador spoke to her—"

"But she might have known earlier? Do you even mean *before* . . . what happened to Bacco?"

"All I'm saying is that the ambassador went into a meeting with her, presumably to tell her what we both know, then left that meeting and was dead almost immediately after."

Mhevet went cold. "But that would mean a cover-up at the highest level. And it makes no sense! She and Bacco were tight; they were close. . . .

You can't mean Rakena Garan was involved in her death?"

"I don't know. I don't know what to think anymore! At the very least, she's been involved in the cover-up. And my point is—I wouldn't trust anyone right now. Not in the constabularies, not in the CIB, and not in the administration. We may as well go and hide in North Torr!"

"I was going to try HARF—" Mhevet stopped as footsteps came clattering overhead. Irian came hurrying down the fire escape, pulling a sleepy little girl behind her.

"I don't know what trouble you're in, Ari," she said, "but there's a police officer at the door asking for you. Coranis is holding him off, but you'd better get going." She glanced at Dygan, then looked away. "If you go down this alley, you'll come to a wire fence. There's a hole cut into it. Squeeze through, and you'll come out onto a path running along the tramlines." She pushed the little girl toward them. "And hurry up!"

They didn't wait around for her to tell them again. Mhevet grabbed the little girl's hand, and the three of them sped off along the alley. As Irian promised, they came out onto a path running along the tramlines. The rain was lashing down.

"We're still too much out in the open," Dygan muttered. "And fairly distinctive . . ."

"Seriously," said Mhevet, "if you can think of anywhere we can go, I'm open to suggestions."

"Let's get under that bridge first."

They dashed through the rain to the cover of the bridge. Mhevet checked on the little girl. She was wide awake, bright-eyed and frightened, and trying to hide it. Mhevet hugged her. "You're doing great," she said.

"They'll never take me alive," the girl said gamely. Her teeth were chattering.

"You bet," said Mhevet, taking off her wet jacket and putting it around the child's shoulders. Better than nothing.

"How did they find us?" Dygan asked.

"I don't know. . . . You left a message on my comm. They must have been able to trace even that."

"In which case . . . You may as well use the comm again."

They looked at each other. "It's a risk," Mhevet said.

There was a shout in the distance. *"I'm going to try down here!"*

"We've not really got a lot of options," Dygan said.

"All right. Here goes nothing."

Mhevet punched in the code. There was some to-ing and fro-ing, and then Fry's voice came out of the comm.

"Investigator? How can I help you?"

"Commander," Mhevet said, "I know this is possibly the most irregular request you'll ever get, but is there any chance that you could beam me and a couple of friends into HARF?" She peered out anxiously into the rain. "Soonish?"

"Investigator," said Fry, "I'm sorry, but I can't help you. All our installations on Prime are closed to Cardassian citizens. Ari, we've been escorting people off the site—"

"Maggie, this is life or death—"

Šmrhová inched closer to Fry. She, Worf, and the commander were in the installation's small communications center. They'd been monitoring reports from other HARF installations across Prime about the lockdown when this call had come through.

"Life or death," Fry murmured.

"Could be a trick," said Šmrhová. "Someone could be forcing her to say all this to get her inside."

"A complicated plan, Lieutenant," said Worf.

"This is Cardassia Prime, sir," Šmrhová replied, and began checking at the companel.

"There have been no signs of any intention to attack the base in that way," Worf said. "All the disorder has been on the streets—"

"A call's out for this woman, Mhevet," Šmrhová said, twisting the screen around so that her superior officer could see. "The constabularies are looking for her. She seems to have kidnapped a child—"

"Maggie, please help!"

Šmrhová listened closely. This really did sound like someone desperate. In the background she heard another voice. "*What's going on? Are they going to help us?*"

"Dygan?" asked Šmrhová, moving around to the comm. "Is that you? Dygan, it's Šmrhová!"

"*Aneta! Aneta, is that you?*"

"Yes, yes it is—Ravel, I thought you were on extended leave. What have you been up to? What's going on?"

"*Aneta, we're in trouble. We need to get somewhere safe. Can you help?*"

The *Enterprise* officers exchanged a look. Šmrhová raised her eyebrows. Worf shrugged.

"Sir," Šmrhová said quietly, "Dygan's practically Starfleet. . . ."

"So he is," Worf replied.

"Ari, I'm sorry," Fry said, "but our orders are to keep the compound closed to all non-Starfleet or Federation personnel. . . ." She stopped speaking. The point had become moot. Dygan had materialized, looking rougher than usual. He was accompanied by two more Cardassians: a female and a little girl. All three were soaking wet and dripping rainwater onto the floor. Fry looked at the trio in shock. "What just happened?"

"Sorry, Commander," Šmrhová said. "I must have leaned on the wrong control."

"Lieutenant," said Fry, "we are under direct orders not to allow any Cardassian citizens on this compound—"

"They were in trouble, sir!" Šmrhová said. "What

else were we supposed to do? Dygan's one of us! You can't expect us to serve alongside someone and then ignore him when he asks me for help!" She gestured around them. "Isn't that the whole point of this place?"

Fry suppressed a small smile. "Well," she said, "you have me there." She turned to Mhevet. "Ari, since you're here—care to introduce me to your friends?"

"Yes, of course—Glinn Ravel Dygan, of the . . ."

"Sixth Order," said Dygan, helpfully. "Although most recently of the *Enterprise*."

"And this one"—Mhevet patted the girl gently on the shoulder—"will be our chief witness should we ever be able to bring the murderer of Aleyni Cam to trial."

Fry drew in a sharp breath. "You know who it was?"

"Yes, we know, but it's complicated." She offered Fry her palm, and Fry pressed her own against it. "I don't know how many rules you've broken bringing us here, Maggie, but you saved this one's life." She pulled the little girl to her. "And ours."

"I see." Fry turned to Šmrhová and Worf. "The *Enterprise*? You've all served together?"

"Yes," said Dygan. He was out of breath.

Šmrhová patted him on the shoulder. "Dygan is one of the finest officers I've served with."

Dygan turned to Šmrhová. "Thanks, Aneta," he said. "I owe you."

"Don't mention it," said Šmrhová. She lowered her voice. "It's easier to ask forgiveness than permission."

The little girl, all ears, giggled. "I like that," she said. "Forgiveness, not permission. I'll remember that."

Ten

Standing at the third-story window of Commander Fry's office, Jean-Luc Picard watched the rain leave red streaks on the plastic glass. It was an ever-changing complex of shifting patterns. Outside, a sodden evening was settling sullenly upon a tired and dispirited city. Here in the temporary safety of the compound, however, all was quiet.

At the desk behind Picard, Glinn Dygan and the Cardassian investigator, Mhevet, were sitting with the little girl between them. Dygan was showing her a series of holo-images.

"What about this man?"

"No, never seen him either. Never seen any of them. Ari, I'm tired! I want to go to bed! I want to go *home*!"

"I know," Mhevet said soothingly. "But you can't go home. Not yet. We'll go through a couple more of these, and then we'll find you somewhere to sleep." She glanced anxiously at Picard, who nodded. He tapped on his combadge and issued a few quick instructions to Šmrhová. *Nursery duty,* he thought, *will serve as preliminary punishment until I find out who is responsible.*

"All right, last few," said Dygan. "How about this one?"

Silence. Picard turned quickly to see the little girl staring at the image in front of her. She poked at it with her small finger, and the picture wavered. "I think I've seen him."

Dygan and Mhevet exchanged a quick look over the child's head.

"Listen," Mhevet said quietly. "It's very important that you're sure. You don't have to recognize any of them. There's nothing to win for recognizing any of them, and you won't be in trouble if you don't recognize any of them. It's much worse if you say you recognize one of them when you don't—"

"No, I've seen him! Definitely! He was the one that was with your friend that time."

"Are you sure?"

"I'm sure. It's the scar. That scar."

The captain, coming to join them, rested his hand gently upon the child's shoulder. "So what do we have here?"

The girl, who for some reason was eager for his approval, looked up quickly. She pointed at the image in front of her: a young Cardassian male with a distinctive white scar running down one side of his face.

"I've seen him!" she said proudly. She shot a quick look at Mhevet. "I'm not lying, Ari. Honestly. You said it was important, so I wouldn't lie. Promise."

Mhevet patted the child's hand. "All right. Brilliant work. You've got a good eye and a great memory. Shall we get you to bed now?"

"Can I have something to eat first?"

Mhevet laughed. "All right. Kitchen first, then bed."

"Wait a minute, Investigator," Picard said. "I have someone lined up for this job." He tapped his combadge. "Lieutenant Šmrhová to Commander Fry's office."

Šmrhová, when she arrived, took on her new task as babysitter with equanimity. She jerked her head to the child. "Come on, kiddo. Let's see what the kitchen can do for us."

When they left, Picard turned to Dygan. "Do you know who that is?"

Dygan nodded. "His name is Colak. He's one of Velok Dekreny's people. He's a nasty piece of work."

"Is he?" asked Mhevet. "I'll enjoy arresting him when the time comes. I'll enjoy seeing Dekreny's face when I arrest him."

"Good work, Dygan, as ever," said Picard.

The glinn switched off his personal comm, and the image of the scarred Cardassian disappeared. "I hope so."

"You've established a direct connection between the extremists in North Torr and the city constabulary," Picard said. "And all signs seem to be that you've found the murderers of Lieutenant Aleyni. I'd say that's a job well done."

"Well," said Dygan. "We'll see."

Picard glanced at Mhevet. "I imagine this must

be a shock for you, Investigator. Did you work closely with Fereny?"

"He was certainly keen to work closely with me," she said. "He asked me constantly about the Aleyni case. I thought it was because he wanted to work on his first murder investigation." She rubbed at tired eyes. "You know, of all the people in the department, he's the last I would have said would be involved with people like Dekreny. Shows how much I know."

Dygan looked at her sympathetically. "The whole point is not to draw attention to yourself."

"Perhaps," she said. "Still, it was on my watch. And we've no guarantee we'll be able to bring either of them to justice. I've no idea what's happening at the constabulary now that Kalanis is out of the way. I wouldn't dare set foot outside this installation right now."

"We'll see what the morning brings," Picard said.

The door opened, and Worf entered. "Another of our guests has arrived, sir," he said. He looked at Dygan and Mhevet with a dry expression. "We are certainly receiving a large number of Cardassian visitors tonight. I've had her taken to one of the small meeting rooms along the corridor from here. It's hardly the most impressive of environments for a guest of her stature, but it is the best that this building can do."

"Thank you, Number One." Picard turned to the two Cardassians. "Well," he said. "Shall we see what our guest makes of your discoveries?"

The two young Cardassians followed Worf out of the door, but Picard held back for a moment. He was thinking about the little girl, the only link in the chain between Aleyni and Fereny, and Fereny and the True Way activists in North Torr. She had looked very small, and very vulnerable. Quickly, he sent a message to his wife:

Kiss René for me.

The captain of the *Enterprise* opened the door to the meeting room. It was indeed something of a bare room: packing cases stood around, the shelves were already empty, and chairs were stacked up in one corner. Sitting down, small but very upright, with the dark window behind her, was Castellan Rakena Garan.

She rose when she saw Picard.

"Captain Picard," she said. "I've had to cancel several pressing appointments this evening to meet you. I know that the current situation grieves us both, but there's very little I can do without some sign of movement from your own people—"

"Castellan Garan," Picard said, taking the seat opposite her, "I'm sorry to have brought you here under false pretenses. I don't want to discuss Starfleet's withdrawal with you. There has, as yet, been no change in policy—"

"Then why, exactly, am I here?"

Picard studied her thoughtfully. All his impressions of her had always been positive. She was strongminded, shrewd, perhaps lacking in sparkle, but clearly a dedicated public servant. *Could she really have been involved in the murder of Bacco?*

"Castellan," he said, "how important is our alliance to you?"

"What?" She stared at him. "You know exactly how important! I've staked my political career on it! I believe it's vital—"

"I am sincerely glad to hear that." He leaned back over his shoulder and called out to the two people waiting in the corridor. "Come in, please."

Dygan came in first, looking faintly embarrassed at being dressed as a rain-soaked street thug for a meeting with his head of state. Garan's eyes widened in dismay, but she masked it quickly, Picard noted. Mhevet, coming in next, looked at the castellan damply but without fear.

"Who are these people?" Garan asked.

"This," said Picard, "is Glinn Ravel Dygan. He was until recently serving on the *Enterprise*."

"Ah, yes. I've heard of you, Glinn Dygan." Garan gave him a quick, tight smile. "All good, I hasten to add."

"Thank you, ma'am. It's a privilege to serve the new Cardassia."

"And this," Picard continued, "is Investigator Arati Mhevet, of the city constabulary."

"Another name that's impressed itself upon me. Reta Kalanis has spoken about you very often, Investigator. I believe she has you in mind as a possible successor. Kalanis and I have been colleagues for a long time, and we worked well together." The castellan gave a heavy sigh. "I hope that this business of her suspension can be resolved as quickly as possible."

"So do I, ma'am," said Mhevet.

The castellan looked around at the three of them. "So, two of Cardassia's finest. Captain, I'm honored to meet them both—but why tonight, and why here, of all places? It hasn't escaped my attention that I am, technically, on Federation soil."

"Two of Cardassia's finest indeed. And, sadly, this is where this meeting has to happen. Both Dygan and Mhevet are, for the moment, under our protection—"

"Protection?" The castellan looked disturbed. "Why would a police investigator and an army glinn need to come here for that? Why are their own people not able to protect them?"

"Because we know," Mhevet said. "We know about the True Way."

Garan stared at her. "Know what about the True Way?"

"At the behest of Ambassador Garak," Picard said, "Glinn Dygan has for the past few months been undercover amongst extremists currently operating out of North Torr—"

"Far be it from me to speak ill of the dead," the castellan said, "but Ambassador Garak had a habit of wildly overstepping his authority."

"Which is our good fortune, at least," Picard said. "By which I mean the good fortune of the Federation. Before the ambassador died, Glinn Dygan was able to tell him that in all likelihood the True Way was responsible for the death of Nanietta Bacco." Picard paused and watched her closely. "I'm sorry to have to speak so bluntly, Castellan."

"I'm sure you're not the only one in this room who is sorry," she said softly.

"When I say 'we know,'" Picard went on, "I'm speaking for the moment of four people only. I've not as yet informed any of my superiors."

She touched her hand against the beads around her neck.

"First of all, I want to establish what you knew, and when. Castellan," he said, "you must realize that this looks very bad. The ambassador came to see you, presumably to tell you what he knew, and within minutes of leaving you, his skimmer was destroyed—" He stopped short at the sight of her fury.

"What do you take me for!" she said angrily. "I knew Nanietta Bacco! I knew her well! We were colleagues—no, we were *friends*! We were trying to bring our civilizations together! How could you think such a thing of me?" She stood up. "Who are you, Captain Picard, to question me? What evidence do you have that one of us murdered Nan Bacco? Yesterday it was Bajoran, today it was a Tzenkethi, tonight it is a Cardassian! Your people are in shock, I understand that, but to throw accusations such as this around is unconscionable!"

"It's true," said Dygan softly.

"Prove it," she said.

"I can," Dygan replied.

"We can already link the city constabulary to extremists operating out of North Torr," said Mhevet. "When we've made the arrests, we'll get the rest of the links in the chain—"

"That's a long way from being able to prove that a member of the True Way murdered Nan Bacco," the castellan said angrily. "What is the True Way, now? What evidence is there that such a group exists? As far as I can tell, as far as the CIB can tell, they were a paranoid fantasy of the late ambassador. A fiction concocted by a man who saw enemies everywhere. I doubt they even exist!"

Somebody spoke from just outside the door. "They're no fantasy, Rakena. Not even I could make them up."

Picard turned to watch the castellan. As the man moved into the light, she put her hand up to cover her mouth.

"Yes, they exist," he said, "but in the shadows. They exist only in the shadows. Their secrecy gives them power because it means they rule by fear, because we fear each other and our intentions toward each other. I know all these games. I mastered them years ago. The True Way holds no fear for me. We must bring them into the light. Let them burn in the hot glare of the sun."

"Garak," she said, sinking back down into her chair.

"Who else?" He took a chair from the stack and placed it down opposite her. "You and I need to talk, Rakena."

*   *   *

As Picard and the other two Cardassians withdrew from the room, Garak sat examining his hands and contemplating what approach he should take with this woman. His tactics necessarily differed from person to person. With Odo, he had resorted to physical violence, whereas Parmak had confessed simply because Garak had sat still and looked at him. Both of those men were courageous, and both of them were very strong. This woman was courageous too, and Garak knew he would be a fool if he underestimated her strength. So what should he do? How did one break someone like this?

When the door was closed, Garak looked up at his castellan.

"Why are you not dead?" she asked.

"Because when I go to the city constabulary and make contact with an undercover agent who tells me that the True Way is responsible for the death of the president of the Federation, I assume the meeting has not gone unnoticed and that the matter of my removal will be a top priority." He shifted in his chair, which was not particularly comfortable. Chairs in little rooms like this were never comfortable, on either side. "I can only be grateful that Captain Picard was willing not only to break a directive disallowing our entry to this establishment, but also to assume that I was not indulging in—what was it? Oh, yes!—'a paranoid fantasy.' I was transported here, to HARF, well before my skimmer exploded."

Garak suppressed a slight shudder. In fact, it had been a matter of seconds, and he'd been fairly shaky ever since. He'd grabbed some sleep here and there, but most of the day had been spent frantically trying to contact Mhevet and Dygan, who had unfortunately— if sensibly—taken his assassination as a signal to go to ground. Garak was not feeling at his most relaxed. But the castellan didn't need to know any of this.

She looked at him steadily. "You can't prove anything."

"No, but you can and will tell me the truth. *Was* it you?"

"Of what am I being accused now? Murdering Bacco? Or attempting to murder you?"

He shrugged. "Take your pick."

"How *dare* you—"

"I know that you've been set on ignoring my advice at whatever cost, Rakena, but on this occasion I would strongly advise you to speak plainly to me. Hitherto we have simply not succeeded in being friends. I would advise you not to make me your enemy."

"What kind of person do you think I am?"

"I think you're the product of a violent and brutal civilization whose leaders have always indulged themselves to excess. Tell me why I shouldn't believe that you are a murderer and an assassin. I know I am."

"*You?*" She was pale gray with rage. "You are all that was worst about the old Cardassia! All that was poisonous and deadly! The Obsidian Order!" She spat out the words. "Central Command! Skrain Dukat!

You were the ones who brought us to the edge. How many died because of men like you? How does a man like you survive?"

Garak didn't reply. He didn't disagree with anything she had said. Softly, he asked, "When did you find out about Bacco?"

"Just before Picard brought the news about President Ishan's shift of policy over the withdrawal. The deputy director of the CIB came to see me."

"The *deputy* director? Not Crell?"

She gave him a cold look.

"No," Garak said. "No, of course not. . . . As a matter of interest, when exactly did Crell stop answering to you? No, you don't have to answer that. I'll work that out for myself." He recalled her sudden moment of distress in the meeting, which he had put down to shock. It had indeed been shock—but of a different kind. "Yes, I see now why that meeting with Picard was so alarming. You must have thought Ishan already knew and was beginning to pull back from us, without even a courtesy call . . ." He examined his nails. "You realize you're going to have to resign?"

"I beg your pardon?"

"Your position really is impossible."

"I have no intention of resigning—!"

"You won't survive this, so you may as well go on your own terms. Rakena, a Cardassian has murdered the president of the Federation. The CIB, if not implicated in some quarters, has, at the least, attempted to cover it up—with your cognizance!"

"*Nobody* close to me had a hand in Nan Bacco's death!"

"No? How did the assassin get on board DS9? How did they get within range?"

There was a pause. Her hand went up to cover her mouth.

"They're not a paranoid fantasy, Rakena," he said. "They think of everything. They mean to control us. They have taken parts of the CIB, and they're taking the constabulary as we speak. And soon they will remove you from your position and put Evek Temet in your place."

She sighed and closed her eyes.

"It would be better if you resigned," he said gently.

"What is the alternative?"

"The alternative," he said, "is that they destroy you."

"I won't let them."

"You won't be able to stop them. Leak after leak after leak . . . Do you want me to map this out for you? It could end with your impeachment."

"I'll fight them all the way."

"You'll lose. And Temet's elevation to castellan will be assured."

"I'm prepared to take that risk."

"I was afraid you'd say that," he said. Again, he studied his nails. "There is another alternative," he said.

"Oh, yes?" She was looking at him with hope in her eyes. Now she was listening. Now she wanted to hear what he could do for her.

"I destroy you first," Garak said.

They stared at each other. Neither of them blinked. "Do your worst," she said.

"Oh, Rakena," he said softly, looking away. "You really shouldn't say things like that."

"Well?" asked Picard, when Garak walked into Fry's office. "Did she know?"

"Not before the act," Garak said. "But soon after." He paced slowly around the room, coming to a halt by the commander's desk. He began to sort through the pile of books stacked there.

"Have you gained any insight into what's happening?" Picard asked.

Garak sighed and put down the book he was holding. "There's plainly some kind of struggle for control happening at the CIB," he said. "Elements there wished to conceal their information about the assassination even from the castellan. Whether because they were implicated or because they were terrified to expose the extent to which they were out of control—I don't know. Possibly both at once, which is alarming. But the deputy director, at least, had the sense to inform the castellan—who then, alas, decided to conceal her knowledge in turn." He rested his hands lightly upon the top of the books. "If only she'd trusted me. . . . But then why should she?"

Picard felt himself relax, slightly. "I must confess it's a great relief to learn Rakena Garan was not involved in any way. But tell me, Garak, what is the hold that the True Way has on your people? Where did they come from?"

"The True Way? Oh, that's a long story. . . . Legend has it that their origins stretch back to our early history, when our society was largely in the control of some very powerful families. Tain's family was one—or so family tradition had it—and that was the start of the Obsidian Order. Whether or not this was true, I don't know, but certainly it was part of what drove Tain, and, I suspect, part of what drives those who consider themselves the True Way." He picked up one of the books, looked inside, then put it back on the pile and resumed prowling, coming to a halt near the door.

"Like the feudalism of Earth's history," Picard said.

"That's correct. The Obsidian Order was created, in part, to end the strife between those families, to put that way of life behind us. It was intended as an instrument of the state: an organization that did not serve a single family, but served them all. The purpose was to put an end to civil war and to provide stability." He gave a low laugh. "And it worked—rather better than perhaps anyone anticipated. It was very good at preventing civil unrest."

"Rather too good, wouldn't you say?"

"In fact, I would say that, now. But this was how Tain justified himself, you see."

"I see." Picard nodded. Despite all, the captain couldn't help being fascinated by this glimpse into the dark, secret heart of Cardassia. "One doesn't commit evil actions in the belief that one is acting wrongly. What allows one to commit such acts is the belief that it will contribute to a greater good."

"Yes, that's largely what's going on inside your head," Garak said. "It's different for the sociopaths, of course. They're just along for the ride."

"The True Way stood for the past?" Picard asked slowly. "The restoration of the great families and their way of life? That was their justification. *Is* their justification."

"Exactly that. This made them the natural enemies of the Order, which was the instrument created to secure the new Cardassian state. I have to say that the True Way's methods were always tediously similar: they'd install their people in key institutions—the Detapa Council, the Order, Central Command—and those people would work to concentrate power in their hands. Always the same, and always a trial to police. A great deal of my work at one point involved preventing the True Way from gaining control of the upper levels of the Obsidian Order hierarchy. . . ."

Garak paused and frowned in recollection. Picard shuddered at the thought of what those purges must have involved.

"You can see," Garak went on, "that they've not changed much, despite the passage of time and the tragedies of our recent past."

"And they survived the Dominion War?"

"Oh, yes—well, something of everything survived

the Dominion War in one way or another. I became aware of them again when Ghemor was alive. They sent a suicide bomber—a teenage girl—to destroy a Federation science project in the Andak Mountains."

"I recall that case," Picard said slowly. "Miles and Keiko O'Brien were there at the time."

"Yes, that's right. If I hadn't been set against the True Way already, I would certainly have been after they threatened Miles O'Brien's family. . . ." Garak smiled down fondly at the floor. "Anyway, we stopped them. But I've been vigilant ever since. I'm all that remains of the Obsidian Order, and watching for the True Way was our primary purpose. . . ." Garak shrugged. "Perhaps they're the same people, or perhaps these are their inheritors, but they need to know that I am still here, and I will never allow them to reestablish themselves. Cardassia is different now, and it will remain different."

"Why was President Bacco targeted?"

Garak sighed. "Who knows what tortuous logic lies behind that crime? Nevertheless, being of a similarly devious cast of mind, I shall attempt an explanation."

"By all means do."

"We are once again at a moment when Cardassian political life hangs in the balance. The Federation is leaving. Democracy is taking root. And if Rakena Garan were to win another term—which she can't now, of course—this would certainly have secured a democratic way of life on Cardassia for . . ." Garak tapped his finger against his cheek. "Well, one hesitates to say 'indefinitely,' but certainly beyond my lifetime and, really, that's the best one can hope for."

"And that's not what the True Way wants," said Picard, understanding. "They want power back in the hands of the elite."

"Yes, indeed. So they conceived a bold plan: one that would, with a single action, reshape our internal politics and external alliances in their interest. And you, Captain—or, more specifically, the Federation—have been the target. Strike at the Federation, and you strike at the new order."

"But why the president?"

"That's a statement of power and reach: 'We have gotten past all your security, all your defenses, and we have killed your beloved leader—and you don't even know who we are.'" He smiled. "A blow to a Federation already suffering a crisis of confidence from the Andorian succession—"

"And framing a Bajoran for the crime only further undermines our confidence in our stability and plays to Cardassian prejudice—"

"Yes, indeed." Garak laughed. "And what 'true' Cardassian wouldn't want to see a Bajoran imprisoned for this?"

"That hasn't quite worked out, though," Picard said. "The Bajoran has been proven not to be guilty."

"No, but I rather imagine they are feeling somewhat emboldened at the moment. They have successfully assassinated your president, they have, as far as they know, successfully assassinated me, and the mood here at home seems to be swinging away from the castellan and her pro-alliance stance. Now, they've set you at odds with the Tzenkethi, and, meanwhile, at home, they maneuver someone friendlier to their interests into the position of castellan."

"Evek Temet."

"Yes, indeed, my new *bête noire*." Garak's face darkened. "With the Federation in chaos, Temet as castellan would be well placed to take an isolationist position: 'We must withdraw from the alliance, avoid other peoples' wars, blah blah blah. . . .' So the Union sits out any ensuing conflict between the powers—and who will be the major power after the dust settles?"

"Cardassia," said Picard.

"Yes, indeed." Garak paused. "It's a bold plan and quite elegant. I might have tried it myself once upon a time."

"It also seems to be working well."

"Relatively well, hitherto," Garak replied. "Fortunately, you and I are now on the case."

"What drives such people?" Picard asked. "Why commit such terrible, destructive crimes?"

Garak looked at him. "Do you want me to answer that?"

"Yes. I think I do."

Garak opened his hands. "Love, Captain. What else?"

"*Love?*"

"For this beautiful, stricken world—"

"Many love their homes, Ambassador, but not all are driven to atrocities because of that love."

"But then there's also the pain, Captain. The pain that comes of seeing one's home wounded and the desire to protect it from coming to such harm ever again." He held his hands close together. "I'm not trying to justify such actions. Not any longer. Never again—never. I'm merely trying to explain them."

A wounded world, Picard thought; yes, that was how it was. A civilization that had harmed itself again and again and was now struggling to put this long cycle of hurt behind itself. But all it took was someone who could not live past the pain.

Garak stirred. "Once again I must apologize on behalf of my people. I find myself doing that far too often. . . ." He fell silent for a moment. "What do you intend to do with this information, Captain?"

Picard pondered this. Regulations required he report this. He imagined speaking to Ishan Anjar and telling that stern and unbending man, a victim of the Occupation, what he knew. He wondered if by withholding the information, the Federation might be pulled into a war with the Typhon Pact.

"If I may," Garak said quietly, "what matters is the alliance. If this destroys the alliance between the Federation and the Union, Bacco's assassins will have achieved what they set out to do."

The captain looked around the room at the half-empty shelves, the packing cases lying open. "I won't make a report until the current situation is resolved," he said.

"You mean with the castellan?"

Picard nodded. "What do you think she intends to do?"

"What she intends to do is neither here nor there. Tomorrow morning she will tell the 'casts that she intends to serve out what remains of her term but that she will not be running for reelection."

"And how do you intend to persuade her of that?"

"I have my methods."

"Garak," Picard said, "I cannot be involved in the removal of the democratically elected leader of another government—"

"No?" Garak looked disappointed. "Why, Captain—you're no fun at all." He sniffed. "Sisko would have been willing."

"Yes, well—I'm not Benjamin Sisko."

Garak gave a measureless smile. "Indeed, no! No, you're not! But you need not trouble yourself. I believe that I may yet be able to persuade the castellan to fall upon her sword." He gestured around the room. "You have merely provided the setting for the crime, Captain. Fear not. Someone else will commit it."

"You know that I'd like to believe that," said Picard. "But you're not that persuasive, Ambassador Garak."

Arati Mhevet, watching Ambassador Garak leave Fry's office, stepped out of the shadows and followed him a little way down the corridor. He soon turned to face her.

"Did you want something, Investigator?"

Slowly, she walked up to him. "I was listening, just now."

"Yes, I know."

"I heard everything you said about the Obsidian Order and its origins."

"I wondered if you might find that of interest."

"I did. . . ." She struggled to say what was on her mind.

"Take your time," he suggested. "What you want to say will be difficult to express, I suspect. I only found a way to say it very recently."

She looked down the corridor. "All my life," she said, "despite everything that happened to our people, despite everything we did, I knew there was something about us that was good. Something worthwhile."

"I agree. Not least that we're almost indestructible. Fortunate, really. But we do take a terribly long time to learn." Garak touched her arm. "Go on."

"And I sensed . . . that at the same time there was something pernicious, something bad, something that was always struggling to dominate. Was that the True Way?"

"The True Way is one form that it takes."

"And the Obsidian Order?"

His eyes were pained. "Came to resemble its enemy, sadly."

"I don't want to be Obsidian Order."

"None of us do." Folding his hands around hers, he gave her a steady, sky-blue look. "But you understand, don't you, that the institutions don't matter? The Obsidian Order, Central Command, the True Way, Starfleet, empires, unions, federations—these are names and names only. They are *tools*. They count for nothing if the purpose is flawed. That was my mistake for a long time—confusing the purpose with the instrument. It took me a long time to learn the truth."

"What is the truth?"

"The truth?" Garak laughed, softly, as if he had never imagined that he would be asked such a question. "The truth is that the institution flourishes only when the people who comprise it flourish. And if the people are sick, the institution will be sick." He squeezed her hand. "If there's anything I could teach you, I'd teach you that."

"I think I knew that. But I became complacent, or frightened, or something. . . . Whatever it was, I held myself back from what was going on."

"Yes," he said, nodding, "that was your mistake, Arati. But it doesn't stop, you understand? It doesn't ever stop. We can never hold ourselves back."

"The True Way. I don't want these people in power."

"Of course you don't. Nobody in their right mind would. The question is now: What are you prepared to do about it?"

Mhevet considered that. "I don't know," she said. "What would you do, sir?"

He let go of her hands. "Young lady, in my case, the more troubling question is: What *wouldn't* I do?"

The castellan was still sitting in the empty meeting room. Outside, the rain was easing up, merely pattering now against the window. The night was passing.

"Rakena," Garak said.

She looked up. She was less angry now, more thoughtful. He knew he had been right to give her some time to think, as he had known that, in her case, honesty was the best policy. Odo he had dominated, and Parmak he had silenced. But he had destroyed this woman with nothing more than the truth.

"It's over, isn't it?" she asked. "I've lost, haven't I?"

Garak sat down, sighing at the hard-backed chair. "I'm afraid so."

Her hands clenched into fists. "Evek Temet! Of all people to become castellan."

"Well," said Garak quietly, "he hasn't won yet."

"But he will if I don't resign?"

"Yes. Either you go now, or you go in a few weeks' time, after Temet and his allies have pulled you to shreds and ensured that they will be your successors. You've given good service, but the best service you can perform for the Union now is to resign. I know it's hard—"

"It's getting less hard." She wiped her hands across her face. "I don't think you can imagine how

I felt when I learned who had killed Bacco. Can you imagine?"

"Yes," he murmured, so she couldn't hear. "I can."

"I'd only just been with her. She was coming here to set a seal upon our alliance, to celebrate better days for both our civilizations. Then I heard she was dead, and then I heard *how*. . . ."

The castellan covered her eyes. Garak leaned forward in his seat and—gently, consolingly—rested his hand upon her arm. "When do we stop being the guilty ones?"

"That's it, isn't it?" she asked. "We seem to exist in a state of perpetual culpability. Sometimes I despair." She finally looked up at him.

"We all want that to end," Garak said. "But it won't end with Evek Temet. It will only continue. And that's no longer good enough for Cardassia. We've suffered a great deal. We deserve something else, and we will get it, if we commit ourselves to achieving it."

"Temet won't stop, will he? He and those who support him? They're taking the constabularies, they're taking the CIB, soon they'll take the Assembly—" Tears were forming in her eyes.

"They won't," Garak said. "I'll make sure of that."

"I tried to stand in their way, Garak. If I go, who will stand in their way?"

Garak closed his eyes for a second to block out what little there was of the light. "I'm working on that."

*   *   *

Garak returned to Fry's office and found only the *Enterprise*'s captain there. He walked wearily over to a cabinet where some bottles and glasses stood. His gray hand hovered over the *kanar*, and then he chose the whiskey and poured himself a liberal measure. "Something for you too, Captain?"

"I believe I'll have the *kanar*."

Garak brought over his drink and then stood looking out of the window into the night, cradling his tumbler in both hands. Picard, coming to stand beside him, lifted his glass close to his face and breathed in deeply the rich floral scent of the alien drink. He sipped. It was not unpleasant, and he could imagine acquiring the taste.

"Has she capitulated?"

"Oh, yes. The way's clear now."

They stood for a while in silence. The rain had stopped and one could even imagine that the sky was brightening. Through the window, Picard could hear the unmistakable sounds of dawn: the steady rise in the hum of traffic—even birdsong, he thought. Some rhythms and patterns to life remain the same, whatever the world.

"You've done me so many favors that I'm ashamed to ask for another," Garak said softly. "But I believe I need to ask one more."

"Naturally. Anything that will aid your world during this crisis—"

"This is more in the way of a personal favor. I need to see my doctor."

Picard turned to him, concerned. "Are you ill, Ambassador?"

"No. But Parmak is . . . Parmak is my conscience, and I am in dire need of absolution. I wonder if you could arrange for him to be brought here."

Picard finished his *kanar* and spoke briefly into his combadge. The matter was quickly arranged. Less than a quarter of an hour passed before Kelas Parmak arrived.

The two men embraced. Parmak, when he could speak, did so with a tragic mixture of relief and reproach.

"How could you do this to me?"

"I'm sorry," Garak said, his voice thick. "Will you forgive me?"

"Forgive you? Oh, Elim. When have I ever *not* forgiven you?"

Eleven

Mhevet woke suddenly, bright morning light upon her. Her head throbbed with the dull ache caused by too little sleep, and her back was out of shape from lying twisted on a camp bed for the night. Stretching out and sitting up, she tried to piece together all that had happened the previous day: the shock of learning about Fereny; the grim drive with Fhret to hide with Coranis and Irian; the dash through the rain; the sudden transportation here, to the compound. And then there was the surreal series of scenes that had unfolded the previous night and the epiphany that had come in the early hours while listening to the ambassador . . .

She heard, out in the corridor, the little girl's voice. "Yes, I want some breakfast, but I want the nice old man to come with me." She heard the human lieutenant, Šmrhová, stifling a laugh and the Klingon officer rumbling in reply, and she assumed the child meant their captain. Mhevet smiled. She would record the girl's statement later, here at HARF, and deposit that evidence with the magistrates.

She got out of bed and went out into the corridor. Someone called after her.

"Investigator!"

Ambassador Garak was standing at the far end of the corridor. He could not, surely, have gone to sleep before her, yet he was managing to look annoyingly alert. Even his clothes still looked tidy, although he was running one finger under his collar, as if something was irritating him. He was holding a cup from which came the distinctive aroma of *rokassa* juice. Good for the nerves.

"I wonder," Garak said, "if we might have a word."

Mhevet nodded and followed him along the corridor. Up close, in the morning light, he did look tired—wrung out, perhaps, was closer to the mark. That, she supposed, was the cost of toppling governments.

"Is the castellan still here?" she asked.

"No. She has a great deal to do this morning." Garak led her into the small meeting room where she and Dygan had met the castellan the previous evening. Dygan was already there, cradling a cup of *raktajino*. Mhevet took the chair beside him. Garak looked at the chairs, sighed, and perched himself instead on the desk.

Garak didn't waste time. "You are of course aware that apart from myself, the castellan, Captain Picard, and a few members of the CIB, you two are the only other people to know who is responsible for the murder of Nan Bacco. As I'm sure you're already aware"—he raised an eye-ridge—"this knowledge puts you in danger."

Mhevet and Dygan swapped a look. No, neither of them would forget that brief, terrified time beneath the bridge with the child in their care and the rain lashing down and no certainty of where they could turn.

"However," the ambassador went on, "it also puts you in a position of power, particularly given what you know about the castellan's unfortunate hesitation in informing our allies. May I ask, therefore, what you intend to do with this information?"

Mhevet stared at him. Dygan, too, gaped. "What do you mean?" he asked.

Garak stretched and rubbed his back. "I mean, Dygan, do you intend to splash the story over the nearest 'cast?"

"Of course not!" Dygan said, hotly.

"I hoped that wasn't in the cards."

"What do you think I'm going to do?" Dygan asked. "I'm not going to say a word to anyone."

"No?"

"No! Besides, I'm not staying. I want to go back to the *Enterprise*." Dygan stared down into his cup. "I don't have the taste for undercover work."

"Taste or not," said Garak, "you'll probably get a medal for what you've done. For unspecified services, of course."

"I don't want a medal," Dygan said quickly, his voice coming out rough. "I don't deserve one. I . . . I did a terrible thing, an unforgivable thing. . . . There was a man, outside a shop, and we went there, and—"

"No, don't tell me this!" Mhevet put her hands over her ears. Garak too spoke quickly and loudly. "Glinn Dygan, have some thought for others! If you must confess to a crime, do it to someone who won't be obliged to arrest you!"

"But I did wrong—"

"You'll be compounding that sin further if you make the two of us accessories after the fact!" Garak shot back.

"You did whatever you had to do to conceal your identity," Mhevet said. "I'm prepared to accept that."

"But I need to—"

"Right now, you need not to put Investigator Mhevet in an impossible position," Garak said, in a voice like steel. "Speak to a counselor, Dygan, or a spiritual adviser, if you're that way inclined. But not to the police and not to me!" Garak sighed and reached for his cup. "I know it's an impossible position to be in," he said softly. "The real fault is mine, putting you there."

"We couldn't have done this without you," Mhevet said.

"Exactly," Garak said. "You kept your nerve when Tret Fereny was hammering at the door, and everything you've done on the *Enterprise* to earn the trust of your fellow officers saved not only your life, but hers"—he nodded at Mhevet—"and the life of that noisy child currently making Captain Picard's breakfast very unrestful."

Dygan didn't look comforted. "I won't be saying anything," he said at last. "I want to put this whole thing behind me."

Garak studied him carefully for a moment, and then he sighed. He turned his attention toward Mhevet.

"Oh, you can rely on me to keep quiet," she said. "I think you know that already. I'm assuming Fereny and Colat are going to be brought to justice?"

"Naturally. And I'm assuming you want to be the one to arrest Fereny?"

"Oh, yes. . . ." she said. "Tell me, sir—do you think whoever murdered Bacco is going to be found?"

"I sincerely hope that's going to be the case."

"Then I can't see what would be gained from making this public."

Garak slumped suddenly, his shoulders sagging down. He closed his eyes. "Well, that is a great relief. It's vital that the castellan's reputation is not destroyed."

"What's going to happen to her?" asked Mhevet.

He opened his eyes. "Watch," he said, "and learn."

"What would you have done," Dygan asked, suddenly, "if one of us had said we were going public with all we knew?"

Garak touched his forehead with one fingertip. "What, really, could I have done?"

"That's not an answer, sir."

"Then, if you require an answer, I would have begged you not to."

"But what if I'd insisted?"

Garak looked at him sadly. "Glinn Dygan, I am a very persuasive man. Believe me—you would have been persuaded. Eventually."

The Cardassian people, watching their media that day, might have been forgiven for losing track of who was where and who did what and who was back in favor and who was now in trouble. Round about mid-morning, the news began to hit the 'casts that Prynok Crell, the head of the Cardassian Intelligence Bureau, had offered his resignation. The cause of this, it seemed, was some messages that had somehow been obtained from the office of the late ambassador to the Federation, in which the ambassador indicated that he was concerned about threats to his life. Crell was not able to offer evidence of having taken the threats sufficiently seriously.

"Well done, Akret," Garak murmured. He was standing in the small command center at HARF, clutching his fifth cup of *rokassa* juice, and watching the 'cast on the wall viewer. Mhevet, standing beside him, was on her third coffee—her own poison.

"What's going to happen at the CIB?" Mhevet asked.

"An inquiry. Internal reorganization. A new director."

"Do you think that Crell will be implicated?" She refrained from mentioning Bacco's name out loud. "In everything that has happened?"

"Far be it from me to second-guess the inquiry, but I don't believe that Crell is involved in that. What I do believe is that he was already hostile toward the castellan and that certain elements were able to exploit that." Garak frowned. "The Fire looms large in all our minds, of course. But those are not the only losses suffered. The war with the Klingons, the deaths at the hands of the Bajoran Resistance . . . We've fought too many enemies. We've lost too many people—and not only at the hands of the Jem'Hadar. How terrible is it that so many have died that we can all too easily forget those people?" His expression hardened. "Cardassia must never go back to that. Still, I'm not sure that Prynok Crell has been well rewarded for his service and his sacrifice. That is surely fertile ground for resentment." He frowned. "I'll have to keep an eye on that."

"Who is lined up to replace him?" asked Mhevet. "If it's just one of his cronies, we're no better off than we were before."

"The deputy seems reliable enough," Garak said. "At least, he was the one to inform the castellan about the True Way, which suggests that he's not under their influence. But the real power will be whoever is brought in to oversee the internal reorganization. And we have someone particular in mind for that."

"Of course I'm delighted that our department has been vindicated," said Reta Kalanis. *"Our officers do a first-rate job under difficult conditions. To find ourselves blamed for something outside our jurisdiction has been tremendously frustrating."*

"Will you be returning to your position as director of the city constabularies, ma'am?"

"In fact, this morning I received an offer of a new position, which I think is going to prove a real challenge—"

"I think," said Garak, "that it will do the CIB good to have an outside person brought in to see what's been going on there. Reta Kalanis is a person of rare courage. I've no doubt she can transform the CIB in the way that she transformed the constabulary." He glanced at his unexpected protégée. "I trust her judgment absolutely."

"I'm glad she's back," Mhevet said. "Very glad. But I still wish she hadn't put me on the Aleyni case. It's only by chance I found out that one of Dekreny's men was involved, and that could have put Dygan's life in danger. If I'd been closer to the ground, I might have discovered that much sooner."

Garak looked at her with pity. "Have you still not worked out what she was doing?"

"What do you mean?"

"You may have spent the past few months denying what was happening around you, but Reta Kalanis certainly didn't make the same mistake. She knew which way the wind was blowing at the constabulary—or at least feared what might happen. Kalanis didn't move you to the Aleyni case," Garak said, "she moved you *away* from your investigations in North Torr. I imagined she reasoned that if she was on her way out, she'd rather have you still inside, and as safely away from anything that might put you out of favor with the new guard as possible. It was even better when you made your displeasure known—people thought you were at odds. Reta Kalanis was trying to protect her legacy, but most of all, she was trying to protect you."

Mhevet pressed her hand against her face. Of course, it all made sense. Kalanis had always looked out for her. She would have to think of a way to apologize.

"This next bit," said Garak, gesturing at the screen, "is going to be hard to stomach. But it's a necessary part of this tale."

Evek Temet appeared, standing on the steps of his family home in Coranum.

"Is it wrong to dislike someone so much?" asked Mhevet.

"Probably. But somehow inevitable."

"*This is shocking news,*" Temet said. "*For the head of the Intelligence Bureau to come out and admit that he failed to listen to warnings that the late ambassador's life was in danger is scandalous. And while the CIB have many questions to answer, I think we should also be demanding answers from the individual who is, ultimately, responsible for overseeing all our institutions of state.*"

He drew himself up.

"Here it comes," said Garak.

"*Castellan Garan has enjoyed an unprecedentedly long period in office, and yet it seems that all she has*" *done with that time is to allow our Union to crumble! An assassination on home soil, problems at the CIB— and a dogged but foolish insistence on shackling our great Union to a power that is struggling to hold itself together. No wonder we too are at the edge of the abyss!"*

"Any second now . . ." said Garak.

"This has been one of the most difficult decisions of my life," Temet said, *"but having taken advice from family, friends, and colleagues, I'm announcing my intention to run for the castellanship in the forthcoming election. The people of the Union will decide whether they prefer this current chaos or if they will put their trust in a candidate who will humbly try to unite us all . . ."*

Garak smiled, unpleasantly. *"Got you,"* he said.

Temet continued in this vein for some time, responding to questions about his intentions for the alliance with a sketch of a much more hard-line policy, and then he posed for the holo-cameras to capture a few pictures of him and his beaming family.

"Oh, *please* . . ." Garak muttered. He thumbed at the controls, looking for another channel. "She should be speaking now. . . ."

Rakena Garan appeared on the viewscreen. *". . . most difficult decision of my life,"* she said, *"but I shall not be seeking reelection for the office of castellan. I wish Evek Temet, and any other candidate who may choose to run for this great office, the very best of luck. . . ."*

Garak said, "Electric blue."

"I beg your pardon?" asked Mhevet.

"Her suit."

"What about her suit?"

"That color is called electric blue." Garak looked Mhevet up and down with a faintly disapproving air. "If we're going to become better acquainted, Investigator, you're going to have to take more interest in fashion."

"I take exactly as much interest in fashion as is healthy. Can you explain what the color of the castellan's suit signifies, sir?"

"It signifies that she finally trusted my judgment about something. Doesn't it look marvelous on her? This will be the main thing people remember about this interview. How good that color looked." He waggled a finger. "Mark my words, Mhevet—by next spring, everybody will be wearing electric blue."

On the screen, the castellan was finishing her speech. *"It has been an honor to serve Cardassia over these past years. I wish my successor, whoever that might be, the greatest of luck. I know that they will already understand what a great privilege it is to hold this office. It has been precisely that—the greatest privilege of my life. Thank you all."*

She turned away from the glare of lights and the torrent of questions to go back inside the Assembly. Mhevet, watching closely, thought she saw a glitter in her eye. "I don't feel like this is much of a victory."

"What more do you want?" Garak asked. "We've exposed corruption in the constabulary, put a break on fifth-column elements inside the CIB, prevented a major crisis from destroying our most significant alliance, and have also, not incidentally, solved your murder case. All in all, I'd call that a fairly good night's work. Were you hoping for something more?"

"But losing the castellan is a huge blow! Who's going to stop Evek Temet?"

"I'm sure a candidate will present himself in due course."

"It's got to be someone impressive. Not her deputy. What's his name?"

"Enevek Vorat. No, not him."

"But Evek Temet is young, handsome, energetic—"

"More reasons to hate him. But, yes, those are certainly attractive qualities to a voter. But others can be equally appealing. Don't worry about this too much, Mhevet. I'm sure that some misguided fool can be persuaded to put their head on the block for the good of Cardassia."

"You do think of everything. . . ." She eyed him thoughtfully. "I have one more question to ask you."

"I'll endeavor to give a satisfactory answer."

"Did you fake that assassination attempt?"

"That would certainly be my style." Garak's smile hardened. "But, no. On this occasion, somebody really did try to kill me."

"The True Way?"

"Who else? They've been watching me for a while now, at least since I interfered with their plans to destroy work happening up in the Andak Mountains.

So I've been watching them. I didn't know for sure when they'd strike, but Captain Picard was most understanding of my anxieties after Bacco's death. The alliance certainly seemed to be the target, and I am closely associated with that alliance. I think the good captain would have preferred me under his protection rather sooner, but I had a great deal to do that could only be done in person."

"You cut it pretty fine."

Garak pushed out a breath.

"Anyone might think you were addicted to risk," Mhevet added, innocently.

Garak threw her a narrow, sideways look.

"I had something of a shaky time after your assassination," she said. "I was terrified we'd all been seen together at the constabulary."

"I did try to reach you, Mhevet. You were incommunicado."

"You bet I was," Mhevet muttered. "Still, I suppose it was helpful when it came to speaking to the castellan that she thought you were dead."

"Yes, resurrection is an excellent trick if you can pull it off. Likely to throw an interviewee off their guard . . . That frightened me, though, thinking that Rakena might have been one of them all along. . . ." He shuddered. "Thinking that it might have been for *years* . . ." He shook himself. "I shouldn't torture myself with these fantasies."

"You do seem to see enemies everywhere."

"I would put it to you that I accurately assess the

reality of my situation. A dear friend of mine has recently been assassinated by these people, and in fact they did also try to murder me."

"But if they've tried once, they're going to try again, surely? Are you going to spend the rest of your life looking over your shoulder?"

"Yes, that's a concern—to me, at any rate. It's not as if I can stay here at HARF forever. The chairs will ruin my back." Garak looked over his shoulder, out of the window. "In the past, I've tried to avoid public scrutiny. A legacy of my training. Blend into the background. Become one with the environment. That has, hitherto, afforded me a considerable degree of safety. But I think those days are coming to an end. So I must adopt new survival strategies."

Give them their due, Garak thought, Ista Nemeny and Edek Mayrat coped admirably with walking into Fry's office and coming face-to-face with him. Mayrat raised an eye-ridge, but Nemeny didn't even blink.

"Aren't you supposed to be dead?" she asked.

Garak held out his hands. "Reports of my demise," he said, "are, as usual, vastly exaggerated. I assume you want the post-death interview? Or shall I contact someone else?"

"How could we possibly refuse?" Expertly, Nemeny began to unpack her equipment, then she checked the light coming in through the window and closed the shutters and turned on overhead lighting.

Mayrat took the pile of books from Fry's desk and began shelving them.

"We should put you in front of these," he said. "It'll make you look authoritative."

Garak frowned. "Do I not already look authoritative?"

"Take whatever help's on offer," Nemeny advised.

Eventually, they were ready. The holo-camera began to roll.

"Ambassador Garak," Mayrat said. "Thank you for your time."

Garak tilted his head. "I'm very glad to be here."

"Yes, indeed, Ambassador—which brings me to my first question. Only two days ago, the Cardassian people were shocked to hear that a skimmer in which you were supposedly traveling had been destroyed. I suspect many of those people will now be astonished to see that you are alive and well."

"But not, I hope, too disappointed," Garak replied.

Mayrat smiled. "One would hope not. What explanation can you offer the Cardassian people, Ambassador?"

Garak adopted a serious expression. "I became aware of a possible threat to my safety shortly after arriving on Cardassia Prime. I notified the relevant people at the CIB. Their response was that they were not apprised of any such threat and that, in their judgment, my security arrangements were more than adequate." He gave a cool smile. "If I were a more suspicious man, I might almost think they wanted me dead."

"Surely not, Ambassador—"

"Fortunately for me," Garak went on, "my friends within the Federation were prepared to take any threat to my life seriously. My particular thanks must go to Captain Jean-Luc Picard of the *Starship Enterprise* who, as you can see, allowed me to take shelter here on Federation soil. Captain Picard is a true friend and ally of the Cardassian people."

"Why did you not share the news of your survival immediately, Ambassador?"

"Truth be told, I was rather frightened by this turn of events. It seemed wise to keep a low profile while preliminary investigations were under way—"

"Then you think you know who was responsible?"

"I couldn't possibly comment on an open case."

"The constabularies are investigating though?"

"I sincerely hope so. Speaking of the constabularies, I'd like to take the opportunity to thank Director Kalanis of the city constabulary for allowing one of her senior investigators the freedom to assist me during this period." That, Garak reflected, while not technically false, played rather fast and loose with the facts, in that Kalanis hadn't formally released Mhevet to him—but the end effect had been the same. "I'm very glad to hear that she has been reinstated."

"Yes, it's been a good day for Director Kalanis—although the fortunes of other senior officials are less rosy at the moment. Prynok Crell, for example."

"It's a shame that Crell didn't listen when I approached him with my concerns. I've extensive prior experience in these matters."

"Would you like to guess why he didn't listen to you?"

Garak pondered this. "No," he said. "I wouldn't."

Mayrat gave him a look. Garak looked steadily back.

"Failings at the top of the CIB have not only cost Prynok Crell his job," Mayrat went on, "but commentators have been suggesting that this is also the reason that the castellan has chosen not to run for reelection. Do you have any further insight into this unexpected decision of hers?"

"I've worked with Castellan Garan for several years now and she has impressed me as a dedicated public servant. Whatever prompted this decision, I'm sure it's been made with the best interests of the Union at heart. The Cardassian people have been lucky to have Rakena Garan as their leader."

Mayrat tilted his head. *That doesn't answer my question.*

Garak tilted his head in turn. *It's the only answer you're getting.*

"This seems to leave the way open," Mayrat said, "for Representative Evek Temet to become our leader. Regular viewers of my program will surely remember your recent, er, *lively* clash with the representative. Would you care to offer an opinion on his candidacy?"

"I'm sure it comes as no surprise when I say that I think that Evek Temet would be a disastrous choice for castellan," Garak said. "He appeals to all our worst impulses: our brutality, our lack of compassion, a suspicion of other species that verges on hatred, on paranoia."

Mayrat was nodding to him to continue. *You've got free rein here, Ambassador.*

"It is my belief that the Cardassian people will not be persuaded by this man," Garak said. "We're wise now. We've learned that the old ways cannot lead to anything other than great suffering. That Cardassia is gone, I am very glad to say, however much Evek Temet wishes it would return." Garak smiled and shook his head and spoke gently. "It won't. It can't. And to return to the old ways would surely finish the task that Dukat and the Jem'Hadar started. I believe . . ." He opened his eyes wide. He was good at not blinking. "I believe that despite all we've lost and all we're still mourning, most of us are looking to the future, not the past. Some of us may still be trapped there—but only some. All it needs is for most of us to say: *No more. Never again. No.* And I believe a majority of us will indeed say 'no' to Evek Temet."

He looked at his interviewer, who seemed to have become caught up in this small speech. *I should do this for a living,* Garak thought.

Mayrat collected himself. "Who do you think would be best placed to defeat Temet in the election, Ambassador? It's difficult to see a candidate among the progressive and radical groups in the Assembly that would be acceptable to them all."

"Yes, that's an unfortunate fact about their coalition at the moment. This is one reason why I've decided to run for the office of castellan myself."

The look on Mayrat's face was beyond comical. It was only a shame the Cardassian people would never see it, as there was only one holo-camera, and Nemeny would surely edit it out. His colleagues would surely enjoy it, though. In a choked voice, Mayrat said, "Can we stop recording for a moment, please, Ista?"

"I think we better had."

Nemeny put down the holo-camera. They both turned to Garak, but before either of them could speak, he pointed across the room. "There's *kanar* over there. I can recommend whiskey for shock, although it's something of an acquired taste."

"You really do enjoy all this, don't you?" asked Mayrat, once he'd downed a decent measure of *kanar*.

"I have few pleasures in life," Garak murmured.

"Rubbish," said Mayrat.

With a nod, Nemeny indicated that the holo-camera was running again.

"That's exciting news, Ambassador," said Mayrat, deadpan. Garak admired his sangfroid. "You were, until recently, not particularly well known in the Union. Perhaps you'd like to take the opportunity to tell the Cardassian people why they should consider you for castellan?"

Garak twitched an eye-ridge up at him. *You really want to give me a platform?*

Mayrat shrugged. *Go ahead.*

"Very well. I am pro-democracy. I am pro-alliance. I believe that the Union stands at a moment of choice: to fall back into the old ways, into the darkness, or to move ahead into a much brighter future. I believe my past experience uniquely equips me to understand the nature of that choice, and my commitment and dedication can lead the Union forward. I have been all that was worst about the old Cardassia, and I have learned a great deal from all those who are best about our new Cardassia." He settled comfortably into this new part. "Of course, talk of alliances and democracy is all very well, but what the people of Cardassia want to know is whether there'll be work, and schools, and education, and health care, and fresh water. My record after the Dominion War speaks for itself, I think. But there's a great more I should like to do for the Cardassian people—if they'll allow me."

"Ambassador Garak," said Mayrat, "thank you very much."

Nemeny signaled that she had stopped recording. Garak rearranged himself in his chair.

"Well," said Mayrat. "You've got my vote."

"I won't hold you to that."

"You can't. It's a secret ballot. But—a choice between you or Evek Temet?" Mayrat shook his head. "No competition."

"The humans have an expression for such a choice," Garak said. "'Better the devil you know.'"

"Except not many people know much about you, do they?"

"I'm sure I can rely on you and your colleagues to remedy that situation," said the newly announced candidate for Cardassia's highest office. "But you're right," he said. "It's a straight choice between me and Temet. Between a future for our people as part of the wider quadrant—or between isolation and infamy."

Nemeny dimmed the lights. "Anyone might think you wanted it to work out that way."

Garak rubbed his eyes. "Believe me," he said. "I didn't."

"I would like to commend your quick thinking last night," Picard said dryly to Worf and Šmrhová. "Your willingness to bring Glinn Dygan and Investigator Mhevet into the compound not only saved their lives, but it saved the life of a child who by chance found herself the only witness to the murder of a fellow officer."

"Lieutenant Šmrhová," said Worf, "has been very concerned throughout the past few days about the security implications of allowing Cardassian personnel onto HARF installations."

Šmrhová shot him a grateful look.

Picard studied his first officer thoughtfully. "I see, Number One," he said. "Well, I'm duty bound to point out that your actions were in direct contravention of an order from the office of the president pro tem that HARF installations were to be closed to all non-Federation personnel."

"We did have Ambassador Garak and his body-guards upstairs at the time, sir," Worf said. "And your instruction was to implement the order within the bounds of reason and compassion."

"That was indeed how I worded the instruction, Number One. Nevertheless, I hope that neither of you will do anything of the sort again."

"Of course not, sir," Šmrhová said, in a subdued voice. "Sorry, sir."

Worf folded his arms and said nothing.

"Until next time, of course," said Picard.

"What I am still trying to understand, Captain," said President Ishan, *"is why the castellan felt that she could not run again for office."*

"My reading of the situation is that there are par-ticular sensitivities within the Cardassian Union con-cerning their intelligence services," Picard said. "The Obsidian Order casts a long shadow over the Car-dassian consciousness. Let us not forget that it was Enabran Tain's decision to step beyond his authority, arm the Obsidian Order, and launch an attack on the Founders' homeworld that lay at the root of the Dominion's antipathy toward Cardassia. The castel-lan, as the leader of the civilian Assembly, plays a cru-cial role in providing a check on the CIB's power. For the castellan to be seen to have lost control over the agency plays into some very particular fears at work on this world. Nobody wants to see an uncontrolled secret police established again within the Union. Rakena Garan made a grave mistake losing control of Prylok Crell."

Picard observed his new president closely. He and Garak had worked for some time on this explanation. He could only hope that Ishan was convinced.

"But if these polls are to be believed," said Ishan slowly, *"the Cardassian people look likely to elect the last surviving member of the Obsidian Order."*

"Yes, sir," said Picard. "A complicated place, Cardassia."

The president reflected upon this. *"I'm not convinced that Garak is the best choice for us,"* he said at last.

"It's not our concern who the Cardassian people choose to be their castellan, but I believe the ambassador is the best choice for the Federation."

"Over Evek Temet?"

"Garak is a good friend to the Federation, sir," Picard said, with conviction. "And I would go so far as to say that a Temet-led Cardassian Union is a disaster in the making for us."

Ishan looked at him sharply. *"How so?"*

"He's isolationist—I would say a borderline xenophobic. My sense is that with Temet leading the Union, its rearmament would quickly accelerate, and the Union might even slip into civil war. There are people here who will not accept Temet as their leader if he pushes certain policies forward. Do we genuinely want an unstable but heavily armed Cardassia on our doorstep? How well has that suited us in the past?"

"But Garak?" said Ishan. *"You can't seriously prefer Garak?"*

"I do," said Picard. "I think Elim Garak is probably the best friend the Federation has on Cardassia." *Damn,* thought Picard, hearing himself. *I genuinely mean that. And, yes, he is a good friend.*

If complicated.

President Ishan sat in quiet thought. *"Much as it pains me to say anything in favor of a former Order man,"* he said eventually, *"I suspect you're right. I certainly don't want to see one of our closest neighbors destabilized, and I suspect Ambassador Garak is probably the best choice to prevent that from happening."*

"In which case, might I offer a suggestion, sir?"

"Go ahead, Captain."

"As a signal of support toward the ambassador, we should indicate that we are prepared to discuss a timetable for the removal of our personnel from Cardassia Prime." Quietly, he said, "They're not Starfleet, sir, not in the main. They are doctors, health workers, educationalists, specialists in social policy. We can make good use of them elsewhere. And, if the worst happens, and the Cardassian Union does elect Evek Temet and moves closer to civil war, we will be putting good people in danger leaving them here."

Ishan pondered this. *"Very well,"* he said at last. *"We'll start moving forward on this again."*

Picard breathed out. *Starfleet would be gone,* he thought, *by the end of the year, before the new castellan was installed.* Rakena Garan would still have the honor of being the castellan who oversaw the liberation of Cardassia. "Thank you, sir. Both Ambassador Garak and Commander Fry will be very pleased to hear that."

Garak saw the final cut of his interview with Mayrat at home, in the company of Parmak. He watched his friend covertly throughout. It was, he thought, rather like watching a dust storm gather. When they reached the part where Garak announced his candidacy for the castellanship, Parmak made a soft hissing noise, which he swiftly cut off, and listened to the rest of the interview in stony silence. Mayrat finished with a long summary of Garak's impeccable credentials for the post:

"With long experience in security matters, an unimpeachable war record, and a lifetime of public service—"

"'Public service'?" Parmak muttered. "That's one way of putting it."

"I liked 'unimpeachable,'" Garak said.

"—not to mention his prior role as adviser—and personal friend—to Alon Ghemor and well-established relations with our major allies, the ambassador is surely an impressive candidate for the role. Other pretenders to the position"—Mayrat looked knowingly at his audi-

ence—"*might struggle to present themselves as equally qualified. And the ambassador's campaign, although new, has been met with positive responses from some significant quarters. The president pro tem of the Federation has already signaled that the delayed withdrawal of Starfleet personnel from Prime is now once again moving forward. . . .*"

The piece ended. Garak waited.

"Well," said Parmak, putting down his glass with a clatter. "I think I can guess whose side he's going to be on throughout the upcoming cavalcade of speeches and meetings."

"I know what you're thinking," Garak said. "I want to assure you that this is not a decision I came to lightly."

Parmak stood up and walked toward the window. The memorials were just about visible in the dusk. "You know your own mind best, of course. I doubt there's anything I could say to stop you doing this. Besides, it all seems well under way already."

Garak put down his glass and stood up. He walked over to join Parmak. Slowly, hesitantly, he put his hand on the other man's arm. "Don't be angry with me. I don't think I could bear that."

"Why would I be angry with you?"

"Why would you not?"

"I'm not *angry* . . . !" Parmak shook his head. "No, I'm not. I'm truly not. But I am worried about you. What I want to know is—are you sure about this, Elim? Are you sure that this is the best choice for you?"

Garak didn't reply for a while. He turned to look out of the window at the battered city that lay before them. Eventually, he said, in a low voice, "I'm less sure of this than I have been of anything in my life, Kelas. You know the kind of man my father was. You know what power did to him. He was monstrous. As monstrous as Dukat—no, more so, because of how long he was able to indulge his excesses. And for years I molded myself in his image. I tried to make myself like him. You know that better than anyone. . . ." He took a deep breath. "Nobody *died* this time, Kelas. At least, not by my hand. I played the game, yes—but I did not initiate it, and I did not . . . I did not do all that I might once have done."

Parmak turned and put his hand upon Garak's shoulder. "You're not like him now," he said. "You haven't been for a long time."

"I hope that's true. I'm terrified it might not be true."

"I know it's true," said Parmak, patting his friend's shoulder. "Do you think you can win?"

Garak gave him a crooked smile.

"Do you *want* to win?"

"I certainly don't want to lose."

"You mean to Temet?"

"I mean at all."

"Will you feel safe out there, out in the public eye?"

"With all that security surrounding me? I'll be the safest I've been since I joined the Obsidian Order.

And . . ." Garak swallowed. "And there's the scrutiny, Kelas. The checks and the balances. Most of all, I'll be safe from myself."

"I see. So you'll be safe, from everyone up to and including yourself. Good. But will you be happy, Elim?"

"Probably not. Have you met the kind of idiot who gets elected to the Assembly? I imagine I'll spend most of my time infuriated. But I certainly won't be bored."

Parmak sighed. "I suspect you won't. And I suspect I won't get bored watching you."

A slow smile curved across the lips of Cardassia's most irrepressible son. "Who knows? It might even turn out to be fun."

Twelve

My dear doctor—a brief note to let you know that I am not dead (yet) but may soon be castellan. Longer letter to follow.

Yours in the pursuit of peace, order, and good government,

EG

Mhevet came up to Fereny on his blind side. Leaning over his shoulder, she whispered, "We can step outside into the corridor, or I can arrest you in front of everyone. The choice is yours, Tret."

He looked up at her, wide-eyed with shock.

"Come on," she said softly, helping him to his feet. "There's no need to make a scene."

When it was all done, she came back up from the holding area. Nobody was working. She walked across the room. They stopped talking and watched her progress.

"There are going to be some changes around here," she said, coming to a halt in front of them. "Listen. I don't care what your politics are. I don't care whether you think we should be friends with the Federation or take the chance to break free of them and find our own way. Chances are the truth lies somewhere in the middle. What I care about is this organization—not for its own sake, but for what it does and how it does it. I don't care what you believe. I only care what you do as a result. And if you lie, and cheat, and murder, then I'm coming after you. Because those days on Cardassia are *over*. We're watching now—people like me—we're watching out for the signs of corruption, and if you're a creature of the shadows, we'll find you, and we'll bring you out into the light, and you'll burn in the glare."

Mhevet looked around. "Have I made myself clear?"

There was a silence.

"Have I made myself clear?"

There was a general noise of agreement. "Thank you for your attention. All right. I want someone to go out to those old industrial units in southeast Torr, and I want someone to go to this address on the west edge. And will somebody else please go and sort out the coffee supply?"

When Mhevet next went into Kalanis's office, she put two bags down onto the other woman's desk.

"I was going to get them ground," she said. "But Lieutenant Šmrhová said no. She said to put them in small bags, freeze them, and only grind them as you need them. Isn't that strange that we never knew to do that? Nobody ever mentioned that. Anyway, these are to say I'm sorry. I didn't realize what you were trying to do, and I must have been an extra worry exactly when you didn't need one."

Kalanis opened one of the bags. They both savored the warm blissful scent that pervaded the room. "Where on Prime did you find these?"

"Lieutenant Šmrhová gave them to me. Apparently I was mainlining the stuff the whole time I was at HARF."

Kalanis dug into the bag and brought out a handful of the beans. She pressed her nose against them and inhaled deeply. "You realize this addiction might become a problem after Starfleet goes?"

"I hope not. I hope some things are here to stay."

Kalanis smiled for the first time in months. "You know I'm moving sideways?"

"Sideways and up, isn't it? Lucky CIB. Keep an eye out for my friend—"

"Erelya Fhret. Yes, I've got plans for her. And for you too." Kalanis pushed a padd across the desk. Mhevet read it and opened her mouth to query the contents.

"It will have to go through the usual channels, of course," Kalanis said. "There's no guarantee. But if you're not this side of the desk in a few weeks' time, I suspect there'll be a lot of questions asked." She gave her protégée a steady look. "Are you ready, Ari? There can be no more hiding away. No more pretending that problems will solve themselves. You'll be a target, a point of focus. People will be gunning for you, trying to catch you out, and trying to get around you to promote their own agendas. And always you'll never be quite sure whether they're simply opportunists or servants of something more shadowy."

Mhevet thought of the conversation she'd had with the ambassador—was it really only the night before?

I don't want to be Obsidian Order.

None of us do.

The old Order was dead, she knew that, and she was glad, because the Order had become the problem, not the solution. But the purpose, the original purpose—to watch the people who served Cardassia, to hold in check their worst instincts—that made sense. *Perhaps the error had been in formalizing this purpose around an institution,* she thought, *and then giving that institution free rein.* In doing so, the Cardassian people had outsourced their consciences and relieved themselves of the burden of self-scrutiny.

We tricked ourselves, she thought, *when we handed this responsibility over to others. It's the duty of each one of us; it's the service we require from one another.*

"I'm ready, Reta," she said.

"Good." Kalanis ran her fingers through the precious beans. "Do you have something to grind these with?"

"No." She hadn't thought of that. "Do you?"

*   *   *

Choosing which book would make a suitable gift for Ambassador Garak had proven a difficult task, and it was not until just before their meeting that Picard made his final decision. Most of his choices had, on reflection, seemed obvious; the others he was sure that Garak would know already. He had wanted to find something obscure, but not too obscure, and worthy of the ambassador's attention. He was, after all, going to be a very busy man for the foreseeable future.

When Garak arrived, the first thing he did was to offer his thanks. "I must express my gratitude for everything that you have done for me over the past few days."

"All I did was to make sure that you were safe, Ambassador. The rest was all your own doing."

"Yes, indeed." Garak raised an eye-ridge. "And I'm willing to accept the consequences of everything I've done over the past few days. But this is not the first time that the Federation has given me sanctuary. I won't forget it."

"I wish you the very best of luck with your forthcoming campaign, Ambassador. You are a friend to the Federation."

"I was a friend of Nan Bacco, Captain. I intend to make sure that her legacy—our alliance—remains intact."

"I spoke to the president before you arrived," Picard said. "He asked me to tell you that as a further gesture of goodwill toward the Union, he will drop the limit on military spending that was proving such an embarrassing aspect of the withdrawal agreement."

A smile twitched across Garak's mouth. "That will rather take the wind out of Temet's sails."

"I believe that may have been the intent."

Garak's eyes narrowed. "Your temporary leader is not, I think, a man naturally disposed to make friendly gestures toward us?"

"No," agreed Picard.

"Which leads me to suspect other hands at work in securing this concession."

"That may have been the case."

"Then again—I am very grateful to you, Captain Picard."

"None of us wishes to see Nan Bacco's legacy squandered," Picard replied. "And it is incumbent upon all of us to ensure that." He waved a hand. "That was the least I could do."

"And . . . may I ask what you intend to do with the information that has caused us all such grief over the past few days?"

That a Cardassian was Bacco's murderer, he meant. Picard tugged his uniform, straightening it. What could he say to President Ishan? A Bajoran: a man who had lived through the horrors of the Occupation, who had inherited a Federation reeling from a profound blow, and who had shown himself willing to make harsh decisions. "I don't know," he said, honestly. "I don't know yet what's for the best."

"I will naturally trust you to make the decision you believe is best for us all," said Garak. "But, please—remember that the alliance is paramount. It's what will secure lasting peace between our civilizations. It's infinitely more important than presidents, or castellans—"

"—or captains," Picard said. "I understand, Ambassador. Thank you for trusting me."

"I cannot think of anyone I could trust more."

Garak made to get up, and Picard reached across his desk for the book. "For your library," he said.

Garak, taking the volume, looked deeply touched. "Captain, how kind of you! I certainly didn't expect my gift to be reciprocated!"

"It's been difficult to select something for a man like you." Picard gestured toward the pile of books he had considered and rejected. "I assumed you already knew *The Prince*."

"I'll send you my annotations," Garak deadpanned.

"And I saw a complete set of Austen in your home."

"Who could be without the sublime Jane?"

"*Doctor Faustus* I suspected you had read."

Garak smiled. "More than once."

"So in the end I chose this. I didn't think you'd know it. But I thought you might enjoy it."

He watched the ambassador examine the book. It had a bright yellow cover with a red dash on the front like a splatter of paint or blood, across which stalked a black cat. The author's name was in black too: Булга́ков. Garak traced his finger across the script and mouthed the syllables.

"I only regret it doesn't have the personal connection of your own gift," Picard said, "but it's a fine edition nonetheless. Do you know it?"

"I don't," said Garak. "What happens?"

"It all starts," said Picard, "when the Devil arrives in Moscow."

To Picard's relief, Garak began to laugh. "Oh, yes? And the cat?"

Picard smiled. "You'll see."

The Riding Club was nearly empty, and those who were there were drinking alone. Who was in the mood for socializing with Nan Bacco dead?

Glinn Dygan, deep in thought, did not notice at first when someone sat down opposite him.

"Hey," Šmrhová said at last. "Are you going to finish that so I can get you another?"

Dygan drained his glass. "I think I should be ordering."

"Don't let me stop you."

Their drinks arrived, and Dygan eyed his balefully. It didn't help, not really. No wonder that there weren't many people here tonight. "You don't let much trouble you, do you, Aneta?"

"That's not true, but I'll take it as a compliment."

"I don't mean to be rude. What I mean is—you don't agonize over decisions. You don't worry about whether something is the right thing or the wrong thing to do. You just get on with it."

"Security doesn't allow for me to take my time to make a decision," Šmrhová said. "That's the quickest way to get myself killed, not to mention anyone who happens to be in my charge. I know right from wrong."

"Did you get into trouble for beaming us into the compound? You know you probably saved our lives."

"I didn't get into trouble."

"No?"

"No. If you want to thank anyone, thank Commander Worf. Anyway, if I did get into trouble, that's my problem, not yours. I'll live with the consequences of my actions." Šmrhová looked at him carefully. "What did you do that's troubling you?"

"What makes you ask that?"

"Weeks undercover on Cardassia Prime? Mixing with some pretty nasty people by all accounts? I can read between the lines."

Dygan frowned. "I don't think I want to say. . . ."

"That's fine too," she said. "You don't have to if you don't want to. I know it's troubling you, but I think it would be worse if it didn't trouble you at all. If you didn't care either way. For what it's worth, I'm sure you did all you could under the circumstances. You're good people, Ravel."

"There was mention of a medal."

"What, for me?" she said, in mock surprise.

"Not this time," he said, and it made him laugh a little.

"Thought not. Will you take it?"

"No."

"There you are then." She lifted her glass. "To all those Cardassian officers who've learned to tell right from wrong."

He tapped his glass against hers. "To all those Starfleet officers who've learned when to bend the rules."

"Long may we flourish."

Arati Mhevet was bending the rules speaking to Fereny without another investigator present, but one more bent rule wouldn't do any harm. And there was the force field between them.

Fereny was lying flat on his back when she went in, but he shifted into a seating position when he saw her. "Come to gloat, Ari?"

"Don't be ridiculous. This is a tragedy. You were a fine constable and had the makings of a fine investigator. What possessed you to get involved with people like Velok Dekreny?"

"I could ask you the same about Elim Garak."

"Perhaps. But I haven't murdered anyone."

"You betrayed your own uncle to the Order. Doesn't that count as murder?"

She didn't react. Of course he would know about that. It was common knowledge around North Torr why she and her family had left.

"Have you ever thought about what happened to him?" Fereny said. "Have you thought about what the Order did to him, once they had him?"

"Yes," she said steadily. "I've thought about that a great deal. We lived in a different world back then, Tret, one that you're barely old enough to remember. Choices like that were a part of our daily lives—"

"That's life under the Order. That's why I want a better way, a truer way—"

"Oh, Tret!" she said sadly. "Is that how they got you? Do you know who these people are? Really? Do you really get what they stand for?"

"They stand for a better Cardassia!" he burst out. "One that doesn't humiliate itself by trying to win the favor of humans, Ferengi, and Klingons! One that will be strong again, better for all of us—"

"Look around you," she said. "Look where you are. You're going to be locked away for the rest of your life. The people you've been working for—they've used you for their own ends. They've walked free while you pay the penalty."

"I did it for Cardassia."

"I'm sure you did. But Cardassia didn't want it done. Cardassia's moved on, Tret. That old Cardassia, where people used people for their own ends, to keep themselves in power—that's dead. We're not going to let it come back."

He turned his face away.

She took a step forward, getting closer to the field. "I know you were blackmailing Aleyni over his marriage, but why? What were you after? Were you trying to get into HARF somehow? Was there something planned for them before they left? An attack? A massacre?"

He looked up at her, and then he started to laugh. He lay down again on his back. "Yes, Ari. That's what it was. We had something special planned. We were going to see them off with a bang."

Mhevet took another step toward him. Something about this didn't ring true. "What was it really, Tret? What did you need Aleyni Cam for?"

But he smiled, and closed his eyes, and wouldn't say anything more. Later, Mhevet got in touch with the people at HARF, but Aleyni's desk was now empty, they told her. Part of the withdrawal, they said. Anything that might have told her more was gone.

She couldn't find Aleyni Zeya either. When she went over to the HARF compound, open again to Cardassian citizens now that the crisis had passed, she found the little house closed and locked up. The neighbor, a young ensign, said that Zeya had packed up and left when the Cardassians had been told to leave the base.

"Surely, Maggie—Commander Fry—would have let her stay?" Mhevet asked. "She was the wife of a Federation citizen—"

"She said she didn't want to stay. Not without Cam."

"Any idea where she might have gone?"

The ensign shrugged. "Family?"

But she didn't have any family. They'd all died in the Fire. This place surely had been her family—

HARF, where she could have a Bajoran husband and live among people who wouldn't judge them for loving each other. Mhevet, heading back to her skimmer, couldn't quite shake the feeling that Aleyni Zeya had been failed in all of this. *Where would she go now? Who would she turn to?* While driving her skimmer off the compound, Mhevet sighed. She was ashamed to say that in some ways she was grateful that Zeya wasn't there. That she wouldn't have to tell her that her husband had been blackmailed on account of his marriage to her. She was saved from that.

Later, Mhevet drove out to the edge of Coranum, where she found a little girl sitting on the steps outside a well-kept tenement. "Hello," she said. "How do you like your new place?"

The little girl shrugged. They'd moved her from home, partly for protection, partly away from her father. "It's all right. Everyone's a bit posh."

"Hungry?" Mhevet asked.

"Always. I'm growing, you know."

Mhevet walked her down the street to the dining house on the corner. "All right," she said, as the girl sat down. "We're going to play a game. Tell me who is sitting behind you—no, don't look! We'll do this from memory! Tell me what they look like and what they're wearing."

The *Enterprise* was breaking orbit, leaving behind a world slowly picking up the pieces. Picard pondered all that had happened. There was no escaping the fact that Bacco was dead—and by a Cardassian hand. But what was to be done?

He had received, the previous day, a message from Iravothra sh'Thalis, the former presider of Andoria, with whom he had worked closely in the period leading up to Andor's secession and her own fall from power.

"I wanted to offer my condolences on the death of Nan Bacco," she said. *"My heart goes out to all of you in the Federation. I hope you are able to remain strong during this terrible time. I hope you do not make the same mistake as Andor and act while in the grip of grief and shock."*

"Computer," said Picard. "Get me a secure channel direct to Admiral Akaar."

When the admiral was on the comm, Picard told him about the True Way and the events of the past few days.

"You understand why I did not report this until now?"

"I do." Akaar sat with his hands covering his face.

"President Ishan is not the kind of man to take this news lightly," Picard said. "We've only just prevented the collapse of our alliance with the Cardassians. To tell him this now may be all it takes to destroy that alliance for good. This would be a grave betrayal of the trust that Garak has put in Starfleet—put in me. As yet there's no firm evidence—"

"Yes," said Akaar. *"Yes. We need to reflect upon this for a while, Jean-Luc. For the moment, this should go no further."*

"In the meantime, sir, do we have new orders? Our purpose here on Cardassia Prime was to bring President Bacco home. I'm assuming that the sad honor now falls to the flagship to bring home her body?"

Akaar shook his head. *"I'm afraid not. Your orders, from the office of the president, are to proceed to Ferenginar."*

"Ferenginar?"

"President Ishan has been impressed by your handling of this crisis and your work keeping the Cardassians in the alliance. He wants to ensure that unfriendly elements among our other allies don't take this opportunity to force a breakaway."

"Have we had any suggestion that this might be occurring on Ferenginar?"

"No," said Akaar, who seemed also to be thinking that these orders were odd, *"but President Ishan keeps his own counsel."*

"Then . . . we'll set course for Ferenginar," Picard said slowly, puzzled by this mission. The conversation ended, and the *Enterprise* moved on, away from Cardassia, and away from Earth.

Returning at last to his office, Garak stood at his desk and looked wearily at the messages that had accumulated while he had been dead. Not even his apparent extinction had stopped them, and the double surprise of his survival and his candidacy for the castellanship meant that they were now coming as thick and fast as a dust storm from the plains. He scanned rapidly through the list of names, trying to determine what was critical and what could wait. One name stood out.

Julian Bashir.

Garak opened the file. He read the message quickly, then a second time more slowly, and then he closed the file. He wondered for a while whether he was angry, and he thought about destroying the letter, and then he realized that he was not angry but grateful, so he stored it instead on a data rod that he tucked away in his pocket. He would read this letter again and again over the coming weeks as Bashir had no doubt intended.

He paced his office for a while, ignoring the gentle but regular chimes from the comm that told him that new messages were arriving, bringing new worries and new trials. Coming to a halt before Ziyal's picture, he touched the frame, very gently, almost a caress.

"I've been trying to do the right thing for a while now," he said to the air. "And, on the whole, it's working fairly well! I haven't murdered anyone in a long time."

He thought about Ravel Dygan and Rakena Garan. Prynok Crell too, despite his misjudgment, had not deserved such a reward for long service and a terrible loss. And then there was Arati Mhevet, whose limits were yet to be tested . . .

"Although it's true there's been collateral damage. Anyway, now it seems I'm going to be castellan. And that concerns me. It's all very well being an ambassador because nobody gives you any real power. That's been a frustration, but it's also been a blessing. But castellans are something different. They have real power."

The scarlet flowers beneath the painting were fading. He would have to get fresh ones brought.

"On the whole, Ziyal, I haven't been good with power. On the whole, I've tended not to know when to stop." One of the petals came away in his hand. "I wish you were here," he said. "You were good at getting me to understand when I ought to stop. You did that for your father too, didn't you? That would be helpful, now."

Garak pondered his past and what the future might bring.

"I'll try not to let you down. I'll try to think what you'd say, and I'll stop doing something if I think you wouldn't like it."

Garak turned and went back to his desk. The petal was still in his hand. Ignoring the outside world, whose demands would be no doubt all-consuming very soon, he opened Picard's book and read the quotation at the front:

"Well now—who are you?"

"I am part of that Power that ever wills Evil and always does good."

"Touché, Captain," he murmured. Tucking the petal inside to mark his place, he put the book aside to read when he was feeling stronger, and he sought solace instead in sublimity. If he must read about those who insisted on shaping the destinies of others, something more comforting was, for the moment, required.

"*Emma Woodhouse,*" he read, "*handsome, clever, and rich, with a comfortable home and happy disposition, seemed to unite some of the best blessings of existence; and had lived nearly twenty-one years in the world with very little to distress or vex her—*"

Epilogue

Twilight Kingdoms

During the Fire

Here, in the cellar beneath his father's house, he could tell himself that he was nowhere, elsewhere, anywhere other than buried beneath a city in flames. He could turn to Preloc and hold in his hands all that was most precious—all that he loved best—about his subtle, brutal, imperishable civilization. He could persuade himself that what he was reading was the truth. He could persuade anyone of anything.

Kira, in the next bed, sighed and put her pillow over her head. It was late, and tomorrow would require great resources, and she needed darkness to sleep. Garak covered the light with his hand but did not stop reading. Damar was long since asleep and snoring softly. They'd joked, when they'd still been trying to pretend that they could be friends with each other, how Damar would sleep through the end of the world. Some joke.

Garak read on. He read of the capture of Qo'noS, and the siege of Paris; he read of firing squads and forced marches, of purges and pogroms, of bonfires of books and buildings, and, at last, in the early hours of the morning, he came to the chapel, where the roses still grew, and a man from a ruined civilization came face-to-face with his conqueror and spoke truth to power.

Softly, silently, Garak began to weep. High above his head, a great empire was burning: his home, and all the people were burning too. *We're finished,* he thought, and felt the terror of a man facing the final darkness. And then: *Never, never, never! I will never give up on you, my Cardassia! You will endure. I don't know what can survive this, but something will— something must! Something stronger. Something better. Something else.*

Preloc had seen this, he realized, and as the thought took hold of him, the book remade itself within his hands. Yes, she had seen this coming and said as much to power as she dared. But that was not who she was addressing with this book. No, Preloc was speaking to those who would be brought to this pass against their will and would suffer. She had wanted them to remember their resilience, their inability to admit defeat, their capacity to endure even when there was no hope left in the world. She had seen that they might one day come to this, and she had known what people would need to survive this. She had written it down before she went into the darkness, and she had left her words for him to read, here, tonight, at the end of things, so that he could take courage from them and bring something worthwhile out of the Fire.

"For the love of the Prophets, Garak," Kira whispered hotly from beneath her pillow, "will you *please* turn off that light?"

Garak touched his fingertips against his lips and then pressed them lightly on the last page of the book. He did not need to read the words. He understood now what mattered about them, and he had taken it to heart.

"I'm done," he said. He closed the book and turned off the light and lay back in the darkness. "Sleep well, Nerys."

After the Fall

"Are you going to stop reading?" asked Parmak.
Garak stretched back comfortably in his chair. "Why would I do that?"

"Because voting is about to end, and then we'll get the exit poll data."

"We already know what that's going to say, Kelas. We've known for weeks."

"Still, you might show an interest."

But Garak read on; not to annoy his companion, whom he loved, but because he was near the end of his book, which he loved too. Breathlessly, he watched Anne Elliot read the letter that Captain Wentworth had written, and, slowly, he began to relax as they put aside their history and escaped the choices of the past. When he came to the end, he closed the book and pressed it between his hands, holding its world to him for as long as he could. She hadn't written anymore, and he wasn't sure who to turn to next. His eye fell upon Picard's gift. *It all starts when the Devil arrives in Moscow,* he thought. *No, not yet. Soon, Captain. But not yet.*

"Please, Elim," Parmak said. "Don't start another one. Come over here. You'll want to see this."

Outside, in the dark garden, they were gathering around the memorials. People had been coming here all day to vote, and Garak himself had, mid-morning, stepped outside amid the whirring of the holo-cameras to cast his own vote in the glare of the public eye. But this was something different. Garak watched, sheltered behind the tinted, transparent aluminum of the window, but they did nothing. They sat down and waited, or stood and waited, and some of them were talking, and some of them were simply waiting, standing amid the silent stones. Nervously, Garak looked around and was much comforted to see the dark figures of his security team moving silently into place.

"I wonder what they're here for," he said. "I wonder what they want."

"Elim," Parmak said patiently, "they're here to see you. They want to be here when your name is called. They want to hear what you have to say."

For a brief, excruciating moment, Garak panicked. The walls seemed to close in on him, and the darkness outside seemed thick and inescapable. He looked around the room for exits and, in desperation, realized that there were none. He pressed his palms against the window and then rested his forehead there too, feeling with relief the cold of the glass. *What in the name of all that I hold dear do I think that I am doing?*

He felt a hand upon his arm, turning him gently but firmly. Eventually, he was face-to-face with Parmak.

"Take a few deep breaths," the doctor suggested. "That's it. Nice and steady. Deep and slow."

Garak leaned his back against the window and did what his doctor ordered. Once he was breathing steadily again, he looked around the room. It was dimly lit, warm, and he was comforted by the sight of his books, his desk, and everything that he had salvaged from the Fire. On the comm, there were messages from friends he hadn't even realized were friends. A huge bunch of red roses and Edosian orchids had arrived that morning with a message from the O'Briens. There was Ziyal's picture, his compass. And, in his pocket, on a data rod, there was a letter from Julian Bashir—sent shortly after Garak had told him he was embarking on this folly, when debates and speeches and public appearances and policy statements had not yet become his daily routine—that he had read again and again throughout.

"Look," said Parmak, pointing to the viewscreen. There was no sound, but the pictures were enough. "That's it. Voting's stopped. All done."

"All only just beginning, I think."

Parmak looked back outside at the stones and the gathering crowd. "What are you going to say to them?"

"I don't know. I'll extemporize."

"You're good at that."

There was a knock at the door. "Ambassador," Akret called. "The exit polls are about to come in. Time to get to work."

"I'll be there in a moment," Garak called back, and then, softly, said to Parmak, "Why do I feel as if I'm about to hear a sentence passed?"

"Why do you feel as if you should?"

They stared at each other. Then Garak looked down at his hands. They were shaking. Parmak, seeing this, took them within his. "You'll be fine. It's all going to be fine."

"I hope so."

"I know so." The doctor leaned in and—quickly, affectionately—pressed his lips against the other man's brow. "I trust you," he said. "I forgive you."

"I haven't done anything yet."

"I know," said Parmak. "I forgive you anyway."

Garak let him have the last word. Later, he stepped out of the shadows and into the light, and the right words came, as they usually did.

Dear Garak,

Firstly, may I express my profound relief at learning that you are not, in fact, dead, but have merely been taking a short sabbatical on Federation soil? I don't know the details, of course, but if it was a trick, Garak, it was not a kind one. We're reeling from one loss. I couldn't have stood another.

Leaving aside the fact that I believed for a brief period that you were beyond the reach of any letter that I might send, I'm conscious of having been a poor correspondent. I am sure you understand how difficult these recent days have been. Everything has changed, and, like everyone else, I'm afraid of what might happen next. I'm afraid of where this grief might take us and what we might become.

Which brings me to my real reason for writing. I wanted to wish you success in your latest venture. Running for castellan! Did you ever see that coming? I admit I didn't, sitting opposite you in the Replimat listening to you slander Shakespeare. I didn't see any of this coming. I suppose I should know better than to underestimate you. Never stop surprising me, Garak. It really will seem like the world has ended.

Because of our long friendship, I hope you'll not be offended by what I have to say next. But I must say it. In your past letters to me, you have written eloquently of the isolation that has been such a condition of your life and how this was what permitted you to lead the life that you led and poison yourself on Cardassia's account. You alone know what you have done for Cardassia, and I have never asked and never will. You wouldn't tell me anyway, not the truth.

But you let me in, Garak. You let me in when you allowed me to help you recover from your addiction to your implant. When you let me stay and listen to what you had to say to Tain before he died. You let me in, and so I have a duty to you: to ask you to look out for yourself, to watch yourself, for any sign that you are becoming like him. When I met him in the Arawak Colony, before I knew who he really was, Tain said that he never had to order you to do anything, and that was what made you special.

From all I hear, you're going to be the next castellan of the Cardassian Union. And I'm terrified for you. I must ask you—beg you—not to isolate yourself. Surround yourself with good people, Garak: people who will speak to you honestly and truthfully and who will tell you when you are doing wrong. Keep them close. Make sure they are never afraid to tell you the truth. Do not be your father's son.

Perhaps I'm speaking out of turn. You'd be well within your rights to be angry with me, to destroy this letter and never speak to me again. I hope that won't be the case. I hope you'll forgive me. These are the words of someone sick at heart at all that has been happening this past week and who thought for a while that you really were dead this time. I'm afraid for myself and my own people as much as I'm afraid for you and for yours. But I want to believe that you—and Cardassia—are coming out of the shadows. It's been a long, hard road for your people, and there's a way to go yet. But perhaps at last it's right for you to have your time in the sun. And while the sun shines on your new Cardassia, and for as long as it shines, and should the shadows ever fall upon you or your world again, I will remain—

Your friend,
Julian Bashir

Acknowledgments

Grateful thanks to my fellow Fallen—David R. George III, Dave Mack, Jim Swallow, and Dayton Ward—for discussion, debate, and all-round brilliance throughout this project. Thanks for being great colleagues and great fun.

Huge thanks to Margaret Clark for asking me to do this book, for letting me have my wicked way with Garak and Picard, and for making this project run so smoothly. Thank you also to Ed Schlesinger for support and assistance throughout writing.

Thank you to colleagues and students at Anglia Ruskin University for being genuinely enthusiastic when I show them the cover of my latest book.

And thank you, as ever, to Matthew, for everything.

About the Author

Una McCormack is the author of four previous *Star Trek* novels: *Cardassia—The Lotus Flower* (which appeared in *Worlds of Star Trek: Deep Space Nine, Volume 1*), *Hollow Men*, *The Never-Ending Sacrifice*, and *Brinkmanship*. She has also written two *Doctor Who* novels, *The King's Dragon* and *The Way Through the Woods*, and numerous short stories. She lives with her partner, Matthew, in Cambridge, England, where she reads, writes, and teaches.